RANCHER'S FORGOTTEN RIVAL

MAISEY YATES

FROM FEUDING TO FALLING

JULES BENNETT

MILLS & BOON

First Published in Great Britain 2022
by Mills & Boon, an imprint of HarperCollins*Publishers* Ltd
1 London Bridge Street, London, SE1 9GF

www.harpercollins.co.uk

HarperCollins*Publishers*
1st Floor, Watermarque Building,
Ringsend Road, Dublin 4, Ireland

Rancher's Forgotten Rival © 2022 Maisey Yates
From Feuding to Falling © 2022 Harlequin Books S.A.

Special thanks and acknowledgement are given to Jules Bennett for her
contribution to the *Texas Cattleman's Club: Fathers and Sons* series.

ISBN: 978-0-263-30322-3

0122

MIX
Paper from
responsible sources
FSC™ C007454

Printed and Bound in Spain using 100% Renewable electricity at
CPI Black Print, Barcelona

RANCHER'S FORGOTTEN RIVAL

MAISEY YATES

Legends of Lone Rock

The Sohappy family has its roots in Lone Rock. So deep that they precede the first European settler to come to North America. The ranch is part of their family heritage, passed on from generation to generation, from father to son.

The ranch has survived flood, famine and the perils of modern life.

In 1955, having no sons to pass the land to, Casper Sohappy passed the land on to his son-in-law. As family legend goes, the son-in-law did have roots, true and deep as the rest of the family. One night, he went out drinking at the local bar. The exact details of that night remain a mystery. But he woke up with a hangover, and a piece of paper indicating he'd lost the stretch of land between Sohappy Ranch and Evergreen Ranch, granting essential water rights to the Carson family.

Since then the Sohappy families and Carson families have feuded.

And when the son-in-law passed on, his son vowed the land would never pass into the hands of someone who didn't carry their family's blood again.

He also vowed to see the Carsons pay for what they'd done.

And the hatred between the families began to go deeper than roots ever could.

One

Chance Carson couldn't complain about his life.

Well, he could. A man could always find a thing to complain about if he was of a mind. But Chance wasn't of that mind. Every day was a gift, in his opinion. The sun rose, the sun set, and he went to bed and woke up and did it all over again, and that was success no matter how it was measured.

Add in the fact that he got to work with his brothers, or take off and compete in the rodeo circuit as he saw fit, and he really did feel like he was living the dream.

And hell, he had to, right?

No one was guaranteed life.

Much less a dream. He knew well the tragedy of a life cut short. It was a different grief to the death of an older person. It changed you. That unfairness.

He'd tried to at least take some good from those changes.

"You look smug," his brother Boone said from his position on his horse.

Five of the brothers were out, riding the range and looking for stragglers.

They had the biggest spread in Lone Rock, Oregon. Evergreen Ranch.

It had been in the family for generations, but had essentially been bare dirt until their dad had made his fortune in the rodeo, and further still as the commissioner of the Pro Rodeo Association. Now it was a thriving cattle ranch with luxury homes adding a touch of civility to the wildness of the surroundings. Courtesy of his family's status and success as rodeo royalty. They competed together, and they worked together. They practically lived together, given that most of them had housing on the ranch.

Though the rodeo hadn't always been a source of family togetherness.

Their sister, Callie, had nearly broken with the family over some of it, making inroads for women who wanted to ride saddle bronc, and now there was a blooming movement happening within the Association.

Chance was all for it.

Well, not as much when it concerned his little sister.

But in general.

He liked a little feminism. Who didn't?

Right now, they were off for the season, and hanging around the ranch, which was a bit more togetherness than they often got.

Flint, Jace, Kit, Boone and himself, all together like when they were kids.

Almost.

Sophie was gone, and there was no getting her back, a pain that he'd had to figure out how to live with. Grief was funny that way. People talked about "getting over it" and he didn't see it that way. It was just learning to live with it, learning where to carry the pain so you could still walk around breathing through it.

Then there was Buck. But his absence was his choice.

Being a prodigal in the Carson family—which was full to the brim with disreputable riffraff—was really something. But Buck had managed it.

But he was focusing on what he had, not what he didn't.

Which was good, since tomorrow he had to head out for a few days, just to see to a meeting with a man about buying another head of cattle.

"I *am* smug. It's another beautiful day in the neighborhood."

"If Mister Rogers were a cowboy…he wouldn't be you," Flint said. "You're an asshole."

"I'm not," Chance said. "I am the cheerfulest motherfucker out there."

"That's not a word."

"Your mom's not a word," Chance said.

"Your mom is *our* mom," Flint pointed out.

"Oh well. It stands. Anyway, I'm just enjoying the day. I'm heading out tomorrow, so I won't be around."

"Right. More cows," Jace said, and if he was trying to look excited about it, he was failing.

"It is what we do," he said.

"Sure," he said.

"You going to have time to come over to the bar tonight?" Jace asked. "Cara has some new beer she's trying out. She was wondering if we could all come taste it."

"I wouldn't mind having a taste of Cara's beer," Kit said.

And that earned him a steely glare from Jace. Cara was Jace's best friend, and it was not *like that*. And hell and damn to any man who wanted to be like that with her. Especially if he was one of Jace's brothers. Not, Chance imagined, because Jace was jealous, just because he knew how they all were. And that was shameless and not looking for a commitment.

"And where exactly are we putting the cattle?"

"You know where," Chance said.

"So, I was just wondering, because I was trying to figure out how long it would be before one of the Sohappy sisters was up in my face."

"Well, Boone," Chance said. "I think you know that Juniper and Shelby will be right at us like clockwork."

"It's like four feet of fence," Boone said.

"Doesn't matter. She thinks our great-great-granddad tricked hers into betting that land in a poker game while he was drunk and she lays into me about it every time we're near each other. And now it's been a fight for…oh, three generations, and our grandfather literally died mad about it." Not that their grandfather had been the most sterling guy, but it was the principle. "And I'm not moving the damn fence. And I'm not letting her badger me into signing something over to her just because of some tall tale that's been passed around the families."

"Well, yeah, because it's like four feet one way and like a mile the other," Kit pointed out. "Plus accusations of sabotage, cattle rustling and all manner of other bullshit."

"And I don't care if she has her panties in a twist about it, it's not my problem. If she wants to try and retroactively prove that her great-great-grandfather wasn't fit to sign over the land, that's on her, she's welcome to do it."

"*She?*" Boone asked. "I thought we were talking about both Sohappy sisters. Weird how it ended up being about the one."

And Chance wasn't at home to any of that. His brother liked to tease him that there was more than just rage between himself and Juniper. But no. Sure, she was beautiful. Both of the Sohappy sisters were beautiful. But ironically named, as far as he was concerned, because he had never seen them do much of anything other than scowl. At least, his direction.

Women loved Chance. He was a charmer. He loved women, so long as it stayed casual, and physical only.

But Shelby and Juniper Sohappy did not love him. And Juniper in particular.

Hell, yeah, Juniper was beautiful.

Long black hair, eyes the color of bitter chocolate, golden-brown skin, high cheekbones...

Shame about her personality.

She'd been a spiteful little scorpion since they were in school. And he didn't call her that to be hollowly mean; she'd once put a scorpion in his backpack when she was ten and he was twelve.

She'd hated him from the time his family had moved to the ranch when he was ten, taking over for his grandfather after his passing.

She'd hated him just because he was a Carson.

And hell, if he'd sometimes responded in kind to her provocations, who could blame him? And if he'd once bid on her at a charity auction and used her to do menial ranch tasks and carry his books at school—which she'd walked out on in the middle of, thanks—again, who could blame him?

Well, she could. And did. But that was beside the point.

And the fact that he'd do it again, even with all the sparks and spite it earned him, well, that was a whole other issue.

He liked sparring with her as much as he wanted to tell her to leave him the hell alone and never come back.

It was like a disease.

Like wanting to pull a girl's pigtails in second grade.

Except his other feelings about her were not remotely childish. Not at all.

"It's pretty bitter," Boone said. "Don't you think we should just get some surveillance done and see if that solves the issue?"

"Our grandfathers didn't. Our fathers didn't."

"Yeah," Boone said. "Grandpa also took cold showers because he thought that instant hot water bullshit made a man soft. I'm not sure 'because it's always been this way' is a good reason to do anything."

"You know," Chance said, "I would like at least one of them to ask nicely."

"And I would love to be standing there when you told her that," Flint said.

"Whatever. Juniper Sohappy and her bad attitude isn't my problem. She knows exactly what she can do if she wants to escalate it. But she isn't interested in that. She's just interested in being in a family feud that seems to always center squarely on me."

Because she could yell at any of his brothers. And never seemed to.

Almost as if she liked yelling at him.

Maybe *yelling* was an overstatement. When they'd run into each other at the market, in the cold beer fridge, each of them picking up some brews, she'd hissed. Like a feral weasel.

Gotta burr in your britches, Juniper?

Just a burr under my saddle. For life. That's you, Carson.

Yeah, I got that.

Flint shrugged. "All right, you may not want Juniper to be your problem, but I have a feeling she'll make it her goal to be."

Chance chuckled. "I'd like to see her try."

"Sure you would."

"You drinking later?" Boone asked.

"Nah. Gonna get an early night in so I can get on the road first thing."

They finished up their work, and his brothers trickled back home. And for some reason, Chance found himself riding toward the fence line, to the part of the property that bordered the Sohappy family's ranch.

It was just a shame, really.

A shame that he didn't see the rattlesnake. A shame that his horse chose to freak the hell out. A shame that his horse was a dirty deserter and ran off somewhere.

And it was a shame that when he fell, he hit his head directly on a rock.

It was raining. Of course it was raining.

Visibility was shit. Juniper had a feeling that she might end up taking calls tonight, whether she was supposed to or not. When the weather got like this, accidents happened. On these windy rural roads it was unavoidable. She wasn't supposed to be on shift tonight. She was supposed to be getting a good night's sleep. She'd gone for twelve hours in a row already.

Then there wasn't enough energy drinks in the world to keep her going at this point.

Maybe she was just being grim.

But it was that damn Chance Carson. The Carsons in general were a pain in the butt, but Chance specifically had gotten under her skin for years. She was two years behind him in school, but it had been enough for them to be in each other's paths quite a bit, and every time they'd ever crossed...

It had been bad.

Then there was the general Carson-ness of it all.

Her parents told her that she was overreacting to the whole border situation, but it mattered to *her*.

It mattered to her grandpa, who had hated the Carsons for as long as she'd been alive, and had told her stories of how they'd set out to undermine the Sohappy family from the beginning. And most of all how Chance's great-great-grandfather had gotten her great-great-grandfather drunk, and conned him into betting a portion of the ranch in a card game.

The legend went that he'd cheated. And he'd taken a valuable piece of the Sohappy ranch away, for nothing.

Your father doesn't love the land, not like you do. And I have no grandson. You're the firstborn of this generation. The ranch is going to go to you.

But Shelby is getting married. Shouldn't Chuck...

You know what happened. When a man was prized over blood. When the ranch passed from our direct line. It has to be you. You must care for it. Nurture it like it was your child.

So she'd taken it on. Rearranged her ambitions. It had been easy, actually. To put off pie-in-the-sky dreams like medical school and pretend they'd never really mattered.

The truth was, it had never been a particularly attainable dream.

So she'd thrown herself into Lone Rock. Into the ranch. Into life here. When she'd decided, at seventeen, that she'd stay, she'd rearranged every thought she'd had about the future.

She'd let her roots go deep.

She was one of the ranchers down at the Thirsty Mule,

hanging with the guys and telling tall tales. She'd earned that place. She could castrate calves and move a herd with the best of them. And could drink most of their sorry asses under the table.

She worked hard, she played hard and she didn't accept double-standard bullshit.

What was good for the goose and all that.

She'd made a life she was proud of, and she'd taken on the EMT job to pay the bills and satisfy the medical itch she'd had when she was younger.

Now she'd educated herself on ways to expand the ranch into something more lucrative.

A horse breeding and boarding facility. And while she liked ranch work in general, horses were her passion.

And if she got the facility going and got people to pay for boarding, then she wouldn't have to work two jobs.

She was having to pay for ranching like it was her hobby, and the only thing that her family just had was this land.

Everything else was an expense. Everything else came out of all the hard work that she put in.

Her dad's soul just wasn't in the land the way it was hers. He cared, but he was devoted to his business, his career.

It was why Juniper had decided against pursuing medical school. Against leaving. Being a doctor was a calling, a vocation, and…

She wouldn't have been able to do both.

So she'd knuckled down and focused on what she could do. And now she was grateful she had. She'd figured out what to do with the ranch that excited her, made her happy.

And she was just fine. Just fine. And she didn't even want things to go differently.

Maybe don't think about that when you're angry and gritty and half-asleep.

Maybe. Yeah, maybe that was a good idea.

The dirt road that led up to her cabin was mud now, and she was feeling pretty annoyed. And when her headlights swept the area as she rounded the corner, she might have thought that her irritation and exhaustion played a role in what she saw.

It looked like a body. A body out there in the field.

Sprawled out flat. But it *couldn't* be. She slammed the brakes on in her truck and stared.

Yes. The rain was pouring down on what was very definitely a male form sprawled out there on the ground.

But why?

How?

She looked around for a second, evaluating the risk level of the situation, because if something had wounded or killed this man, she didn't want to be next.

She wasn't about to be the first fifteen minutes of a crime scene investigation show.

But she didn't see anything, and there were no points for sitting there wondering about it. Juniper got out of the truck and ran out to that spot in the field. And her heart hit her breastbone.

It was Chance.

Chance Carson.

She knelt down and felt for a pulse. She found one. Thank God. He drove her nuts, but she did not want him to die. At least, not on the border between Carson and Sohappy land. That would be unforgivably inconvenient.

She could call someone, but not here. There was no cell service right out in this spot in the ranch.

But she had her truck.

She rolled him onto his back and did a quick assessment for spinal injuries. None of that. But he was out cold. And what the hell was he doing out here anyway?

She couldn't tell what the hell had happened. But she had some medical equipment in her truck.

She ran back to the road, then pulled her truck out to the field, getting it as close as possible to him. He didn't rouse.

Shit.

She had a board in the back of her truck, and with great effort, she rolled him onto it, strapped him to it and used it to drag him over to the bed of the truck. He was strapped securely in like a mummy in a sarcophagus, so she propped the top up against the tailgate, then lifted up the end by his feet, and pushed him back into the bed of the truck.

"Sorry," she said, slamming the tailgate shut. Was she, though? She wasn't sure.

Well, she was sorry that he was hurt.

Her cabin was the closest place that she could get him dry, warm and examined. She was a medical professional, after all, and he certainly wasn't the first person with a head injury she'd ever dealt with.

The road to the cabin was bumpy, and she winced every time she hit a big pothole. She really didn't want to *kill* Chance Carson. He might think so, but not even she was that petty. At the end of the day, land was land, and it wasn't a human life.

It might feel like it was sometimes. It might feel like looking at this place was the same as opening a vein and letting all her hopes and dreams run red and free.

But it was land.

He was a human being.

Even if he was the human being who left her angrier, hotter, more stirred up and just plain trembly.

She hadn't realized quite how tense she was until her little cabin came into view, and then her shoulders relaxed immeasurably.

She just didn't like driving with him in the bed of the truck like that. It was unnerving.

She got as close to the front door as she could, and felt a little bit exhausted and sweaty staring at his inert form in the back of the truck, still on the board.

She could get him down there, to the front door, but it was just going to be a little bit of a trick. She eased her shoulders upward and rolled them, then grabbed the end of the board, doing her best to lower it gently down to the ground, getting him out much the same way as she had gotten him in. And then she... Well, she dragged him. Up the front steps, slowly, methodically, careful not to jostle him.

She got him into the front room of the house and looked around. Then she took all the cushions off the couch and laid them down on the floor. She unstrapped him from the gurney and rolled him onto the cushions.

He groaned.

Well, at least there was a sign of life.

His clothes were soaking wet, but she was not stripping him naked. No. She had lines, and they were definitely around stripping Chance Carson naked.

Her heart bumped up into her throat.

Well. Dreams weren't anything to get too worked up about. Granted, her grandmother would disagree.

But that didn't matter. Juniper didn't put any stock in them. And the fact that she had dreamed a time or two about what it might be like to rip Chance Carson's clothes from his body at the end of an invigorating argument was... It was immaterial. She didn't think about it consciously. She didn't marinate on it or anything. It was her subconscious mixing up its passions. That was all.

She opened one of his eyes and shined a flashlight in it, then the other. "You are concussed," she said. "Sorry, my friend." She was going to have to observe him. Well, *someone* would.

She could take him down to the hospital…

Suddenly, a hard, masculine hand shot up and grabbed her around the wrist. "What's going on?"

His voice was rusty and hard. And she was…

On fire.

Her heart was racing, her skin suffused with heat. He had never…touched her before. In a panic, she pulled away and he released his hold, but the impression of his hand on her skin still remained.

"I…"

"Where am I?"

"You're at my house. I found you in a field. Can you tell me what happened?"

"I don't know what happened," he said.

"You don't know what happened?"

"That's what I said."

"Right. Okay. You don't know what happened."

"Yes," he said.

"That doesn't matter. It doesn't matter what happened. Can you see all right?" She put her finger off to his left, then his right, and watched as he tracked the movement. "That seems to be fine."

"Yeah," he agreed.

"No double vision?"

"No," he said.

"You definitely hit your head," she said.

"Right," he said.

"I'm just trying to figure out how serious it is."

"You a doctor?"

"No. I'm an EMT…" He knew that. Chance Carson knew that she was an EMT. Everybody did. "Do you know who I am?"

"No. Should I?"

Oh. Well. Holy crap. Chance Carson didn't know who she was.

"Juniper," she said slowly. "Juniper Sohappy."

"Name doesn't mean anything to me. Sorry."

"What's your name?"

His brow creased. "You know… I don't know."

He didn't know his name? Juniper couldn't wrap her head around that. He could be lying, of course. Though, to what end she didn't know, but how could you ever know with a Carson?

Wasn't her whole family history a testament to that?

If he was lying, she wasn't going to give him the satisfaction of tricking her. She…

She stopped herself just as she was about to open her mouth.

If he was lying, it might be funny to go along with it, see how long it took him to reveal himself.

And if he wasn't?

She thought back to the humiliation of when he'd had her working his land. Of every insult over the years, of everything.

She was going to keep an eye on him tonight, make sure he didn't lapse off and die of his head injury. And she was more than qualified to do it. She also knew if he really was suffering from some temporary memory loss from the fall he'd taken, it would resolve quickly enough and you weren't supposed to go heaping facts on people while their mind sorted things out.

What would it hurt if she taught him a little something in the meantime?

"You don't remember your name?" she pressed.

"No," he said, his eyes blank, and she looked hard to see if he was being genuine. "I don't remember anything."

Two

It was the damnedest thing, and he hadn't realized it until his pretty little rescuer had asked the question.

What's your name?

He didn't have a clue. Reflexively, he reached toward his back pocket, and felt that there was no wallet there. Which meant no ID.

Somehow he knew *that*.

"You can't remember," she pressed.

Her dark eyes were intense, and he couldn't quite get the read on them.

"No," he said.

But his head hurt like a son of a bitch. And apparently he knew enough to know that. But this wasn't normal, that he didn't like it.

"Chance," she said. "You don't know?"

"Chance," he said. "That's not a name."

"It is," she said. "Your name."

"Oh." He tried to see if it rang any bells, but it didn't. It didn't ring any at all.

Didn't bring to mind anything. There was just a big expanse of blankness.

"Well, you clearly know me. Who am I?"

"You… You work for me. You work here," she said.

He let that settle over him. "Okay."

"That doesn't ring any bells?"

"No," he said.

"You're… You're a cowboy," she said.

That felt right. It didn't ring bells, but it felt right.

And apparently he worked on her ranch.

And he didn't know who this woman was, but she was the most beautiful thing he'd ever seen. Well, he didn't know all the things he'd seen. But he knew that. Somehow. Instantly. Electrically.

But it was more than beauty. It was deep.

He could swear he did know her, and that she mattered. That she was singular, significant. That she was the woman who occupied his thoughts, his fantasies.

"A ranch hand," he said.

"Well. Yes. But you know, you had such a hard time lately and… Anyway."

"A hard time?"

"I'd rather not tax you, Chance."

"You'd rather not…"

"You had a head injury," she said slowly.

"Yeah," he said. He rubbed the back of his head and felt dried blood.

"I don't think you need stitches," she said. "But it's pretty bad."

"Well. I don't have any context for that. Or if I've ever been… Hurt very bad before? How does this stuff work? Why can I remember… How to talk? But I can't remember who I am."

"Head injuries are complicated," she said. "That much I know. I can't say as I've ever run into anyone with amnesia…"

"It's not amnesia."

"I think it is."

And one thing he knew for certain right then and there was that he was not the kind of man who was used to being without his faculties. He wasn't the kind of man who wasn't used to being in control.

This was something he hadn't experienced before. And he didn't like it. Not in the least.

"I could drive you down to the hospital…"

"No," he said.

"No?"

"No. I don't want to move. I'm not… I'm not gonna die."

"No," she said. "And I have… Look, you definitely need someone to stay with you. You can't go back and sleep on your own."

Something fired in his blood, and he wondered then if… If there was something between him and Juniper.

Because it seemed fair to think there might be, considering the way she got a response out of him even when he was in this poor of shape.

"I'll sit up with you," she said.

"Would I be alone otherwise?"

"Look, what you get up to with people is none of my business, but you don't live with anyone."

"Okay," he said.

So they weren't together. Had they been? Had he touched her? Kissed her? Held her naked in his arms?

The thought sent a surge of heat through him.

But he supposed it was just that she was his... His boss. That was strange, he didn't feel like he was the sort of man who had a boss. But he wondered if maybe he just wasn't the best judge of that sort of thing.

Maybe no man felt like he should have a boss deep down, but most people did. Because they had to.

"You should probably try to stay awake," she said.

"I'm so tired," he said. And that immediately felt... It was a strange thing, that admission. It was honest, but there was something about the admission of what was akin to vulnerability that didn't sit right with him. So whatever kind of man he was, he didn't truck with that sort of thing.

"I'll fix you some food," she said.

"Well, I don't want you to do that," he said.

"I need you to work it so that you are in a sitting position as soon as possible," she said. "You've got a concussion, and I don't want you dying on me."

"Can I help with anything?"

"No. I'm going to make you fry bread, and you need to stay away."

"If I've had it before, I can't remember."

"You probably have," she said. "But likely my mother's. Which is better than mine."

"I bet not." He didn't know why he said that. He just bet that he would rather have something made by Juniper than by... Maybe anybody else.

"I have dough ready to go." She took a bowl from the fridge and uncovered it, then took a large jug of oil from a cabinet beneath her stove, got a large pan and put a generous measure of the oil in it.

She waited, bustling around the room doing what appeared to be busywork to keep from having to look at him. He didn't know why he knew that, only that he did.

Then she took a small wooden cylinder from a container on the counter and retrieved dough balls from the bowl, rolling each of them out quickly, before dropping them into the hot oil.

Her movements were practiced and eased, whatever she said about her mother doing a better job. And as the smell filled the room, his stomach started to growl.

She put a wooden spoon into the pan and did something he couldn't see, then a couple of minutes later removed the dough, which was now golden and glistening.

She placed the bread in a stack on a plate and put what looked like a heap of powdered sugar over the top.

"I'm not giving you alcohol," she said. "Not with a head injury."

"Well, I don't even know if I want alcohol." Except he found that he did. But he wondered if that was a good thing or not. Maybe he was one of those people who didn't drink in moderation. Maybe he had a problem. Maybe that was part of the troubles that she'd been talking about him having.

He didn't know, and he hadn't known for all of twenty minutes and it was starting to frustrate the hell out of him already.

There were too many unanswered questions in a moment. He had no idea what he was going to do if he eventually walked out of Juniper's cabin and found that he still didn't have any answers.

"Here," she said. "I'll give you a pop."

"A pop?"

She grinned. "A soda. My grandpa always called it that. So I do too. I don't actually know why. I think his wife was from the Midwest."

"You don't know for sure?"

"No, not about the crap on my dad's side. Because he

had a few wives. On my mom's side, yes. My grandparents that are still here on the ranch have been together for sixty-five years."

"Hell," he said. "That's a long time."

"Yeah. I guess so. My mom's family has had this land for generations."

"Family ranch?"

"Yes. And it's very important to us." The sentence was heavy, and he couldn't quite say why.

"Do you work on the ranch, or just as an EMT?"

She laughed. "Just an EMT? I'll give you a pass because you just hit your head."

"That isn't what I meant. I meant... How do you find the time?"

"You make time to do what you need to. To do what you love. That's how it works. You do what needs to be done. At least, if you're worth anything."

"And you do what needs doing," he said. He had no trouble imagining it.

She brought a Coke and a plate of fry bread to where he was on the floor. "But you have to sit up," she said.

She reached out, and grabbed his hand, and helped him.

And maybe he should be embarrassed about that. But the only real thought he had was just how surprisingly soft her hands were, given that she was a woman who clearly worked hard. He had expected something different.

Surprising softness.

That was what he would remember.

Would he remember? Would he forget all this when everything else came back to him? He didn't know, and there was no way to know, so he just needed to quit thinking about it.

"How long have I worked here?"

Because what the hell else was there to do but ask questions about himself?

"A while," she said. "Eight months."

"Right. Where do I come from?"

She looked to the side. "Honestly, I don't really know. Sorry. You haven't shared a whole lot. I just know that you were going through a bit of a rough time. And we... Well, we've given you a lot to do, and focus on. Kind of a new start."

"That's nice of you."

"Yeah."

He didn't know why he needed a new start. And that was disconcerting as hell. Because that could mean a whole lot of things. He didn't know what kind of person he was. If he was a good one. If he was genuine in his appreciation for what this family had done for him, or if he was a con man. It was near impossible to know. And he didn't like that. Here she was, making him food—damned delicious food—and offering him beverages and to sit up with him all night, and he didn't even know what his intent was toward her. Or if he had any way of ever knowing.

"What about you?"

He wanted to know something. And if he couldn't know something conc rete about himself, maybe he could learn something about the woman sitting across from him.

She looked confused, surprised. He wondered now if they'd ever talked before. If he'd ever asked her about herself. "Like I said, I'm an EMT."

"How did you get into that?"

A funny little smile crossed her face, the dimple to one side of her lip creasing her cheek. "My sister got hurt. When we were kids. We were playing out in the woods and she fell and she broke her leg. I wanted to be able to help her. I didn't know how, though. I didn't know how to help her, and that ate at me. I didn't know what to do to fix her. I asked my grandmother to teach me some things. Basic survival skills. She did, and I just got really into it. I thought maybe I'd…you know, go into medicine, be a doctor. But there's a need out here. I'm actually based out of the fire department. The rural fire department handles a lot of the medical emergencies. We're the first responders, until somebody can get here from the hospital. There isn't a hospital for forty miles."

"Wow," he said.

"Yeah. I don't know. I just like knowing how to fix things, more than I really wanted to help people, I guess." She laughed. "I mean, I like helping people, don't get me wrong. But my original motivation was… I wanted to be able to fix myself. Because, isolated like we are, we can't count on anyone else. It's like you and me right here. I can't call from my cabin. I don't have cell service. We would have to go down to the main house, and it's quite a drive. So… It just makes more sense for me to treat you here. And I know how."

"It's not serious?"

She laughed. "Well, I didn't think so until you didn't remember anything. I'm a little more concerned now. But as far as what I can tell? You're okay."

"What about the ranch?"

"It's been in my family for generations. It's… It's important to me. It isn't important to my dad, and it's the most important thing to my grandpa, and someone has to…carry the torch, I guess. That's me. My dad's a contractor. And the house that he's made for us there is amazing. And he makes enough money from it to support us. But he isn't interested in growing the actual ranch. He has his passion. And... The ranch is what my grandfather loves. He had horses. But that's all gone away now because he can't take care of things the way that he used to."

Conviction and passion rang in her voice, something that spoke to even deeper truths than she was admitting. It made him want to dig deep.

And he had no reason to question himself. Because he knew nothing. Why shouldn't he know everything about her?

"Does your grandfather still live on the ranch?"

"Yes. He and my grandmother still live in the original house. Not the grandfather that's had a lot of wives."

"I understand that."

"But... You know, there's this big family feud," she said.

"Family feud."

"Yeah. With us and... The neighbors. They're... They're dishonest is what they are. Crooks. They've been disputing the border of the land forever. But it's ours. In fact, years ago, all this land was ours. But my great-great-grandfather fell on hard times and he had to sell off a portion of it. And it just hits me wrong the Carsons are trying to take more. More than what we even had to get rid of back all those years ago."

She looked at him expectantly, as if she was very curious what he would say about that.

"Well, sounds like some bullshit to me. Why are they trying to take your land?"

"They're greedy," she said. "They never think they have enough. And it started with the great-great-grandfathers. When...when theirs took mine out drinking and got him to sign over a portion of the land that... It's very important. It sparked a major feud. Anyway. It's just important. And it's frustrating when something that matters so much to you is being badly used by a bunch of idiots who don't even really have ranching in their blood."

"They don't?"

Her lip curled. "They're showmen. Rodeo cowboys. My ancestors didn't believe in owning land. But the rules changed, and now we have to live by those rules. To have more taken from you is…"

"It's unconscionable," he said.

Land mattered. That he knew. That he felt in his blood, in his bones. With certainty. He didn't know why or how he felt it so deeply, only that he did.

It was real. That sense of ownership. It was real and it mattered.

"I've always thought so."

She sat down with him, and took a piece of bread from the platter.

"This is my favorite," she said, taking a bite. "My sister likes it with cinnamon sugar."

"I doubt you can go wrong," he said.

"Not in my opinion," she said. "My grandparents met in Arizona. This is my grandmother's family recipe. She moved out here to be with him when she was only eighteen. And her parents were furious. I can't imagine. She got married at eighteen. It seems almost ridiculous."

"Does it?"

She scrunched her face. "Don't you think?"

"I don't know. I don't know how I feel about marriage," he said.

Right now, he could see the benefit of it. You could hole up in a cozy cabin with a woman, she could cook you food and sit on the floor and talk to you. He didn't know anything except this moment with Juniper, and it felt like something important. It felt like something real. And he could imagine spending every day after this here.

That was probably the amnesia. Maybe. Maybe he was a commitment-minded man.

Maybe he was married. Maybe he had left a wife and children somewhere.

The idea was disconcerting.

"Maybe I should drive you down to the main house..."

"No," he said.

Something about expanding the scope of his reality didn't feel... It didn't feel right just now.

"Why not?"

"Honestly... I don't know. But the thing is, I don't know anything. I don't know anything, and the idea of jumping into... A lot doesn't sit well with me."

"Okay," she said slowly. "Then I'll sit with you."

Three

Juniper felt like a jerk. Well, it fluctuated. But right now she did. It was why she'd offered to at least take him down to her parents' place. Where they could tell her she was being awful and maybe help take control of this situation.

But he'd said no, and she was happy to back out. She knew why she'd let her own meanness goad her into this.

She'd been thinking about the time he'd bought her services in that high school auction and had made her work on his ranch. Mucking stalls and all things she was accustomed to, but working his land was anathema to her and he knew it.

And now she was sitting here cooking her grandmother's recipes for him, and in general sharing things with him she knew she shouldn't.

But he was still Chance.

And he'd been…well, unapologetically a jerk to her for

the past twenty years, so what was so wrong with getting a little back while taking care of him?

Bottom line, she'd saved him.

And she really didn't think it was the right thing to do to explain everything to him. At least, she felt like she knew that from somewhere. She had given him his name, and she had talked about the Carsons, and nothing seemed to jog his memory. That concerned her, but so did the wild look in his eye when she had said that they ought to take him back to the main house. The fact of the matter was, she didn't know what had happened to him. He didn't know what had happened to him.

That thought made a shiver of disquiet race through her. Maybe there was danger out there. It was likely he had fallen off his horse...

But for all she knew, there was something else to it.

Anyway, there was no harm keeping him for the night. Keeping him settled here.

She really didn't think he was in any physical danger from his injury. If she did, she would've run him down to the hospital right away. But it just didn't seem likely. She knew enough about head injuries to evaluate him, and the fact that he was up and talking was a good sign. His speech was clear and coherent, and it wasn't slurred. His eye movement tracked, and they looked clear—no visible bleeds or anything. He seemed completely with it. Except for the whole *not remembering who he was.*

"Thank you," he said, taking another piece of bread.

And her heart did something weird.

Chance Carson had never been nice to her a day in her life. And now he was being... Well, he was being very nice.

And he looked disheveled and handsome, and she

did wonder again if she should help him strip out of his wet clothes…

Probably not. Probably that was a really bad idea.

She needed to stop thinking of him out of his clothes.

She looked at him, and her heart did something very strange. And it was the heart reaction that really bothered her. Because a regrettable physical reaction to Chance wasn't completely unheard of. He was a good-looking man, and the fact that she noticed was inevitable to an extent. But she had to remember that he was her enemy. Her enemy. The Carsons were her enemy.

Fortified with that, she took a breath. And then took another piece of bread.

"Did you always know you wanted to stay here?" he asked.

And she wondered why he was asking her so many questions.

Maybe it was because he was trying to orient himself in a certain space and time. She could understand that.

What she really didn't know was why she was answering them.

"I… Yeah, I guess so. I've always been very close to my grandparents. And the land means everything to them. It's really hard to make a good living ranching. Especially if you don't have a lot of capital to invest to begin with. I want to move into hire and horse breeding. That's really where there's a shot of making some money."

"And money is important to you?"

He asked the question earnestly enough, there was nothing behind it. How could there be? He was a man who didn't remember anything. Just a big, beautiful log. He reminded her of Brendan Fraser in *George of the Jungle* right now.

That movie had been responsible for a certain level of awakening in her youth.

But she had never figured she'd meet a man who didn't understand the way the world worked, who was gorgeous and full-grown on top of it.

"It's not money so much as… Succeeding. Making my grandfather proud. I… I sacrificed some of my dreams and learned to make this my dream and I need it to matter." And she didn't know why she told him that. Hell, she could've made everything up, and he never would've known the difference. Even if he remembered everything, he wouldn't know the difference. She had known who Chance Carson was all of her life, but they did not know each other.

Amnesia or not, he wouldn't be able to pick her life story out of a lineup. So why she was telling him now, over her grandmother's recipe, she didn't know.

"Because your dad wasn't able to do it with the ranch?"

"I don't know that he wasn't able to do it. He just didn't care. But it's ours. It's our heritage. It's…"

"And that's important to you," he said.

"Yes," she said. But what lay beneath the surface of that affirmation was the fact that her grandfather was important to her.

The most important person in her life. And she just didn't know if she'd done enough to make him proud. She had done her best. To be the heir. The first girl to inherit the responsibility of working the land, of being the one in charge. She had plans and she wanted him to approve and to be proud and…

He was in his nineties. She didn't have limitless time.

"I just love him," she said.

"Your grandfather?"

She realized that she hadn't given any context for what she had just said, but that he had picked up on it anyway.

"Yes," she said. "My grandfather. I love him more than anything. I love him... He made me who I am. He taught me to ride. He taught me everything there is to know about this place. About what we can grow here. About what we can use that grows naturally. About how free you can feel out in the middle of nowhere with no one around to talk to. How you can just be. Just you. And the ground and the trees and the sky."

"What happened with your sister that made you want to be an EMT?"

She laughed. Entirely unexpected. "Yeah. Thank God for Shelby and her broken leg."

"Why not stay an EMT?"

"I won't have time. And anyway, eventually, the ranch should be self-supporting. It's not like I'm making a ton of money with what I'm doing. It's just enough. Enough to make sure that I'm supported. Enough to make sure I have some to invest in."

"And is this where you live?"

"Yes. All the time. Rent free. Which helps. Everything of mine goes back into the ranch. I have been fixing the same pair of boots for two years so that I don't have to fork out any money that I might need."

"That's commitment."

"Yeah, well. When it's your legacy, you just do."

She hadn't meant to spill all this to him. Honestly, she never would've talked to him under normal circumstances. She never would have spent any sincerity on him whatsoever. She yawned.

And he looked at her with... Concern.

"Are you going to be all right?"

"I'm going to keep you from dying."

"Wow. Nice of you. I don't think I'm going to die, though."

"I don't think you are either. Otherwise I would've forced your ass down to the hospital. I think we've got it under control."

She hoped she did.

"I don't want to go to the hospital," he said.

And it was a strange sort of fear in his eyes that made her want to listen.

She squinted. "Do you remember something about the hospital?"

He frowned. "I don't know. It just feels like a place I don't want to be. I don't know why. But look, I don't remember anything. I don't know if I'm a good man, I don't know if I'm a bad man. I don't know if I'm on the run from the law or from the Mafia. Or from a wife."

"Maybe you aren't on the run," she pointed out.

She'd planned to mess with him tonight, but she wasn't going to hold him here. In the morning, he really did need to go somewhere. But he might just remember. He might.

His expression went opaque. "I just feel like I might be."

She sat with that. Because she knew that Chance wasn't on the run. Not strictly. But it made her wonder. Because he seemed confident in a few things, not many, and she wondered if there was a grain of truth to them or if he was just drinking his bathwater. If amnesiacs didn't actually have any kind of sense of their former life.

"Well," she said. "I can only respect that."

"Thanks. Makes me feel like I might know something."

"Well, good. Unexpected silver linings." She had another piece of bread.

"What if we take turns sleeping?" he asked.

"That seems like a potentially dangerous idea."

"Or we set an alarm. You can check on me and make sure I'm not dead."

"Great."

She was tired, though. She had been exhausted when she pulled in at the end of the shift, and it was gone nearly one in the morning now.

At least her radio hadn't gone off. She didn't think he was severe. And as long as they kept on checking in…

"All right," she said. "Let me get some sleeping bags."

She went down the hall and retrieved two sleeping bags from her closet. She laid them out on the floor. He seemed more mobile now, but she was unbearably conscious of how cold he must be.

"I swear I'm not trying to get you naked," she said, wincing slightly. "But before we settle in, we need to get you out of these clothes."

It was the look on his face that got her. Charming and a little bit wicked all at once. As if he didn't mind one bit if what she was trying to do was get him naked, after all.

"You got a blanket for me?"

"Yes," she said. "Go to the back. To my room. Strip off, and I can get your clothes washed and dried."

"That's awfully nice of you."

"What's the point of saving you from a head injury if you die of hypothermia?"

"Well, that is a good point."

She went to the hall closet and grabbed a Pendleton blanket, big and woolly with bright geometric patterns on it, and flung it in his direction. "You can hunker down in this."

"Sure thing."

He went into her bedroom, and she paced for a moment. And when he came back out, he was holding the clothes and wrapped in the blanket, a disconcerting measure of masculine shoulder and chest revealed.

"Sorry I don't have any extra men's clothes." She migrated to the washer and dryer that were in the hallway. She chucked his clothes into the washer without examining them too closely. She didn't want to think about handling Chance Carson's underwear. Lord have mercy.

"I'm shocked you don't have an extra pair of men's jeans laying around somewhere."

"I'm not that kind of girl."

"Too proper to take a man home?"

"Too commitment phobic to let him keep a pair of jeans here. Or let him leave them behind. Once his ass is out of my bed, every trace of him better be gone, and if it's not, I'll just throw it in my burn pile."

It was true enough. The thing about taking on the mantle of being the heir to the ranch was that she had decided to go ahead and adopt all the perks that came along with it. She wasn't going to get married or have a family. She didn't care what anybody thought of her. She was going to behave the way the cowboys did. So when she wanted sex, she got it. She didn't do boyfriends. She didn't do relationships. She was a law unto herself, and that was how she liked it. Well, it could be argued that she was also a law unto her grandfather and her obligations to the ranch. And if they chafed a little more now than they had at one time…

The equine facility was the answer. It would give her a chance to show her grandfather that her own unique spin on things was right. It would give her a chance to keep her promise and then some. And it would fulfill her. The thing was, her grandfather had always been supportive of her. He was judgmental about a whole host of other people, so she knew what was involved in disappointing him. And she never wanted to do it. But she had promised him that she could do this. That she could be the thing that his own son hadn't been able to be, and she had liked that. That she had basically moved into being his favorite because she had made this vow.

And then she had discovered how difficult it was going to be to keep. The older she got, the more she questioned whether or not this was all there was to her life on the ranch. So change was the answer. Putting a stamp on it that was uniquely hers was the answer.

But then she got distracted by his shoulders and she forgot why she was thinking about her grandfather at all.

"I respect that," he said.

"You don't remember anything. How would you know not to respect it?"

He laughed. "I guess that's a good point. But I have the feeling that I'm a man who scratches an itch when the need takes him."

They looked at each other, and their eyes caught and held. And it was just a little bit too hot. She looked away, her heart pounding fast.

"Well."

"You got a deck of playing cards?"

"Are you kidding me? I have a tablet and a streaming service, we can just watch a movie."

"No way. You've already gotten the pants off me, we might as well play a rousing round of Go Fish."

"Wow."

She went back to her closet and rummaged until she came up with an unopened pack of playing cards. She tossed them to him, and he undid the cellophane on the outside, then pulled the cards out, shuffling them with ease and skill.

"You know how to shuffle cards," she said.

"Apparently. And I know how to play Go Fish."

"That's weird," she said.

"You're telling me."

He dealt the cards, and she sat across from him. And of course when he held his own cards up the blanket fell, down to his waist, revealing his whole chest.

Good grief.

If she had been told that she would be sitting with a bare-ass-naked Chance Carson in her house someday, she would have told whoever said that that they were crazy, and then gone to her room and cried because it would've made her hotter than she would have ever liked to admit.

That was the problem. Chance had always made her hotter than she wanted to admit.

He soundly destroyed her at the game, which piqued her temper, and she realized she had to keep it in check because he didn't know that they were rivals, not when it came to anything, so being generally persnickety regarding her loss had to have limits on it.

But by the time he beat her in round three, she chucked her cards at him. "I think you're cheating."

"Why would you think that?"

And he looked wicked, his blue eyes twinkling, his smile suggesting that he had never cheated at anything in his life. And he was a man who had the ability to tell himself that, because he had no memories.

No baggage. What a gift that was for a man like him, she bet.

"You're feral," he said.

"I am not."

"A little bit."

"Not."

"Come get your cards now, you gone and thrown a fit."

The cards were sitting in his lap. And he didn't think

that she'd get them. Which meant that she absolutely had to.

She licked her lips, then she reached across the space, and somewhere along the way, she forgot exactly what her motivation was. If it was to prove her mettle, or if it was to be seductive.

She wouldn't say that seductive was normally in her wheelhouse. She was a woman who took a straightforward approach to sex. Because it just made sense.

It was easy enough. There was no fuss or muss required. She never felt the need to dress up or try to be anything she wasn't. But she bit her lip, looking up at him. And then slowly swiped a card from his lap. And the fire in his eyes leaped.

And she scrambled. She grabbed the remaining cards and fell back, realizing that she was overplaying her hand, no pun intended.

"Maybe Go Fish should be done now."

"I'm pretty tuckered out," he said.

"Well, let me put your clothes in the dryer."

"I don't mind sleeping nude," he said, shrugging.

Her face went hot—like she was some inexperienced virgin, and she went to transfer his clothes to the dryer, and by the time she got back, he was in the sleeping bag. In her sleeping bag, bare-ass naked. And she thought, just for a moment, about what it would be like to join him.

"We better hit the hay," she said. And she got down into her own sleeping bag. "You sleep first. I'll watch something with headphones. I'll set a timer and wake you up and make sure that you're all right."

"I feel well taken care of," he said, grinning at her.

He was so unbothered by all of it. And it turned out that, with or without memories, that was the thing that bothered her about Chance Carson the most.

He made her extremely bothered. And she wasn't sure that she could ever do the same to him in equal measure. Then she reached out and touched his forehead. "Just checking," she whispered. His jaw went hard, his blue eyes hot. And she could well imagine what was going on down in that sleeping bag. And just like that, she felt much better. Because maybe, just maybe, he was a lot more bothered by her than she thought.

And why exactly did you feel the need to prove that?

Why exactly anything. It didn't matter, though, because in the morning, all would be well. She could send him packing on back to his ranch, and forget that this ever happened. Forget that they had ever sat across from each other playing cards while he was naked. Forget that she had ever given in to the impulse to flirt.

Forget that she had ever let herself fully acknowledge the attraction that she felt to Chance Carson.

Yeah. In the morning, everything would be fine.

Four

When he woke up the next morning, he opened his eyes and felt a sense of urgency. And it took a full thirty seconds for him to realize he had no idea what the urgency was directed at. Because he didn't know who he was.

Chance.

The name echoed in his mind as he went and got yesterday's clothes out of the dryer and pulled them on.

His name was Chance, but it didn't really tell him anything that that was his name. Except that his parents had some weird tastes in names. He closed his eyes again and tried to picture... Anything. But all he could see was the liquid dark eyes of the woman who had taken care of him last night. The woman who had fed him.

Watched over him.

And when he opened his eyes and looked to his right, there she was. Her dark hair had fallen into her face, and her beautiful features were obscured. But that didn't mean there wasn't plenty to look at. He stood, and he felt dizzy, and his head hurt like a son of a bitch. But he supposed amnesia was never going to be painless.

Not that he ever had occasion to think about it before. He didn't think. He couldn't actually be sure. Since he couldn't be sure about any damn thing.

But he knew this place. He knew this woman. And he held on to that as tightly as possible.

He was a ranch hand. He walked toward the door and opened it, looked out the cabin, stunned by the view directly in front of him. The little cabin seemed to be built into the side of a mountain. Overlooking a vast and beautiful view below. The pine trees grew up tall and proud, and the patchwork of bright and dark green mountains seemed to stretch on endlessly. He could see notes of desert out before them too, flat, rocky outcroppings and deposits of porous-looking lava rock.

And it felt… It felt curiously like home. He had to wonder if he was from here originally, or if it was just that he had gotten accustomed to this place. If this was just the place he had decided to settle. But it felt too deeply ingrained to be anything quite so transient as a recent move.

It felt like something else. Something more. He took a step down the porch, and closer to the edge of the mountain, taking in a deep breath.

There was something about the air in his lungs that felt right. It felt right. In ways that he could never fathom. In ways that he could never explain.

Then he started to look around. For something to do. For anything to do. Maybe if he got back to the task at hand, any task, he would feel more like himself. He didn't know why but he had the sense that he wasn't idle. That he wasn't the kind of man to sit around and let grass grow beneath his feet.

He had a feeling that he had chosen a life of manual labor. That it was something that appealed to him. That it was something that made him feel centered. And since he couldn't really be one with himself at the moment, he would take being one with his surroundings. He would take anything, really.

He saw a stack of wood, all logs, big old rounds, and there was an ax out there.

He could chop wood. For some reason, he had no concerns about whether or not he could chop wood. And before he could put any thought to it, his body went into action. He set one log up longways on top of a larger one, then picked up the ax.

He split it with one fluid motion.

It was easy. The motion fluid, and he was right. There was something about it that made him feel accomplished. That made him feel like he was himself. Even if he couldn't remember anything, even if he didn't know who that was, or practically what it meant, he was himself. He was himself and that mattered.

So he started burning through those logs, as quickly as he could, till his shoulders and chest, the back of his arms, burned like hell.

Until he could hardly breathe, but he was getting a big old pile built up the side of him. And he didn't know why, but he had a feeling that if... If someone could see him, they would be making fun of him. For being extreme. For... For whatever thing it was that was in him that made him like this. Because this was him. He knew that. It was the weirdest thing. Like a word being on the tip of his tongue and him not quite being able to figure out what it was.

"Hey."

He looked up and saw Juniper standing there. She was

wearing the same clothes from the night before, her dark hair a wild tangle. She made him ache. Not to know more about his life beyond this place. She made him ache to stay here. "What are you doing?"

"Cutting wood," he said.

"Do you think it's a good idea to be up cutting wood?"

"You're the EMT. I'm sure you can tell me whether or not it's a good idea."

"I don't think so," she said. "Hey…"

"It made me feel better," he said, cutting her off.

"It did?"

"Yes. It made me feel a little bit more like myself, whatever that is. In fact, whatever chores you have."

"Look," she said. "I need to take you somewhere. Your memory still hasn't come back and it made sense for you to be here last night, but going forward…"

"No," he said. "Do you know what anybody does about amnesia?"

She looked down. "As far as I know, they wait for it to resolve."

"Then let's wait for it to resolve. Here. I want to wait for it to resolve here." She looked hesitant. "Look," he said. "I don't know any details about myself. But I just know that I don't want to leave here. I don't know why. But it might be important."

"Chance," she said, her tone firm. "I'm not a doctor. I'm an EMT and you…"

"I don't want to," he said, his tone hard.

He didn't know why he was so certain he needed to be here. That he needed to be with her. The world was one entire lesson he had to learn, but for some reason, this place—she—felt like the one he had to learn first.

And he might have no real basis for that conviction, but it was strong and clear and real.

"Do you have jobs for me to do? Can I be useful here?"

She hesitated. "Oh. Oh. Well. Yes," she said. "The wood. Thank you. And… Well, I've been working on restoring one of the barns."

"You have been?"

"Yeah," she said.

"Well, let me come help with that."

"Chance…"

"I am a man who knows what he wants," he said. "Even if I'm not a man who knows who he is. And I don't think I take kindly to being told what to do."

She sighed. "No. But right now what you are is a very confident man with no memory."

"I have the feeling that I'm very confident," he said.

And she bit her lip as if she wanted to say something. Yet again, he wondered at the actual details of her relationship to him. He had a response to her that seemed to be bigger than just boss-employee. But then, it could be that he had been attracted to her already, and it was just that it was exacerbated by the fact that now he couldn't remember their roles.

"I have to get ready," she said. "You will probably also need a change of clothes."

"Yeah," he said. "That is true."

He didn't want to leave here, though. Didn't want to go to his home, or lean-to, or whatever it might be. She seemed to realize that.

"Why don't you go in and have a shower?"

"Sure."

"I'll… I'll be back with whatever you need."

Juniper was cursing herself all the way down to Shelby's place. And she knew that she would be cursing herself even more once Shelby heard what she wanted, because she was going to be pissed off at her.

Chance wanted to stay. And it was one thing to haul his dead weight, but quite another to think about forcing his big, muscular frame—*oh dammit, Juniper, can you not objectify the man even in this?*—out her front door if he didn't want to go.

But what if his family worried? Granted, there were lots of Carsons and they seemed to come and go as they pleased, and she had no idea how often they all communicated.

But Chance didn't have a phone or wallet or anything on him.

You could just tell him the truth...

No, she couldn't. It could harm him. Like waking a sleepwalker.

Also, he'd know you were a liar and all the nice things that happened last night would disappear.

That wasn't the problem.

It was the cognitive issues. That was it.

"Hey," she said when she rolled up to the door.

Shelby had chin-length hair, and rounder eyes than Juniper. She also had grooves by her mouth from frowning. She was younger, but life had really worn itself into her face. Juniper doubted it had been avoidable. Shelby had had a rough couple of years. And a better moisturizer would hardly have kept the evidence of her pain away.

"Can I come in?"

"Why?"

Juniper smiled brightly. "Can't I just come visit my sister in the morning?"

"You can," Shelby said, narrowing her eyes. "You *don't.*"

"I need to borrow some clothes."

"I am four inches shorter than you, Juniper."

She felt bad now, her heart squeezing. "No. I need to borrow some of Chuck's clothes." She softened her voice when she spoke of her former brother-in-law.

"Oh," Shelby said, her expression going blank for just a moment before she suddenly brightened. "Why? You got some dude naked up at your place?"

Juniper rolled her eyes. "Well. Yes."

"And he needs clothes?" Shelby smirked. "Are you a *quitter*?"

She couldn't help but laugh. Because of course her sister would take it there. "I have stuff to do. I can't lounge around naked all day."

"I wasn't suggesting lounging, J."

"I'm *aware*," Juniper said.

"Why doesn't he have a change of clothes?"

Juniper let out an exasperated sigh. "Look. It's complicated. Just indulge me. Just give me something for a man to wear."

"All right." Shelby stepped away from the door and let Juniper into the small, cozy house. It wasn't as old as her cabin, which had been built in the 1920s. This was straight out of the '70s with wood paneling and shag carpeting. It was the house they'd spent part of their childhood in, until their dad had built the sprawling, modern home their parents lived in now.

Even if it was a little dated, Juniper would always find it warm and lovely. Homey. She wondered how Shelby felt now, though. It was supposed to be her home. Her family home, and now...

Well, *now*.

Shelby led them back to her room, and suddenly, Juniper felt strangely uncomfortable.

Everything in there was untouched. Just as it had been. And Chuck's clothes were still in the closet.

"You know, you don't have to loan me anything if…"

"I need to get rid of it," she said. "It doesn't matter whether they're hanging here or not. He's gone. He's not going to come back. I'm not going to have a séance with his favorite flannel and get him to come say *hey* from the beyond."

"I know. But if you want to keep his clothes and not have another man in them…"

"It's you. It's not me. If it were me having a sexual partner who needed some clothes, that would be weird. And I would not do that." The very fact that her room was exactly as it had been, with her wedding picture on the nightstand and a closet full of his clothes, told her that there wasn't any chance of that, since there were no men coming over anyway.

"I just… I don't know when I'd be able to get these back and…"

"I'll just give you a pair of black jeans and a black shirt. I couldn't tell you the difference between those anyway. They're all the damn same. The man had no fashion sense."

He had also been quite a bit shorter than Chance, but Juniper wasn't going to say anything. Beggars couldn't be choosers, and anyway, she wasn't bringing up the fact that it was Chance Carson who needed the clothes. All the better to let her sister think that she had picked up a guy for an uncharacteristic one-nighter.

"You're not fucking around with Jamie, are you?" she asked.

"What?" The lovely blond man that she often worked shifts with had a boyfriend. But clearly her sister didn't know that.

"You were on shift last night," Shelby pointed out.

"Right," she said. "No, look, it's not like that. It's not… No. Not Jamie. Whatever. Don't worry about it."

"I can't help it. I do worry about you. You're my only sister. And you've been… Very moody lately."

"I am not moody," she said.

"Yeah, you are," Shelby said. "You're a moody beast."

"Hey, you're the baby. I'm the one that's supposed to worry about you. Anyway, you're the prime example of stability?"

"No." Shelby shrugged. "But I have an excuse."

"Sure. Play the grief card." Gallows humor was really the only way to cope. At least, the only way Juniper and Shelby had found.

"Glaaaaadly," Shelby said, drawing the word out and finishing it with a smile. "I have to get some benefit out of this."

She didn't think the clothes would be a great fit for Chance.

Not that she was an expert on his body. Not that she had been looking. A lot. Since she was thirteen years old.

No.

Well. She *wished* that were true. She wished that she were wholly and totally immune to Chance and his looks.

And really, she wished that she were immune to the god-awful pettiness that had made her decide she was going to play this game with him.

But there's a point to it.

Maybe there was. Maybe there really was. Maybe it was possible for him to begin to understand just why all of this was so important to her.

Maybe he could understand why the land was so important to them. Maybe without all the baggage from his own family, all of the ridiculousness, and the ridiculous male ego nonsense that had been entrenched in him over the course of their feud... That was it. It was that there was so much nonsense between them.

So much.

And maybe with all of this there would be less.

He'd seemed...human last night. And that made her feel something shift in her chest. She didn't like it.

Except, of course, when he remembered and... No. She wasn't going to think about that. He would've gotten to know her maybe a little bit and by then she would be... Humanized or something.

"What is that look on your face?" Shelby asked.

"What look?"

Her lips curved upward. "Your visitor must've been something else in the sack."

She shifted uncomfortably. "Why do you say that?"

"Because you are *spacey*."

Juniper snorted. "I don't get spacey over men."

That was true. She'd had a few boyfriends, but they hadn't been serious. And she hadn't been heartbroken when the relationship had ended. Hadn't missed them in her life or her bed.

Sex... It didn't matter that much to her. She had other things to worry about. Other things to focus on.

Her sister had been *so* in love with Chuck. He had been her one and only.

And she had acted sort of interested in the idea that Juniper had been able to have more than one partner.

But Juniper didn't see sex as anything more than a basic itch that occasionally needed scratching. And she had found often that it wasn't really all that scratched when all was said and done.

All to build up a little fanfare.

Minimal fireworks.

She didn't really know how to pretend that there had been epic fireworks.

Though, apparently, the distraction level caused by Chance was something that her sister imagined might be fireworks. Well, in fairness, it wasn't Chance himself that she found so distracting. It was the fact that she was lying to him. And that he had amnesia.

Yeah. That.

"Thanks."

"Want to have a coffee?" Shelby asked.

"I should… Get back. With clothes."

Shelby looked a little disappointed and Juniper went ahead and threw that disappointment right onto her guilt pile.

But Chance was *without spare clothing in her house* and that had to be solved.

"Right. Okay."

She scurried back out, got into her truck and began to drive back to the cabin.

And when she scampered into the house, she did so just as the bathroom door was opening, and Chance came out in nothing but a towel.

Juniper's jaw practically hit the floor. Maybe if any of the men that she'd been with had looked like this…

His body was unreal. She'd noticed that last night. Well. She'd noticed it a long time ago. But it still took her breath away. Broad shoulders, well-defined muscular chest, narrow waist with abs her grandmother could have grated cheese on for enchiladas.

All covered in dark hair that made her fingers itch with the desire to test the texture. The desire to touch them.

"Sorry," he said. "I didn't mean to ambush you."

He was *glistening*.

It was, like, not even fair.

"It's fine," she said. She took a step toward him and handed him the clothes, feeling like she could straight up sense the heat coming off of his body.

He disappeared into the bathroom, and she sat there, unbearably aware of her heart pounding in her ears.

When he reappeared, it was in black jeans that were two inches too short.

"Thank God for boots," he said.

"Sorry," she said. "They were my... They were my brother-in-law's. He wasn't as tall as you."

"Wasn't?"

Dammit. She hadn't meant to bring all this up.

"My brother-in-law, Chuck, died in a car accident a couple of years ago. My poor sister... She was devastated. She loved him. I mean." She rolled her eyes at herself. This was never easy to talk about, and it wasn't getting easier. "Obviously she loved her husband. It's just they were childhood sweethearts. It was deeper than it is for a lot of people. He was the only one for her."

"That's sad," he said. He didn't say anything for a long time. "Kind of amazing, to have the one for you. Even if just for a little bit."

She stared at him, and she didn't know if he was like this all the time, or if this was something to do with having all the... The *Chance* wiped away.

But maybe the Chance was there. Maybe she just didn't know him.

This is supposed to be making him like you, not the other way around.

She cleared her throat. "Yeah. I mean... I don't think she would've traded it for anything. It's just really sad."

"Of course it is."

She shook her head. "I mean, I know it sounds really dumb. But it is."

"You're an EMT," he said.

She nodded.

"Were you called to the scene of the accident?"

That he'd connected those two things, and then gone ahead and asked the hard question... It made her chest hurt. Made it hard to breathe.

She took a breath. "I... Yes. Jamie, my partner. He... He recognized Chuck. He knew. He told me not to come any closer. I was desperate to, but he said... Chuck was already gone. He spared me from the worst of it. I'm thankful." She tried to swallow, her whole body seizing up. Sometimes she was angry that she'd had to do it. Sometimes she was grateful. She could never decide which. "But I will never be over having to tell Shelby."

"Has that impacted your relationship?"

"If anything, it brought us closer. I was there for her during the hardest night of her life. I had to give her the worst news. Nobody should have to tell their sister that. And yet... Who else but your sister should tell you? Who else but your sister should be there to hold you?"

"That's an amazing perspective," he said.

"Maybe. We didn't have a choice. So we just make the best out of it. You ready?"

"Yep."

Without speaking, they walked out of the house and to her truck.

When they were closed inside the vehicle, she realized she had made another error. She hadn't fully considered what it would be like to be closed in the space with him. Hadn't fully considered the way he might smell. Or what it would feel like to be in such close proximity to him.

Her breathing became more rapid. And she felt like an idiot. Like a straight-up idiot.

And now she was basically hyperventilating. Her heart was going a thousand miles a minute, her senses were... Swamped with him.

He had used her soap. He had no other options. And it was just a generic bar brand, and it smelled so good coming off of his skin.

Like there was some magical Chance additive that had gone into it. It was him. His skin. The pheromones.

She wouldn't say she had wondered. What it would be like. If when they were done fighting they just... Fell into each other. If they tore each other's clothes off, and finished it that way. On the ground. On the floor of her cabin. Nowhere in her fantasies had they ever managed to make it to a bed. No, she and Chance Carson would never make it to a bed. They were destined to be against the wall, on the floor...

Nowhere, idiot.

Nowhere. They would never have sex anywhere.

He had never shown any indication that he might want to. Ever. And that was good. It was good.

"The barn is up here," she said, because she had to distract herself.

Good God, she had to distract herself.

"What kind of work are you doing?"

"Well, I've been reroofing."

"Reroofing?"

"Yeah," she said.

"By yourself?"

"Partly. I mean, mostly."

"Was I helping you with this?"

"No. We've mostly been... We have some cows. Not that many. And some horses, which is what I'm building up. And you mostly help with that kind of thing. Cows are mostly your thing."

The thing was, she didn't have any idea what Chance knew how to fix or anything. So she had to make sure that her lie was something he already knew how to do. Which was cattle ranching. She had a feeling he'd have the muscle memory for that. Not that she would actually let him get down to get anywhere near the cows. No. That was not going to be a thing.

"Well, I'm pretty confident I can swing a hammer as well as I can swing an ax."

"I appreciate it."

They pulled up to the old barn, and she suddenly felt self-conscious. It was nothing like the kind of barn that would be on the Carson spread. Where everything was new and perfectly kept. But then, he didn't remember that. So maybe he wouldn't judge hers quite so harshly.

He surveyed the place, and she watched his expression closely. "There's a lot of work to be done," he said.

"I know," she said.

"Don't take it personal," he said.

"About taking it personal. It's just that I have done a lot of work."

"I'm sure you have."

They got out of the truck, and she felt irrationally annoyed, and that made it feel a lot more like the Chance that she knew. It helped temper the attraction. That was the problem. He hadn't been annoying. So the way that she felt when he was around hadn't defused the fact that she wanted to punch him in his ridiculously handsome face. And now all was well. All was right with the world.

She understood herself when she wanted to punch Chance Carson in the face.

Maybe that was sad. But she didn't much care.

It was fair. It was more than fair.

She went over to the base of the ladder and picked up some tools. "Let's go," she said.

"All right," he replied.

He began to climb up the ladder ahead of her, hammer gripped in his hand. She suddenly worried about having him up there. And she wondered if she was being a little bit cavalier about his safety.

But physically, he seemed just fine. Everything seemed to be in fair working order, and it seemed as if he was capable of ladder climbing.

She came up behind him and found herself staring directly at his ass. It wasn't the first time she had looked at Chance's ass. But it was the first time she'd had such a prime view.

"You checking me out back there?"

Her head snapped up. "What?"

That had sounded more like Chance. Cocky. Exceptionally male.

"Are you checking me out?"

"I'm thinking about roof tile," she said.

"Sure," he said.

He looked back behind him, and he winked. The bastard winked.

She felt tetchy. But at least she wasn't mired in the sadness of a few moments earlier.

But then he got up onto the roof and was towering above her, and she scrambled up behind him, standing up as quickly as she could so she wasn't kneeling at his feet.

That was a bit on the nose.

"We got the nail guns all ready to go," she said. "So…"

"Let's get to it, I guess."

And he did. Making her own time on the roofing look sad.

"So you know how to do this," she said.

"I guess so. It's like the wood," he said. "I didn't know for sure if I'd ever done it before, but my body knew how to do it. So, I guess there are just some things that are like that." He looked up, and his eyes caught hers and held.

And she couldn't help but think of all the other things a person's body might actually remember how to do.

Oh. She didn't need to be thinking about that right now.

Remember how he's your sworn enemy, and you're just looking at his ass?

Yeah. She was sort of a disgrace, all things considered.

"Sorry about your brother-in-law," he said, between nails.

"Me too."

"You married?" he asked.

She huffed. "Have you seen a husband around?"

"No."

She really didn't need to be playing this brand of getting-to-know-you with Chance. And yet… She couldn't resist him.

"Ever been married?" he asked.

"Nope. Not even close."

"Why not?"

She shrugged. "Don't see the point of it. I think it's kind of bullshit, actually. I mean for me. Not for everybody else. My parents are in love. My grandparents are in love. My sister was really in love."

"So why is it bullshit?"

"It's just not for me. I don't think that I have the capacity for it. I don't know. I've never been all that worked up about any of the men I've hooked up with. Anyway, it doesn't work. Not doing what I want to do. A man can get a wife, I guess, to run his house while he works the land. I have to figure out how to do it all, and I've never met a person I wanted to try to fit into all that. On top of that, I just don't see how it would work practically." She swallowed hard. "I wouldn't respect a man who didn't have the drive I did. I couldn't be with a man who didn't have land. If he has his own land, he won't be coming to live on mine. And I certainly won't leave."

"A man ain't no kind of man unless he has land? I feel like I've heard that somewhere."

Of course, Chance didn't think he had land. But he did. A lot of it.

And that's your fault that he doesn't know, because you're a lying liar.

Yes, she was a lying liar. She felt kinda bad.

But not enough to *quit* lying.

Not enough to…

Not have him. Not have this anymore.

"Something like that."

"But?"

"If I was with a man who had the kind of ambition I did, if I was with a man who had land, then what would we do with mine? I just don't think things can work that way. Shelby and Chuck built their lives around each other. It wasn't about a ranch, or a career, for either of them. It was just about this life that they wanted to share. Everything was about each other. For my parents, it was about my dad. His business. My mom wanted to be a home-maker, and that was what she loved. She took care of us, she does beadwork, and just kind of works around all of her household duties. It's not anything she was ever ambitious with. My grandmother is kind of an extreme home-maker. She did everything joyfully, but busily. Always working. My grandfather was that way with the ranch. They share the homestead. And they were contributing toward it. If she had been doing that in one place, while he had been doing it with another, it would not work."

"And you wouldn't be happy with your horses on a different plot of land."

"No. I couldn't be. That's the thing. This is Sohappy land. And that means something to me. The heritage of it means something to me. I decided to pour myself into this at the expense of everything. I could never... I could never walk away from it."

"So, because of all that, you can't find a man who brings out strong feelings in you."

"Basically. I think that's the problem. I just... I'm not built for it."

"I wish I could tell you my story," he said. "The reasons that I think love and marriage are bullshit. But I don't even know if I think that."

"You probably do," she said. "Men who look like you..."

"Look like me?"

"Did you get a chance to look in the mirror?" she asked.

"Yeah," he said, lifting a shoulder.

"So you must know you're good-looking," she said. "I mean..." She waved her arm up and down.

"Thanks," he said. "I guess I didn't really think about it."

"Well, there's no point beating around the bush."

He laughed. "I guess not. You think I'm trouble?"

"I *know* you're trouble," she said.

And his eyes met hers again, and it felt hot and weighty, and she didn't like it.

"Just better keep moving before it gets warm," he said.

"It's funny," she said, letting herself become distracted. "It's funny the things you know."

"Yeah. I guess it is. Still don't know anything about

myself." And she could feel him staring at her, long and hard, and she didn't look back. "I feel like there's something there," he said. "Between us."

Oh, that was so dangerous. And it made breathing nearly impossible, and she hated him for it as much as she wanted to launch herself into his arms.

That, at least, was normal.

But she wondered…treacherously, she wondered… if that meant that without all the anger, without all the memories, without everything…

If he felt this.

If he had.

"You work for me," she said.

"Right."

And then they let that subject drop.

They worked until the heat of the day was too much, then they climbed down. Juniper went to the bed of the truck and took out a cooler, where she had packed a couple of boiled eggs and ham sandwiches.

"I don't know if you like ham," she said, handing him a sandwich.

"Neither do I," he responded. He took a bite of the sandwich. "I do," he said. "I'm hungry as hell."

She realized that one sandwich probably wasn't going to be enough for him.

"You can have my boiled egg," she said.

A paltry offer, really. One egg. But all things considered, she owed it to him.

The lying being considered?

"Awfully nice of you."

"Well," she said dryly. "You don't know anything about me, but I am *very nice*. That's what people say about me."

"Why do I get the feeling that's not strictly true?"

She shrugged. "I don't know. Not my fault if people are sometimes incorrect."

"I don't know much, really. Literally. But I sense that a lot of people are not as observational as they should be."

"I would agree. People get entrenched in their own ways. Their own beliefs, and they never really look at anyone else. They never look around. And never challenge themselves."

She was speaking of him, of course. Him and his outrageous prejudice against her. Him and his certainty that his ancestors were being truthful about who owned that section of land.

But she felt it. She felt it resonated in her own heart. In her own chest.

And she hated that.

This was all supposed to be about him. About getting him to see things in a new way, about getting him to respect her and her family.

It wasn't supposed to change her.

"Now we get to go inside and replace the floorboards."

"Sounds like a party."

Inside, there were planks that she had precut the other day with her skill saw. They were measured out ready to go, they just needed to be nailed in.

"Fun with power tools," he commented.

She huffed a laugh.

And what was really strange was that she was having fun with him. That spending the afternoon with him was better than spending it alone.

It's not him, though.

And she would do well to remember that.

"Have I met your grandfather?" he asked, out of the blue.

"Yes," she answered truthfully.

"Does he like me?"

Well. She wasn't sure if she should answer that truthfully.

"You're taking an awfully long time. I'm wondering if I'm not going to like the answer."

"He doesn't like very many people. Or rather, I should say he's not impressed with very many people."

That was true. Her grandfather was as crotchety as they came, and he had opinions. Big opinions about who was good, who was worthy of respect and whether or not he had to pay it to them.

She liked that about him.

He was a curmudgeon. He didn't let anyone know he had a soft spot, right at the center of his soul, that he reserved for the sky, the river and the land itself. That he was a man who loved the earth he'd walked on all his life more than most people loved anything.

He might not show his feelings, but he had them.

And it was so important to her—so very important—that she honored the trust that hard, stubborn old man had put in her.

He'd bypassed his son as the heir to the ranch.

He'd bypassed his son-in-law.

His belief was in her and it had been clear and bright from the beginning. And she'd taken the reins and promised to ride hard and true.

It was only now that sometimes…

Sometimes she wondered if she could love this ranch and this ranch alone.

Too late now.

"He doesn't have much use for you," she said. "But… That is actually true of most people. And my grandfather… He loves his family. He loves his dogs. He loves his land. Otherwise… Well, his feelings aren't all that strong."

He laughed. "I can respect that. As long as he's good to you. And recognizes how wonderful it is to have earned your admiration. I have a feeling a man could spend his whole life trying to get that, Juniper."

"Really," she said, her throat suddenly feeling dry. "What makes you think that?"

"You just seem like the kind of woman that doesn't impress easily. I like that about you. You seem like you're a whole thing."

"I am."

It was sweaty work, but they finished the flooring, and her stomach was growling ridiculously by the time they finished.

"I'm starving," he said.

"Luckily," she said, "I have some meals my grandmother made me in the freezer. I'll just heat up a double portion."

"I will never say no to a grandmother's cooking. Another thing I know deep in my soul."

"Great."

"And what are we getting tonight?"

"Stew. And bread. It's wonderful. She makes her own sourdough."

"And you don't cook?"

"No." And then she felt a kick of sadness inside of her heart, because she didn't cook because her grandmother did. Shelby did, thankfully, but she did sometimes wonder where the recipes would go when Grandma was gone.

"It's amazing that she still bakes," she said softly. "She's ninety, and she hasn't slowed down. But I worry. I worry it won't be long before she does. That's just life, isn't it?"

Maybe that was the problem lately. Time was marching on relentlessly. Chuck was gone and it marched on. Her grandparents were getting older and older and it marched on.

She was…just her. Just here.

And it marched on.

"I don't have a lot of specific memories about how life is," he said slowly. "But it seems to me that life really is like that."

Her chest got tight. "I guess I should ask for her recipes. But part of me doesn't want to. Because sometimes I think maybe when she's gone we don't deserve to have her food anymore. We should feel the absence there too."

"But it's heritage, right? Like the land."

"Like the land," she agreed.

They got in the truck and drove back to her cabin. And she was thankful that she hadn't run into anyone from her family. They didn't often come out this far, but it wasn't unreasonable to think that they might come to bring her some food at midday. It happened occasionally.

Her mom might not bake quite like her grandmother, but she would often bring bologna and mustard, or some chocolate chip cookies.

She didn't want to explain why she had Chance Carson working with her. And why Chance Carson didn't know who he was. And why Chance Carson thought they were maybe friends, and that he was an employee of the ranch.

No. She really didn't want to get into all that.

"It's a nice evening," he said.

"Yeah," she agreed.

"I notice you have a firepit out there. You want to eat dinner outside?"

And… She found that she did. She wanted to sit with him by the fire, and she wasn't even certain why.

"Yeah. In fact, maybe I'll get out the Dutch oven and heat the stew over the fire."

"Sounds great."

He'd said that to her more than once today.

Sounds great.

And it did funny things to her chest. Because Chance had never said that anything sounded great to her before. She might have said it to him, but that could've been when he asked if she would see something over his dead body.

Sounds great.

Except, when she had found what she thought might be his dead body, she hadn't done a dance or anything like that. In fact, she had helped him.

That made her feel a little better about her eternal soul. Sometimes she had wondered.

He got the fire going. Another one of those things he remembered, apparently. And she got the big Dutch oven, and the frozen block of stew, and got it set on a grate over the firepit.

There were little camp chairs that she set by the fire ring, and she brought out a couple of beers and handed one to him.

It didn't take long for the stew to start bubbling, and then she ladled it into tin camping bowls, and they sat and ate.

"Is this elk?" he asked.

She frowned. "Yes. How did you know that?"

"I've had it before. I mean, I just know. I don't know. I guess it's something I've had before."

"Obviously," she said. "Common out this way."

"Right."

"My dad is a big bow hunter. So we always have meat. I imagine that…" She almost said she imagined his dad was too. In fact, she was sure of it. But she shouldn't go saying things like that. Not when she was doing her best not to give him details about anything. Because it was the right thing to do, really. For the handling of the amnesia. But also she didn't need to go implicating herself in anything.

"I imagine you would've had it before." That finish was lame. And she knew it. But if he was suspicious, he didn't say anything. She stared into the fire, and then over the flames at him.

Dusk had begun to fall, and stars were punching their way through the curtain of blue velvet above, and as it darkened, they grew stronger. The light shining all the clearer for the darkness around it.

"It's a beautiful night," she said.

"Yeah. Such a strange time of year," he said. "Beautiful. But there's something sad. In these hours just before darkness. When it's warm still but the sun has gone away. I don't know why."

She stared at him, like she'd never seen him before, and she knew that he wouldn't even find it all that weird. He didn't know that she had seen him most days for a good portion of her life. Whether it was catching a glimpse of him across the Thirsty Mule on a crowded Saturday night, or in the grocery store, or when she saw him, silhouetted by the sun, riding across Carson land.

Those moments when she wanted to hate him but felt something else instead.

"But you just know that?"

He seemed to be wrestling with it. Or concentrating hard, like it was a feat to hang on to it.

"It's a feeling. It's a feeling that I have as strong as anything."

"I see. Well… I guess maybe it's long nights?"

He shook his head and stared past her for a while. And she had the feeling when he spoke again, he wasn't speaking to her, but using words as a way to write this truth on his heart. So he wouldn't lose it. "It's something more than that. I can see a little girl. A little girl and… She's not mine. Because I'm a little boy. She's very sick."

"Oh."

"That's why I don't want to go to the doctor." He sounded far away then. "She went to the doctor all the time. Hospitals. So many hospitals. All the time. A never-ending rotation of them. When she died, it was late spring like this. One of these long nights."

The sounds around them were amplified. The flames licking over the wood, cracking. The crickets, insistent, rhythmic, somewhere in the darkness.

"Who was it?"

She didn't know. This was a story about the Carson family she didn't know.

"I don't know. I just know that I see her. And that when you asked me if I wanted to go to the hospital, I thought no. That's where people go to die. And she's why I think that. Because she was a little girl, and one day she went into the hospital and she never came out."

An overwhelming, heavy sadness pervaded Juniper's chest.

"You know, I take people to the hospital every day," she said. "They don't just go there to die. They go there to be healed. I understand that there can be bad traumatic memories connected to that. But… But the hospital can be a good thing."

"Logically I know that. But…"

"I'm sorry," she said. "I'm sorry that the first memory you're having is so sad."

"I think it's probably the strongest one I have. Because

I think I felt that sadness inside of me before I ever saw her face. What a hell of a thing. That I almost died. Out there in the field. When…"

"When what?" she whispered.

"My parents have been through enough," he said. "She must've been my sister."

"Oh." The word left her body in a gust.

He knew what it was like to lose someone. He was… human.

Just the same as she was.

Just the same as they all were.

The Carsons and Sohappys weren't so different.

She was hoping he might see that during this time, but she hadn't expected it would be her own lesson.

She…she had never heard anything about that and she didn't know why he thought it. Or if it was true. And it still settled hard in her chest.

He was getting way too close to remembering things, and it was getting… Dicey. It was one thing to think that she wanted to endear herself to him this way, but him sharing something personal like this, something he never would've shared otherwise, it felt like a violation. And she had never thought that she would feel like she violated Chance Carson. But this was different. The situation with his sister.

No. He had a sister. And she was alive and well.

Callie Carson was much younger than him, and she had gone off and married a rodeo cowboy who lived in Gold Valley.

But the way he was talking about it, it sounded like he was younger.

She felt hungry for more, but at the same time she didn't want to press him. For so many reasons, but maybe the biggest one was her heart felt so tender right now. For him.

That wasn't supposed to happen.

"All right," he said.

He stood up, and she stood at the same time, ready to take his bowl from him.

"I can take the dishes."

"Oh no, that's okay," he said, and she put her hand on the bowl, and her fingertips brushed his, and their eyes locked.

And she felt a frisson of something magical go through her. Something hot and delicious and sticky like cayenne honey, flowing all the way through her veins.

And she could hardly breathe around it. She could hardly think. All she could do was stare. And feel the thundering rhythm of her heart, like a herd of wild mustangs, the kind that you could find out here in Eastern Oregon, and she was sure that he could hear it too.

And then, gradually, that didn't worry her. Because she could see in the look on his face that he was... Hungry.

Hungry for her.

And she had to wonder if this was new, or if it had been there before.

Just like it was for her.

Maybe they felt the same.

She'd always thought she and Chance Carson felt absolutely different. About everything. But maybe not.

Maybe they felt the same.

Maybe they always had.

She opened her mouth to say something, but then he lowered his head and kissed her.

It was like an electric shock. His mouth was hot and

firm, his lips certain and miraculous as they moved against hers.

She clung to him, instinctively, and it wasn't until she heard the bowl clatter to the ground that she realized she had let go of the metal vessel. And she was glad it wasn't glass.

But it was a metaphor. A metaphor for how precarious this was. Because she was forgetting. And she was letting herself get caught up in all the wrong things.

But she couldn't help but be caught up now. In his hold, in the searing kiss, the magical pressure of his mouth on hers. She'd had any number of kisses. But they had just been something to do.

Because when you thought a man was attractive, you might as well kiss him. Because even though it wasn't like she had gone to bed with that many men, she had never found it to be that big of a deal, and if she was in a relationship, she was all right taking it to its natural conclusion.

A kiss had never scalded her like fire, searing her and leaving her feeling empty, a hollowed-out vessel forged by flame.

But his did.

She was so hot. Everywhere. And she ached. Not just between her legs, but in her chest. It hurt how badly she wanted to be close to him.

How much she wanted to tear away their clothing that stood between them, how much she wanted to press herself flush against him with nothing between them.

She had never wanted like this. This quickly. This violently.

It was a sickness.

But it was a beautiful one.

She clung to his shirt, then pushed her fingers through

his hair, arching against him, rubbing her breasts against his solid chest like a cat.

He growled, and then rolled his hips forward, and she could feel the insistence of that hard length between them.

On the floor. Against the wall.

She had thought about this.

And she wanted him. But… He didn't know who she was.

He didn't know who he was.

She jerked away. Horrified. And she realized that she was snared in a net entirely of her own making.

"I'm sorry," she said. "I'm sorry. You work for me and…"

"But that's not all there is between us, is there?" he asked, his voice going husky.

No. Of course it wasn't all there was between them.

Of course it wasn't.

But she couldn't say that. She couldn't explain. Anyway, the explanation didn't make things any clearer. The explanation was even more confusing. He wasn't her employee. And they weren't having a secret assignation.

They were enemies. Caught between a family feud, and nothing more. Two people who had driven each other nuts for an age. Not anything deeper than that. How could they be?

"It's just… I'm sorry. It's not right. It's not right."

"I'm a man," he said. "And I know that. For certain. Whether or not I have all my memories. I know how to cut wood. I know how to fix a roof. I know how to put in a floor. I think I can figure out how to…"

"That's not what I'm worried about. I am worried about taking advantage of you."

As she stood there with her head coming up to the

middle of his chest, she realized that what she was saying sounded ridiculous. But she understood.

Way to go, Juniper. Caught in the net of your own idiocy.

"I'm sorry I…"

"It's all right," he said. "Look, I can leave if you want. I don't need to stay here. I can go back to my own cabin if it…"

"No. I'm fine. I don't… It's not you. I promise."

"I'm not going to hurt you," he said.

"I know that," she said. "I trust that. You have never… You've never given me any indication that you would. No matter… No matter what. Even if we were fighting."

"All right." He nodded slowly. "As long as you trust that."

"I do."

Five

Sleeping on the living room floor in Juniper's place was more uncomfortable tonight than it had been the other night. Because he was hard as a rock and unlikely to find sleep. But he had meant what he'd said to her. He wouldn't make any advances on her. No matter what. Not if she wasn't interested.

It was hilarious, her being worried about his consent. He had made his pretty clear. But then, she had concerns about his memory. Or whatever.

Even if we were fighting.

That word came flooding back to him.

Fighting? Had they fought? The way she said that made it sound like they had. Sometime.

And he couldn't help but wonder why. What about. She had acted like she only vaguely knew him, but he was starting to get the impression that wasn't true.

He was up before the sunrise and set about fixing coffee and eggs.

Juniper woke up not long after, dressed in utilitarian gear, clearly ready for her shift as an EMT.

He found her fascinating. And beautiful.

"I'll see you later," she said. "I have to work. I... I'll bring you back some more clothes."

"Sure," he said.

"Sorry you just had the one spare outfit. Sorry about... Everything."

"None of it's your fault."

"How are you feeling about staying here?" she asked.

"It's still what I want," he said. "If you don't mind."

"No," she said. "Not at all. If this is where you want to be, then... Great. I... I'm happy to have you."

"Hey, can I head over to the barn and do some finish work for you today?"

"Sure," she said.

"I'd like to keep helping out. I'd like to make myself useful in my invalid state."

"I appreciate it. You don't need to do that."

"But I enjoy it," he said.

And that was that.

He left the cabin and went out walking. There wasn't a vehicle left up at her cabin, so it was up to him to make it there on foot, but he didn't mind. He remembered the route to get down there, and it was a pleasant walk.

The stormy weather of a few days ago had vanished now. Spring flowers making themselves known, dots of yellow and orange in a brilliant field of green.

His mind was pleasantly empty. And right now, it felt pleasant. It was strange, how he knew that this was different, even though he couldn't quite remember what it was like to have his mind be full. Last night had maybe been a preview of that. He had been so preoccupied thinking about the things that had happened with Juniper, that thing that was niggling at him that she'd said, that he hadn't fully marinated on that memory from his childhood. The little girl. His sister. He was sure. Even though he didn't know her name. Even though he didn't really know his own name—not beyond what Juniper had told him—he felt a sense of certainty over the images there. In the feelings they created. He had been a child. There was something different about his eyes and those memories. And there was something about the pain in his chest. The way that it bruised. As if it was a fresh betrayal brought on by life. Not just another of life's bullshit moves.

No, this had been something unique. Something special. The pain that was the first of its kind. Back when the world seemed bright and full of possibility, this had been his first indicator that things could go terribly, horribly wrong.

It had shaped him, this pain. It had changed him. There was a before, and there was an after.

Even without his memories, he was still living in the after.

But he chose to focus on the day around him, and not on those memories, and he wondered if that was what he did. If he was the kind of man who didn't dwell on hurt, if he was the kind of man who simply walked forward.

He walked across the field and made his way over to the barn. He climbed the ladder, ready to do the work now. He began to nail more tiles into the roof surface, and right as he was finishing one section, he stood, and his boot heel wrapped around the edge of the cord. He pitched forward, and he saw the ground far below rising up to meet him. But he didn't fall. He caught himself.

But still, it took him back to a moment, and suddenly, he could see another fall in his head.

He had fallen off the horse. His horse. He had fallen off of his horse and hit his head on the ground. While he had been riding the line between Carson land and Sohappy land.

Carson land.

He had been on Carson land, because he was a Carson. And Juniper Sohappy was his rival.

By the time Juniper pulled into her sister's property, she was exhausted. She had stopped at the Thirsty Mule and had picked up burgers to go, and had had a difficult time making eye contact with Cara Thompson, who was Jace Carson's best friend, so even though she would never be outright rude to Juniper while she was in the woman's place of business, she didn't like Juniper, and she didn't do a very good job of hiding that fact.

If only she knew. If only she knew that Juniper had Chance squirreled away up at her cabin, and Chance didn't know who he was.

She had worried about his family and their concern for him before, but now that she knew about their loss, it…

It ate at her.

As soon as Juniper closed the door to her truck, her sister's front door flung open, and her sister came bounding outside. "What the hell?"

"What?"

"I saw Chance Carson up on the roof of your barn today, wearing Chuck's clothing. And so you have to answer my question."

"I do not guarantee that I will answer your question," Juniper said, her mouth going dry.

"Are you going to pound town with Chance Carson?"

"Don't say *pound town*," Juniper said, practically covering her ears.

"Doing the horizontal Macarena?"

"Stop it."

"*Screwing.* Are you *screwing* him?"

"I am… I am not *screwing* Chance Carson."

Of course, the truth was so ridiculous she should probably stick with the story that she was…banging the man, because her sister was never going to believe that Chance Carson had amnesia, and that she had lied to him, and they were currently doing a modern-day dramatic reenactment of *Overboard* with him as Goldie Hawn to her Kurt Russell.

No. That wouldn't go over very well at all.

But she had to try and explain. Somehow.

"He…" She scrunched her face. "He got hurt."

"He got hurt?"

"Yes."

"Why was he naked at your house?" she pressed.

"He wasn't naked at my house specifically. I mean, he has been. You know, when he was showering or changing his clothes. Not *with me*. But he fell. Off of his horse or something, the details are fuzzy. And I found him in the field unconscious. I took him back to the cabin because it was the middle of the night and we're so far away from the hospital, and I am a professional, so I looked at his head, and he had a concussion…"

"None of this explains what he is doing there, and why he is wearing my husband's clothes."

She hedged. "He can't remember anything."

"He can't *remember anything*?"

"No," she said. "Least of all that he hates me. I mean, that he hates all of us."

"Oh, Juniper."

"I might have… I might have a little bit told him that he's working for me."

"Do you have a death wish?" Shelby practically shrieked that question.

"No. I don't have a death wish. I don't wish to be dead at all."

Shelby's dark eyes were wide. "He's going to kill you."

"No, he isn't."

"When he finds out that you were lying to him, that you made him do menial tasks for you while he didn't remember who he was, he is going to *kill you*. Strangle you with his big, capable, roof-repairing hands."

"You are being a drama queen." But there was a thread of truth to her words that disquieted Juniper.

"I'm not being a drama queen, you're being a sociopath. And, I grant you, Juniper, I really admire the brand of crazy that you're being. Because this is petty on a level that I could never even aspire to. And I value pettiness. I value it with all of my being. I am so deeply impressed by this, but I worry for your safety. Because if you are by yourself when he finds out…" She suddenly stopped talking, and her eyes went wide. "But are you *sleeping with him, though*?"

"I'm *not* sleeping with him," she said.

"Not even a little?"

"How do you *a little* sleep with someone?"

Shelby huffed a laugh. "Oh please. You're the one who has had multiple sex partners."

"Don't say it like that!"

"More than me anyway, and I think you know exactly how you can a little bit sleep with someone. Are you sucking his…"

"No." She needed Shelby to not finish that sentence. Badly. "I kissed him. Once. I told him that it couldn't hap-

pen again. Because I'm not actually a sociopath, Shelby, and I cannot sleep with a man who thinks that he works for me, when he is in fact my mortal enemy. I will screw with my mortal enemy all the livelong day, but I will not take advantage of him physically in that way."

"Well, thank God you have some scruples remaining in you. But this is deeply disconcerting."

"I don't know what to tell you. I just… It just happened, it tumbled out of my mouth. I was very tired, and then there was no going back."

"I don't even know what to say."

"Get me some clothes for him, or…"

"He's going to have to walk around the cabin naked."

Her face went flushed. She could feel it. "No," she said. "He will not be walking around naked."

But what a visual that was.

"I have deep concerns for your safety. You need to have your walkie-talkie on you at all times. When he finds out, and he literally tries to kill you."

"He isn't. He isn't going to try to kill me. He's… Look, the worst part is I kind of like Chance. I mean, Chance without his memories."

"It's *not* Chance," Shelby said insistently. "We're not who we are without our memories. If I didn't remember all the horrible shit that happened in my life over the last couple of years that…"

"It might be nicer?"

She sighed wearily. "It might be nicer. But I probably wouldn't be me. And the minute that he remembers, he will be him, and he's going to go back to being the person that he always was. This isn't really him. You have to remember that."

"I know. I promise you I'm not going to get hurt."

Shelby sighed. "Right." She said nothing for a moment. "But how good of a kisser is he?"

There was a keen sort of interest shining in Shelby's eyes and Juniper knew why. But they never talked about it. Ever. It was an unspoken law.

Never mention Kit Carson, or the way Shelby looked at him.

So she didn't. Even though she wanted to.

Juniper growled. "Just get me some clothes, please."

Shelby returned with a stack of clothes and handed it to her with a skeptical expression. Juniper snatched them close to her chest and looked at her sister's hopeful expression.

"He kisses like a dream," she relented.

"Oh, that is really good to know. The Carson men are... Well, they are problematic."

"Agreed."

"So are you," she said.

"Noted," Juniper shouted as she ran out of the house, ignoring her sister's further calls to not get murdered by Chance.

She got into her truck and drove back up to the cabin. And when she got there, Chance was standing in the doorway.

But it wasn't Chance, the man that she had spent the past several days with.

It was Chance Carson.

The *real* Chance Carson.

And he did in fact look like he might have murder on his mind.

Six

He could see the moment she registered what was going on. He could see the second she realized that she was looking at him. Really him, not the man that she had been playing around with for the past few days.

No.

She was well aware of who she was looking at in that moment, and he was fascinated. What would she do? How would she try to talk herself out of this? Would she? In his experience, Juniper was confrontational. A hellcat if ever there was one, and the little creature was more likely to bite than anything else.

He looked at her face, and he waited. Then she held up a bag that was in her hand and smiled. "I brought hamburgers."

Interesting. That's how she was going to play it.

She was going to make him say it.

"I'm not in the mood for hamburgers," he said, crossing his arms and leaning against the post on the porch.

"That's too bad," she said, her grin somehow brightening. "I would've gotten you a salad if I would've known."

"I don't want a salad."

"Well. I guess there is some middle ground between a hamburger and a salad. But I didn't realize. I'm sorry."

"You know what I would like?" he said.

"What exactly?"

"I'd like an explanation."

Her eyes darted left, then right, and she put him in the mind of seeing her as a scared bull, trying to figure out which way to scurry.

There was no way to scurry. Not from him.

"Well, I finished my shift, I am quite tired, but I stopped at the Thirsty Mule anyway to grab some hamburgers from Cara. You don't know who Cara is, though." That smile became all the more determined.

"I don't?"

"Not as far as I know," she said, smiling sweetly back.

And that was the thing, the weirdest thing. What hit him then was that while he hadn't known who she was, she had known who he was the entire time. She had been well aware that he was Chance Carson, that they theoretically hated each other, and she had kissed him.

Enthusiastically.

Had pressed that tight little body up against him and practically begged for his touch. In fact... He had a feeling that if it hadn't been for his memory loss, she would've taken it all the way.

She had weird lines, did Juniper. Apparently, there was no issue lying to him and using him for manual labor, but she wasn't going to take advantage of him sexually.

He supposed he should be grateful for that. Not that he would've felt overly taken advantage of.

"Not as far as you know," he repeated. "You know, I've been thinking," he said.

"Have you?"

"Yes. I've been thinking about the kiss the other night."

"Oh."

"It was good."

"I… Yes." Her face was scarlet red, and he could see her doing the dance. He could see her uncertainty. Maybe she wasn't entirely sure if he remembered or not, and it was making her nervous. Making her uncomfortable. Good.

He took a step toward her. "I'm not in the mood for hamburgers. I'm in the mood for another kiss."

He knew that his voice had a dangerous edge, and he could see her respond to it. Could see her pupils widen, could see her breath get shallow. She was afraid of him, but she was also intrigued. She was aroused. Turned on, and more than a little bit interested by what was happening between them.

He felt a smile curve his lips, and he knew it wasn't a kind one.

"I told you it wasn't a good idea," she said.

"Right," he said. "You're so worried about taking advantage of me."

Rage thrummed through his veins as he advanced on her, as he moved to cup the back of her head with his hand.

Her hair was so soft. She was soft.

And he never would've thought that Juniper Sohappy was soft.

He'd've thought she would be like embracing a cactus. All prickles and spikes, and maybe hard steel underneath.

But no. She was a woman.

She smelled like honeysuckle and the warmth of the sun. She was impossibly beautiful. And he wanted her.

And dammit, he felt owed.

She had been screwing with him. Laughing her ass off having him do her chores while he couldn't remember anything.

All over a piece of land?

And he had told her things that... Things he didn't talk about. Because he didn't remember that he didn't talk about them.

It was a damn shame.

But nothing he couldn't correct by getting some of his own back.

He watched as her pulse fluttered wildly at the base of her throat.

She was a beautiful creature. He wanted to lick her there. Run his tongue along the smooth column of her neck.

And he realized right then that what he wanted more than anything, more than punishing her, more than making her pay, was to make her scream.

Beneath him. Above him. However she wanted it.

He had buried that. All these years he had buried that. He had acknowledged that she was beautiful, but he had never allowed himself to fully give in to the desire that arced between them every time they fought. But her kissing him back had proved that she felt the same, and it had opened the floodgates of his own need.

And honestly, the worse she was, the more of a little weasel she was, the more he wanted her. Angry and hard and complicated.

Chance didn't do angry, he didn't do hard, he didn't do complicated.

Chance liked a bar hookup with a pretty, easy girl who didn't have any connections to his actual life. Chance liked a woman who was there for a good time, not a long time. He liked to keep it easy. Because he didn't like complications. Because complications meant entanglements, and entanglements meant attachments, and attachments were just something he wasn't willing to do.

For all the reasons he remembered now. Deeply. Keenly.

"Don't you want to kiss me again just a little bit?"

"No. I was being stupid. I was being crazy. And I…"

He closed the distance between them, kissing her hard.

And there was no way that she wouldn't be able to read the difference between this and the previous kiss. Because they were nothing alike. In this kiss, he poured all of his frustration. All of his rage that she had tapped into something emotional inside of him that he preferred to never acknowledge. Into this kiss, he put every ounce of withheld desire. All of the need that he had chosen to shove down deep for all of these years. Because he couldn't sleep with Juniper. She was the bane of his existence. She was…

She was the damned sexiest woman he had ever held in his arms, and his body felt like it was on fire.

He had never been so angry at a woman in his entire life, and at the same time he was utterly and completely helpless to battle the desire that he felt for her.

So he kissed her. Kissed her hard, held her face and angled her head just so he could take it deep. His tongue sliding against hers, stoking the fire in his midsection that left him shaken to his core.

And he didn't do shaken. He didn't do anything like this. "Kiss me back," he demanded.

And she whimpered, wrapping her arms around his neck. He felt the bag of burgers hit him square between the shoulder blades, but he didn't really care.

He arched his pelvis against hers, let her feel the intensity of his arousal.

"Chance…"

"Tell me," he said.

"Chance…"

"Tell me what you did," he said, reaching down and cupping her breasts, squeezing one, rubbing his thumb over her nipple until she gasped with desire.

"Tell me what you did, Juniper."

"I didn't… I didn't do anything."

He arched his hips forward, grinding the evidence of his arousal against the cleft between her thighs, and she shook, shuddered.

"You're a little liar," he said.

"And you," she said against his mouth, "are a fucking asshole."

"Am I? Am I the one who lied to a man that couldn't remember who he was?"

"Am I the person that is trying to steal somebody's land out from underneath them?"

"I told you to get a fucking surveyor, Juniper," he said, curling his fist into her hair and pulling, angling her head back as he kissed her deeper. "Did you think about doing that?"

"You pay for it," she spit, then launched herself up on her toes and kissed him again.

He picked her up, just a couple of inches off the ground, and walked them both backward into the house. He slammed the door behind them, grabbed the bag of hamburgers from her hands and flung them down onto the couch.

Then he set her back down, staring down into her eyes. "Too far," he said. "You went too far."

"I saved your ass, Chance."

"Well, thank you for not leaving me out there to get eaten by coyotes, what a fantastic example of your humanitarianism. You truly are the best of us, Juniper."

"Screw you," she said.

"I'd rather screw *you*," he said.

And he grabbed the top button on that EMT uniform and flipped it open.

Then he did the next button, and the next, revealing golden-brown curves that made his mouth water.

"You always knew it would end here, didn't you?" he asked.

"You're such a bastard," she said, reaching out, her hands working the buckle on his belt. She undid the snap on his jeans, then reached inside, and the breath hissed through his teeth that she curled her fingers around his cock, squeezing him tight.

"Such a bastard," she said, but this time the words had no heat.

And her mouth dropped open, a small whimper escaping. She licked her lips, then looked up at him. "You're so big," she said.

And that did it. That absolutely undid him. Juniper looking at him and talking about his size, the venom gone from her voice... There were spare few novelties left in the world for him.

He had experienced loss, grief, he'd had well more than his share of sex, but this... This was a truly new experience.

And he hated that he was betraying to her that he was

so damned basic. That all it took to get his engine revved was for a woman to say something like that.

Not a *woman. Her.*

It's the fact that it's her.

"And you are the sexiest little demon I've ever seen," he said. "Shame about your personality."

"Shame about yours," she said, still gripping him tight and running her hand up and down his aching shaft.

"Let's get you out of this," he said, undoing the rest of the buttons on her top and flinging it down to the ground.

Her bra was simple, black, but displayed her glorious cleavage to perfection.

He lowered his head, licking the plump skin there, tugging down one side of her bra and revealing her nipple, sucking it deep into his mouth until her head fell back and she gasped.

She held on to his head as he sucked, teased her. With his other hand, he smoothed down her back, moving to grab her ass, squeezing her as he continued to tease her.

He could feel her begin to tremble. Her whole body on a razor's edge.

"You're gonna call my name so many times that neither of us will ever forget it," he said against her mouth.

"I'll make sure to spell mine," she said. "That way it gets in there good."

He did away with the matching navy pants she was wearing, and with the bulky uniform dispensed with, he could see that she was all woman, all curves.

Her underwear did not match her bra, and there was something about that that got him hot.

This wasn't a woman who had been expecting to have sex.

Black bra, white panties with little red roses.

"Cute," he said. "I didn't take you for a delicate little flowers kind of girl."

"It's not that deep. I bought a package, white, beige and floral."

"You are something else," he said.

"Don't fall in love with me."

He laughed. And kissed her again. "No worries," he said. "I'm not in any danger. We're going to have a lot of fun, though."

And he hauled her up off the ground again, this time lifting her completely so that she could wrap her legs around his waist.

While he walked her back to her bedroom, she grabbed the back of his shirt and tugged it up over his head. He let go of her with one arm, then the other, so that she could free the entire garment. Then she cast it onto the ground. She put her hands on the center of his chest, running her fingers down his body.

"It is such a nice chest," she said.

"I like yours too." He reached around and unhooked her bra, freeing her breasts and revealing them to his gaze. "Fuck," he said. "You're so damn sexy."

"Good," she said, and she had that same wicked smile on her face that he felt on his own when she'd said he was so big.

There was just something about it. Knowing that the person who hated you more than anything was completely spellbound by your body. Couldn't do anything to fight this. Because, dammit, if they could, they would. She had done something that was unforgivable. But he didn't like her anyway.

Sure, for a minute, he thought he did. But then he remembered himself. And it had been different. It was all different.

And he wasn't worried about it.

He was going to have her.

He was going to have his way with her until neither of them could walk.

He flung her down onto the bed, then kicked off his boots and took the rest of his clothes off along with it.

Her eyes went round. She gripped the edges of her underwear, and she made them down her legs, leaving her spread out and naked for him on the bed.

He growled and came down over her. "Little witch."

"Asshole," she said, putting her hand on his face.

And then he kissed her. With all the pent-up hunger inside of him. And this wasn't as angry as the rest. Because he was past anger now. All the fire in his blood was desire. And he was desperate for wanting her. She sighed and arched against him, her legs falling open, and he put his hands between her thighs, stroking the wet seam of her body, moving his thumb in a circle over that sensitized bud there.

And then he pushed a finger into her, then another, working her as he kissed her. Until he couldn't take it anymore.

He didn't take a slow, leisurely trip down her body. He just moved quickly, dragging her hips up to his face and licking her deep, making her body arch up off the bed. "Yes," he said, lapping at her with all the need inside of him.

He tasted her, licked her, sucked her until she was sobbing, until she was begging. He pushed two fingers inside of her and stroked her until she whimpered. He added a third slowly and she started to shake, her thigh muscles trembling as he sucked her deep into his mouth while pushing deep.

And she broke. She grabbed hold of his hair, pulling

hard as her internal muscles pulsed around his fingers. As her release ripped through her, seemingly going on and on.

He was so hard he could scarcely stand it.

He had never believed in blue balls before, but he did now.

If he didn't have her, he was going to combust. Or something was going to fall off. And he didn't want that.

"Please tell me you have some condoms," he said. "I don't have any of my shit."

"I do," she said.

She hurried off the bed and into the bathroom, and he heard her rummaging around. It took her a minute, but she finally returned with a strip of protection.

"It's been a while," she said. "I don't really need to just keep them by the bed."

"I'm not judging either way. I'm just glad that you have them."

It hadn't been a while for him. Or maybe it had. Maybe it had been forever. Maybe this was the first time. Maybe this was the only thing that mattered.

He wasn't sure anymore. Everything was mixed up and jumbled up inside of his head, and the only thing that really made sense was her.

She went back down onto the bed, and he took one of her arms and pinned it up over her head. Then he did the same with the second, the pose trapping her beneath him and raising her breasts up like an offering. He lowered his head to them again, sucked one briefly into his mouth, then another.

He positioned himself at the entrance of her body, and she was so tight and wet he groaned.

"Please," she begged. "Chance."

"Say it again."

"Please, Chance," she said.

And he thrust home. She arched up off the bed, a rough cry rising in her throat. And she met his every stroke, thrust for thrust.

Her nails digging into his skin as he drove them both to the edge of sanity.

And then when he couldn't hold on anymore, he pressed his face into her neck and bit her.

And that was when he felt her lose her grip.

Her climax took him off guard, the force of it tearing through him like a wildfire. Her internal muscles clenched tight around his cock, and he lost it completely.

He moved his hand down to her hips, gripped her tightly as he thrust into her three more times, hard and fast, before spilling himself.

"Juniper," he said, unable to hold back the exultation of her name. Unable to do anything but simply... Praise her.

He lay down beside her, his chest pitching with the effort of breathing.

"Hell," he said.

"I can't move," she said. "You killed me."

And then she laughed.

"What?"

"My sister said you would kill me."

"Your fucking sister knows?"

"My fucking sister *saw you*," she said. "I ended up having to tell her."

"You owe me," he said.

"I'm... I what?"

"I'm not kidding. You crossed the line."

"We have to talk about this right now. Have you ever heard of an afterglow?"

"I don't think you get an afterglow with hate sex," he said.

"Was it hate sex? Or was it just undeniable sex?"

"A good question," he said. Because he had to wonder if maybe it was more undeniable than he would like. He had to wonder if maybe they'd been headed this direction the whole time. So maybe not as directly, all things considered.

"In what way do I owe you?"

"You're going to have to come work for me."

"I am not working for Carsons," she said.

"You have no choice. You slept with me. You lied to me. And there are quite a few things I could do with that."

"Are you… Blackmailing me?"

He hadn't really intended to. And he didn't quite know what all was going on inside of him just at the moment.

But it seemed reasonable. It seemed reasonable, the idea that he would bring her to Carson land and force her to do the same amount of labor that he'd done for her.

Or maybe it's not that at all. Maybe you're just trying to get your own back because you spilled your guts about Sophie and now she knows.

"I'm not working for you."

"I could probably call the police, Juniper."

"And tell them what? You had amnesia and I made you work for me? Yeah. I'm sure that Deputy Morton would be very interested in that. She is my friend, by the way."

"Then maybe your grandfather would be interested to know that you have a hard time keeping your hands off me."

"You… You're horrible," she said. "I cannot believe that I just did that with you."

"You can't?"

Their eyes met, and she looked away.

"Maybe you should just do it because you feel bad."

"I will never feel bad for you. I will never feel bad for any Carson."

"Let me know when you have a day off coming up," he said.

She rolled out of bed and stepped away from him, and he watched the gentle jiggle and that rounded curve of her ass as she stalked into the bathroom.

She was soft. Curvy. He liked it.

And he hadn't had sex with her to enact any kind of revenge. It was just that it was… Convenient.

She came back in a moment later, fully dressed. "How about this?" she said. "I'll come work for you. I will debase myself as your farm girl. But in the end, you agree to look into what happened between our great-great-grandfathers. And into the way the card game happened. If your family has a record…"

"I'm sorry, I don't think you're in a position to negotiate," he said.

"Maybe not," she said.

And he realized that they were at the end of everything. Of common sense, of dignity. He had been filled with an insane amount of rage, and rightly so. But it had led here. And now he was trying to use it against her. And maybe they did need to settle it, once and for all. But his pride wouldn't allow him to do it for nothing.

"All right, Juniper Sohappy, you have yourself a deal."

"You know I don't have time to come work for you."

"I know. Maybe use some vacation time."

"You…"

"You'll get your evidence, if it exists."

"Good," she said.

"Get time off."

"Get out of my house," she said.

"Now… I'm going to need a ride," he said.

She reached over to the nightstand, grabbed her keys and threw them at him. "I'll have my sister drive me, and I'll pick up the truck tomorrow when I report for work."

"Well, then. See you bright and early."

And he began to collect his clothes, and he had a feeling it was going to take a hell of a long time to sort through everything that had happened over the last few days.

Seven

She had to submit for time off and she was furious about it. But that was a good thing, because when she wasn't furious she felt overcome by the memories of what it had been like to be in bed with Chance.

The way that he had touched her, the way that he had… The way that he had filled her.

And that bastard had gone ahead and proved her own fantasies were wrong. Oh, it had been intense. It had been angry. But he carried her right to bed, and there was something in that, when her previous, shame-filled fantasies had always been centered around them not making it to a bed.

No, it infuriated her.

And also left her hot and bothered in a way that…

Sex had never been like that for her.

Forget multiorgasmic, she had never even been consistently orgasmic. And even then, often it had felt muted.

She had always been more concerned about how she looked, the way that she was reacting. All these little things that really shouldn't matter, but did.

And she found herself stalking over to Shelby's house, because she was going to have to explain her absence. And she... Well, she would rather have Shelby be the keeper of the information, and not her parents. And definitely not her grandparents.

"Still alive, I see," Shelby said.

She laughed bitterly. "Oh yes. But he knows."

"Oh no," Shelby said. "What happened?"

And she felt... She didn't want to talk about sleeping with him.

Because what did it say about her? She had been... She had been angry and so turned on when they had been fighting. She should've resisted him, but it had never even entered her mind to do that. She had just... She had just wanted him. And what kind of insanity was that? Just wanting a man who so clearly hated her. The malice in his eyes as he had advanced on her...

But then he'd kissed her. And gradually the quality of the heat between them had changed.

Gradually it had become about something else.

And by the time he had buried his head between her legs and...

Well, she could honestly say no man had ever done that quite like that before.

He was a beast.

And she had... She had loved it. She had always sort of considered herself practical about sex. Not that she would say she wasn't sexual. She got the urge like anyone else. Just that it wasn't a driving factor in her life, or anything she needed all that frequently.

But after all that with him, she was ruminating on it quite a bit more than she would like to admit.

"Well, I am being blackmailed," she said.

Shelby sputtered over her coffee. "You're being blackmailed."

"I guess that's a little bit dramatic. But he is making me work for him. Tit for tat."

"Well," Shelby said. "All things considered… It could be worse."

"Don't tell me you're taking his side."

"There's not really a side here. You play games with dangerous predators and you win… Well, you win whatever the predator is going to do."

"You don't know anything about this. You don't know anything about predators."

She laughed. "Maybe not. But I'm smart enough to know I wouldn't screw around with one of the Carsons."

"Right. Well. So I'm just imagining the fact that your cheeks get pink when Kit Carson goes by?"

She felt guilty. She really did. Because Kit Carson was a closed subject, and Juniper knew it, and yet here she was, talking about him.

"There's nothing between me and Kit Carson," Shelby said.

"Doesn't mean you don't look at him."

"I'm not dead," Shelby said. "That's the thing."

And she knew that she was dancing dangerously close to things that she ought not to touch.

"Fine. I just wanted to let you know, in case anyone asked. I am doing some work on a friend's ranch."

"A friend."

"Well." She sighed. "And I'll get Chuck's clothes back for you."

"Thanks," Shelby said. "I probably shouldn't hold on to them."

"You love him," Juniper said.

"I do," Shelby agreed. "I do love him, but I think that that isn't… Isn't helping. It doesn't do anything. It doesn't bring him back." She shook her head. "Any more than hanging on to his clothes or his pocket knives or… Or anything."

"It doesn't make it go away," Juniper said.

"No," Shelby said. "It doesn't. It would give me more space, though."

"Well, I guess at a certain point you'll decide what you need more. His things or space."

"True," Shelby said. "Right now… I don't really need the space. You be careful."

"What do you mean? You keep acting like Chance is dangerous. We may not like each other, we may be involved in a feud, but…"

"No, the problem is I think you do like him. I think you always have. You have a conflict with him. But if you didn't…"

"It doesn't matter. I do. Grandpa hated Chance's grandfather. Until Chance makes it right, what Grandpa feels like…"

"Why is it up to Chance to make it right? And why is it up to you to fix it? Your great-great-grandfather caused all this bullshit."

"It was Chance Carson's great-great-grandfather and…"

"Hey, maybe he cheated him. Maybe he took advantage. What happened happened."

"That's easy for you to say, Shelby. This isn't up to you."

"Why is it up to you?"

She nearly exploded. "Because I promised. I promised

him. And I said it would be easy and I could do it. I have to be the one because there isn't another one."

Shelby looked like she pitied her then, and Juniper could hardly stand it. "If our great-great-grandfather couldn't fix it. Or our great-grandfather. Or our grandfather. Or our father... Why do you think you can?"

Because then she'd know. She was right.

She'd done right.

"Because," she said, knowing she sounded frustrated and childish. "Because somewhere, deep down, I kind of assume he *does* care about what's right."

"I see. And it's not just about the Carsons, it's about him. That's what it always comes back to. The way the two of you fight about this."

"It does not always come back to the two of us."

"It does, Juniper. It always has. Like I said, what if there was no feud? How would you feel then?"

"It doesn't matter."

"You kissed him."

"Well, yes," she said, her cheeks going hot.

"And?"

"It doesn't matter. Because he is who he is, and I'm who I am. And all that matters is that this might finally settle things between us. He agreed to get the property assessed. Based on old records..."

"You don't have the money for that."

"He does. He agreed to pay."

Shelby arched a brow and crossed her arms. "I'm worried what that's gonna cost you."

"Again, you're acting like..."

"It's your emotions, Juniper. I am worried about your emotions. I am worried that you have feelings for this man. And if you spend more time with him, something is going to happen and..."

Juniper's face went hot.

Shelby's eyes narrowed. "Something already did. You're not telling me something."

"It doesn't matter."

And then her sister's eyes widened. Comically. "You *slept with him*."

"Maybe. Well, there was no sleep. He stormed out after."

"Oh."

And suddenly, Shelby took on the manner of an indecisive squirrel. Her body jerked one way, then another, and Juniper wondered what the hell was happening with her sister.

"What?"

"I'm trying to decide something."

"What are you trying to decide?"

"I'm trying to decide if I want to know the details."

"Why?"

"Because I would be lying if I said that I wasn't curious about…well. There are a lot of Carson men."

Juniper narrowed her eyes. "Kit. You are curious about Kit. And you think hearing about his brother will give you insight."

"Why are you fixated on Kit?"

"Because you're fixated on Kit. I'm not an idiot. He has made you into a little bit of a stuttering mess since you were sixteen."

Her sister's face flushed, but this time it was with anger. "I was with Chuck when I was sixteen. The fact that I got embarrassed around an inarguably cute boy is not an indicator of anything."

Except she thought it probably was. She thought it always had been.

But there was no having the discussion. And maybe

there was really no point. Juniper had never been very good at letting things go. The entire incident with Chance being a prime example of that.

"Tell me you've never had a sex dream about him."

"Get out of my house," Shelby said, only a little bit kidding.

"It's really big," Juniper said.

Shelby bit her lip. "Thank God."

"Right?"

There would've been nothing sadder. Nothing sadder at all than evidence that all those tall, handsome men were over there and they were... Lacking.

But she could say with certainty, Chance was not lacking at all.

"It's just good to know," Shelby said pragmatically. "That there are some things in the universe that make sense."

"I guess. Though, if I hadn't made a very bad choice and slept with a Carson, I might've found it amusing if they had all been cursed with teeny-weenies."

"Yeah. But a handsome man is a handsome man. And a waste of all that...would be a waste of all that. Feud or not."

"Yeah. Fair," she said.

"I'll cover for you."

"Thank you."

"Don't have sex with him again."

"I won't. It was a onetime thing. The truth is, it had been... Brewing. And the whole explosion when he got his memory back was the tipping point. And I don't think it's going to combust like that again."

"It better not. Protect yourself."

"Aye, aye, captain."

And as she left her sister's house, she purposed in her

mind to let go of fantasies of Chance. She purposed in her mind to rid herself of impure thoughts entirely.

She was going to work. She was going to keep the goal in mind.

With any luck, this feud would finally be over. Or maybe it would still simmer beneath the surface, but she would be proved right.

And as far as she was concerned, Chance Carson could die mad.

Eight

"I don't see any cattle."

That was Chance's greeting when he got back to Evergreen Ranch.

"Well, that's because I didn't go get them," Chance said. "Where the hell is my horse, by the way?"

"Hell if I know," Kit said. "Keep track of your shit."

"Yeah, I don't know," Jace said.

"Is she here?"

"Why don't you know?" Boone asked.

Well, he was going to enjoy *this*.

"I don't know," he said, "because I have had amnesia."

His brothers exchanged a glance. Seated around the table outside one of the barns, where they all took their lunch, they had been eating sandwiches and planning the day when Chance showed up.

He had stopped off at his cabin and taken a very long shower.

Put on some of his own clothes that actually fit, and tried to make absolutely certain that he had his thoughts together.

"You do not have amnesia," Boone said. "That is idiotic. That's like the time we told Kit that Dad was going to sell him to a traveling band to play the washboard and set him out at the edge of the property at ten p.m. He believed it because he was eight. We're not eight."

"I did," he said. "I spent days not knowing who I was, and I don't know what happened to my horse."

His brothers looked at each other. "Seriously," Boone said.

"Seriously. I don't know what happened to my horse, who I can only assume ran back here. But I'm a little concerned about her."

"Well. I don't know. It's entirely possible one of the hands did something with her."

"Great," he said. "Not only did you assholes never try to contact me, and get concerned about me, you don't know where my horse is."

Flint frowned. "Where *have* you been?"

"It's a long story," he said. "However, it ends with the fact that Juniper Sohappy is going to be working here. She owes me."

"Well, I need to hear the long story," Kit said, kicking back in his chair. "Because you're claiming to have been struck down with amnesia and now I hear Juniper Sohappy is involved. So it is story fuckin' time."

This was the part he was looking forward to less.

"Fine. She found me, she rescued me. But I didn't remember who I was. And she told me that I was her ranch hand."

Boone just about fell out of his chair. Kit was laughing so hard that Chance thought he might choke, while

Jace was shaking his head, his eyes wide. "Well, damn," Jace said.

"Yeah. So."

He noticed they were happy to believe the amnesia thing now.

"I knew she hated you," Boone said, wiping tears off his face, "but that is really something. So she held you hostage all this time?"

"Yeah. Torture every hour."

"Really." Boone and Flint looked at each other.

"Shut the fuck up," Chance said. But he couldn't even really be mad, because they were right.

He had in fact slept with her. That was in fact a thing that had happened.

"We'll behave ourselves," Flint said. "When she gets here. Unless you don't want us to. Which would be fair."

"She and I have an agreement."

He wasn't going to get into the whole thing with the card game and looking for evidence that may not exist.

Because then they really would ask what the hell he was doing.

Because why he had agreed to meet any of her demands, he really couldn't explain. She didn't deserve it. That was the thing. That was the bottom line. She didn't have any kind of high ground. She didn't have any kind of upper hand. It made no earthly sense that he was giving it to her.

"I'll see you guys around. I'll be devising torture for Juniper."

"Return torture," Boone said. "My favorite."

"You're a dick," Chance said as he walked away.

And right when he got to the main through road for the barn, Juniper pulled in.

"Howdy," he said when she rolled her window down. "Welcome to Evergreen Ranch."

"Thanks," she responded.

"You can park over this way."

Thankfully his brothers had cleared out by the time he got to the barn. He didn't want to deal with them on top of having to deal with her.

"All the trainees start here," he said.

She rolled her eyes, then rolled the window of the truck up. She killed the engine and got out, and his gut went tight at the sight of her.

She was wearing a tight black tank top and a pair of formfitting jeans.

Much more flattering than the EMT uniform.

And he knew what her body looked like underneath all that now.

Knew that the promise of the spark that had burned between them all this time was barely even a preview of what it could be like between them.

He was a lot taller than her, nearly a whole foot, he reckoned. And yet they had fit together perfectly.

And he was trying to keep his mind on the task at hand, and not on her, but it was difficult. Because last night was still fresh in his mind.

"I'm investigating to see if my horse actually made it back," he said.

"Oh," she said. "I didn't know you fell off your horse."

"I did. I can't remember quite what happened. Something. Something must've spooked her. She's a good mount, and normally steady, but…"

They went into the barn and went down the stalls. Most of them were empty, because his brothers had taken their horses out for the day, but there she was.

"Geneva, you turncoat," he said. "You left me to die."

"Now, you leave her alone," Juniper said. "I think she's a discerning woman."

"She's not discerning of shit," Chance said, shaking his head. "She's a termite is what she is."

"I won't hear a word said against her."

"You can choose any of the horses that are left," he said. "Lefty is pretty good. Cheech has a bad temper."

"Well, so do I. I guess I'll settle for Cheech."

She did so, and while they were getting ready, she ran her hands over the horse lovingly. "Ex-rodeo horses?"

"For the most part. Not all."

"I never did know how I felt about the rodeo."

"Believe me when I tell you, nobody cares more about their animals than the people who breed them for those events. They're worth more than the cowboys. Trust me."

"I guess I can understand that. In the sense that I know a lot of people don't get that cattle ranchers care about cows more than just about anybody."

"Damn straight," he said. "We're connected to the way everything in the world works. To the way it's fueled. Life, death and the cost of all of it."

"I never would've thought we have something in common."

"Well, there you go, we have a couple things in common. Caring about our animals, and a mutual enjoyment of having sex with each other."

She frowned deeply. "How do you know I enjoyed it?"

"Please. You were basically putty."

"Maybe I'm easy," she said.

"Somehow, I don't think so. Somehow, I think you're a little bit of a tough nut, Juniper Sohappy. And I think I cracked you."

"Please. Men really do think highly of themselves."

"I think pretty highly of you too."

"So highly that you're forcing me to do manual labor for you?"

"Payback for the work I did for you."

"Fine," she said. "That's fair enough."

"Yeah. Sometimes I am. And if you would stop being mad at me for the sake of it, you might see that."

He got on his horse, and she mounted behind him, and the two of them took off, with him leading the way.

They walked the horses down over a bare rocky ridge that ran along the river.

This was high desert.

The rocks ran the gamut from pale tan to adobe red.

The sagebrush that was scattered throughout the landscape was scrubby and vile. The deer liked to eat it, but it gave them a particular flavor that Chance had never been fond of.

Because of course he actually did know the taste of venison, the taste of elk and the different regions where they tasted different, because of what they ate.

Because now he understood himself, and his memories, and it was no longer a mystery.

He felt a strange… A strange stab of envy for the man he had been just two days ago who hadn't known a damn thing. Who had been strangely excited by the things that he knew, and unencumbered by… Everything. The only thing he had known for sure was Juniper.

And that had been interesting.

To say the least.

Great. He missed being a simpleton. That was really something.

He shook his head.

"There's a whole bunch of lava rock down in here, and you can find agates," he said. "Me and my brothers used to spend hours down here hunting rocks. It was our favorite spot to go."

"I can imagine you running wild around here. And getting into all kinds of scrapes," she said.

"Oh hell, yeah. One time Boone got bitten by a rattlesnake."

"Really?"

"Yeah. Oh man, he held off on telling Mom and Dad as long as possible, because he was sure that he was going to get his hide tanned. And he was right. Dad was so pissed off."

"He was mad that Boone got bitten by a rattlesnake. At *Boone*."

"Yeah. We weren't watching. We weren't being responsible. We knew better."

"Still, that seems a little odd."

"It's just that they had so much to worry about, what with…"

He cut himself off. Because he didn't really intend to talk about Sophie.

He never did. It was just that he had already told her, in a roundabout way. And that was the problem.

He had already explained certain aspects of that part of his past, even without the details.

And it had made him feel freer now.

"Well, at the time my parents had a lot on their plate."

"Right. Well, I never got bitten by a snake. But Shelby and I used to run all over the ranch too. It's funny, how we didn't really run into each other."

"You stay to your side, we stay to ours. It stands to reason."

"Yeah." She chewed her bottom lip. "My grandfather really hated yours."

"A lot of people did," Chance said. "He was a difficult bastard. It doesn't surprise me that your grandfather hated him. I'm not sure that any of us were ever especially fond."

"Really?"

He shook his head. "Yeah. I don't know. To hear my dad tell it, he was mean. Mean as a snake."

"That isn't how I imagined you would feel. And if that's true…why do you care so much about the land? I know why I do. I love my grandfather, what matters to him matters to me."

"Because we're not carrying this on for him," Chance said. "We're carrying it on for us. To be more, bigger, better than the name he established for us. To be stewards of the land and everything that inhabits it." He grinned. "To get rich."

"Ha!" She belted that laugh and it echoed around them.

"Hey, in my estimation, my grandfather did one valuable thing. He had my father. And whatever his father was like, I don't know, but it's because of them that we are here. My mom and dad… They're good parents. Getting mad about rattlesnakes notwithstanding. They love us."

"Yeah. So do mine. We just want different things. We care about different things."

"You care about the ranch," he said.

"Yes," she said. "Just about to the exclusion of everything else, if I'm honest."

"Why do you care about it so much?"

"I remember once in school I was doing a group project, and this kid got mad at me for having an opinion. And he told me to go back to where I belong. You know, my country." She held her arm out in front of her, showing her brown skin. "And I didn't know what to say at the time. All these things stuck in my throat, chief of which were how stupid he was. But… I realize that the ranch was where I was from. It rooted me. Grounded me. And even when people were ignorant or assholes or whatever... They can't take that from me. I belong here. I love it here."

Chance's stomach turned. "You might've told him to go back to where he came from."

She laughed. "Yeah. I thought about it later. Unfortunately, at the time I was just... Shocked. And sad. But the truth is, even though I didn't give him the thousand comebacks that I have inside of me now, I found my sense of resolve that day."

"I'm sorry that happened to you."

"Don't you think there's a little bit of that in this whole dispute?"

He stopped his horse and turned to face her. "Not for me."

"With our grandparents."

He looked surprised. "I don't... Probably. Probably. I can't say no."

"I think your grandfather, your great-grandfather, thought they deserved it more. Because they think they're more important."

"I'm sorry," he said. "It never occurred to me."

"Why would it?"

The simple question was a stinging indictment.

"Look, this is dumb. Why don't we figure out how to share?"

"No," she said. "I want to know. I really want to know. If you have paperwork that says anything about the ownership transfer, I want to see it. If you have family history. I don't want you to give me something because you feel guilty. And if...if he lost it fairly, if there's a way to know that..." She sucked in a breath. "I'll buy it back."

"You don't have the money," he said pointedly, and he saw her flinch as he did.

"I know. But I'll figure it out."

"What if there are no answers, anywhere?"

"There have to be some," she said. "Talking helps."

"Usually we just end up yelling."

"Yeah, I guess this is a step toward being functional adults. What a novel concept."

"We behaved like adults the other night," he pointed out.

And he regretted that, because he didn't need to bring it up. It just made it far too easy to imagine everything that had passed between them. And how damned good it was.

"Right," she said. "Except the aftermath."

"You have to admit," he said, because the reminder of her behavior brought him right back to reality, if nothing else would, "that what you did was…"

"All right. Lying to you wasn't my best move. But honestly, I couldn't tell you everything. You're not supposed to do that, because of shock. I needed you to have realizations on your own. Also, I sat up with you all night, I made sure that you were okay. I didn't leave you out in the middle of that field."

"I know," he said.

"What bothers you the most? That you did some labor for free? Or that I had to take care of you? Because I think maybe that's part of the problem. That and the fact that maybe you don't hate me."

"If I don't hate you, then you really don't hate me," he said.

"Well, I had to see you as a human being for a few days."

"Must've been a trial," he said.

"No. It wasn't. That's the problem."

"Well, I didn't know who you were."

"I wanted you to understand," she said. "I wanted you to understand why it was important. Not with all of what you think you know sitting there in your head. So I'm sorry if I made a weird choice. I'm sorry if I made a bad choice. But the land means the world to me. My grandfather means the world to me."

"And what would your grandfather say if he knew about us?"

"There's not an us," she said.

"I meant the fucking, Juniper, but I was trying to be a gentleman."

"He'd die," Juniper said, looking at him straight on. "Then and there. My grandfather will not be knowing about us. Not ever. He can't. I've given up too much to have a romp in the sack ruin my relationship with him."

"A romp in the sack? Wow."

"Oh, don't give me that, it's not like sex is sacred to you."

He looked at her long and hard, and what he hated most was that the word she'd used just now felt more right for this thing between them than any other he could think of.

He said nothing. He just snorted. "Well, I'm not in any hurry to spread it around."

"My sister knows," Juniper said. "But I can't keep anything from her. It doesn't work."

"My brothers know too, but it's not because they're insightful, it's just because they're assholes, and I didn't tell them anything. But they're going to think what they think no matter what. And they've always thought that…"

"They've always thought what?"

Sacred.

No, just sex. And sex he'd wanted for a long time, in

fact. Maybe that was why it was notable. Maybe that was the only real reason why.

"They've always thought that I wanted you."

"I see," she said. "And are they right?"

"What do you think?"

"What's your favorite spot on the whole ranch?" she asked.

He looked around and pointed down at the watering hole below. "That spot. All the good agates are there. And you can jump right in from those rocks. And the water goes way over your head. You feel like you're never going to touch the bottom. We used to play here all the time."

"It's nice," she said.

"Yeah. That's one of the last memories I have of all of us together. Before Buck…"

"What happened to Buck? I barely remember him, because he's older."

"He had that accident. He… He didn't want to stay after that."

He could never understand his brother's decision to leave.

Buck hadn't been the one drinking. He'd been badly injured all the same.

But it had something to do with his friend's death, he knew that.

But he had never understood what required Buck to leave home, to leave his entire family when they all would've supported him. But it was like he just didn't want to be here anymore.

And his absence had created some strange, hard feelings around town.

Especially with the family of his friend.

"Yeah. It's been rough without him. But I have a surplus of brothers."

"Well, you were all close."

And he thought about Sophie again, in spite of his best efforts.

"Yeah," he said. "We are close. We don't take family for granted. You can't take family for granted when…"

He stopped talking. And she didn't push him.

"How close are we to the border of your land?"

He knew she would know.

"Not far. Maybe two hundred yards."

"I want you to show me your favorite spot."

"I haven't done any work so far," she pointed out.

And he realized that he'd lost the thread of what today was supposed to be. He was supposed to be punishing her or something. He was supposed to be making her work. And they should've gone the rest of the way along this trail to get to the fence that needed fixing. But they could also do it later. They could do it later and it would be just fine.

But suddenly none of it seemed as important as this.

And it wasn't just because he was attracted to her, though he was. There was something else.

Something about the way the sun glinted off of her hair, and the way she smiled. Or the way she frowned.

There was just something about her.

"Show me," he said.

"Okay," she responded. "If you really want me to."

"I do."

She moved her horse forward, leading the way, jogging the animal down the side of the trail.

He laughed and took off after her. It was an easy ride. Not for beginners. It was for people like them, who knew what they were doing, knew the land and knew how to push the limits.

"You actually ride in the rodeo?" she asked when

they were on a flatter part of the trail, moving into the more lush part of the land, pine trees suddenly becoming thicker and more prevalent.

"Yep," he said. "I can't say that I was the best. But I had a good time. Saddle bronc, mostly. That is generally my family's game."

"Oh. Not bulls."

"Boone rode bulls."

"Maybe I should've slept with Boone."

He shot her a look, and she grinned.

"Oh, so it's like that," he said.

"I'm a woman of discerning tastes," she said.

And he didn't think they had ever gone this long without acting like they were going to kill each other. So that was something.

They pushed their way through the trees, and the trail narrowed. "This is out way far away from anywhere my parents ever go to. And my grandpa quit moving through the whole property a long time ago. His mobility just isn't what it used to be. But this was my and Shelby's secret spot. The trees seem to grow over the trail, like a rounded entrance into some kind of enchanted world, and we imagined that if you were a child, that was exactly what you would see."

Especially what two girls would see.

"We always said there were fairies," she said. "There was a movie about that. Fairies in an English garden? And we were obsessed with it. And we used to imagine that they were here. I love this place."

There were purple flowers and ferns growing beneath the trees, and it was just entirely different to the landscape they had just come from.

There was running water nearby, and it took him a

while to realize that it was a stream. It probably fed into the larger river that they had just come from.

And at the end of the stream was a little pool. "Not deep enough to jump in," she said. "But perfect for floating. Which is what we used to do."

"It's beautiful," he said.

"This place means so much to me," she said.

Then she got a mischievous glint in her eye, turned around and pulled her shirt up over her head.

She didn't know what she was thinking. Stripping while still on the back of a horse. It was crazy. And she had decided that she wasn't going to touch him again. Because it was foolishness. Absolute lunacy.

Because it wasn't anything that she needed to do, and it was in fact something she absolutely shouldn't do.

But then, she didn't know why they were out spending time together. Riding around their favorite childhood spots rather than working or sniping.

And then she'd done that.

Oh well. She was committed now. She dismounted, unhooked her bra and threw it down where the shirt was. Then she stripped off the rest of the way and slipped into the translucent green water. It was like an emerald here under the trees, and the still pool with its large rounded stones at the bottom had always ignited her imagination. Had always made her feel like she was part of something wonderful. Part of something bigger than herself.

Part of something magic.

Her grandmother believed so strongly that there were things in the world that no one could understand. That nature itself had breath, and it was constantly speaking to them, flowing through them.

And it was here that Juniper could feel that for herself.

Here that she felt touched in a spiritual way. And she had brought Chance to this spot. She really didn't know what she'd been thinking.

She felt vulnerable, exposed, and it wasn't just because she was naked.

"Join me?" she asked.

He got off his horse and pulled his shirt up over his head, revealing that delicious body to her gaze.

How could she ever go back? To hating him. She wanted to. It was simple.

Even just admiring his body, she had hated him.

But now he had touched her. And he was a generous lover, she couldn't overlook that. And what it said about him.

He wasn't a man who just took. He was a man who gave with talented fingers and a wicked tongue. He was a man who seemed to derive as much pleasure from hers as he did from his own.

That's just sex. It has nothing to do with the content of his character.

Well, that was a good reminder. But it wasn't doing much to penetrate her thinking right now.

He was completely naked in a moment, and then he joined her in the pool, his eyes intent on hers.

"Normally, I wouldn't be too thrilled about being in a pool of cold water in front of a beautiful woman. But thankfully, your beauty far outweighs the cold."

"Well. That is… Bizarrely flattering," she said.

"In the absence of anything else, always take bizarrely flattering."

"I'm not sure what to make of this," she said. "Given that you're my mortal enemy and all."

"Yeah, why me specifically?"

She knew the answer to that question. Because she

was supposed to hate the Carsons, and from the first moment she had ever seen Chance Carson, hate was not the dominant emotion. She had been fascinated by him. She had been completely and utterly transfixed from day one, and there was something about the directive given to her by her grandfather, and that feeling that had made her feel violently angry with him in that first moment. When she had been eight and he was ten.

She remembered it so clearly. It may not make sense. And it may not be fair, but it was the truth.

She had liked him, and she wasn't allowed to. And she loved her grandfather more than she loved any other person on earth, and wanting a Carson was a violation of their family. Of their name.

Of all the promises she'd made to be worthy of being the one who took over the family legacy.

So she had done her best to turn that all into anger. She had done her best to turn it all into outrage.

But it hadn't worked. At least, not consistently.

And here she was. Naked in the water with him again.

"Chance..."

"You're beautiful," he said, closing the distance between them. And he kissed her lips, the heat of his body cutting through the icy water and making her tremble.

He wrapped his strong arms around her, crushing her breasts to his chest. "Dangerous," he gritted against her mouth.

"Why?"

"I don't have a condom."

"I'm on the pill," she said. "As long as you're... As long as you're good."

He nodded. "Yeah."

"Me too."

The fact of the matter was, she always doubled up on

her protection. This felt alarming and like a step into something new. But she wanted him. And she didn't want to wait for him. Because if they waited, they might come to their senses. If they waited, then they might realize that they shouldn't do this.

But she didn't want that realization. She wanted to feel him against her. Inside of her. She wanted to kiss him until neither of them could breathe. She wanted to chase down her pleasure with him.

Only him.

"I always use…"

"Me too," she said.

He understood. He didn't say anything, but he understood. That she'd never let a man do this before. And she felt breathless with the anticipation of it.

She waited for him to shift their positions and surge inside of her, but he didn't. Instead, he angled his head and kissed her. It was maddeningly, achingly slow, something completely different to the way they had come together in anger only recently. It was painful, almost. The care that he took with each corner of her lips. To make sure he kissed every inch. And then he began to look into her. Slowly. She moaned as he took the kiss deeper and deeper. As the desire between them became a burgeoning flame, and he kept it banked. It was the control. The absolute, maddening control that got her.

Because she felt like she was going to vibrate out of her skin, and he seemed to enjoy it. Didn't seem bothered. Not in the least.

His big hands roamed over her body, all of her curves, and he made them feel beautiful. Made them feel precious. She wasn't toned. Wasn't insanely physically fit, but she liked the way that it felt when he squeezed her tight; he made her softness feel sexy, and it was a novelty.

It was more than a novelty. She couldn't pretend that's all it was. Some simple fascination and nothing more. No. It was everything.

This moment was everything.

She moved her hands down his chest, his damp chest hair. He was just really beautiful.

And she was going to take this moment and drink it all in. Drink him in, because she didn't know if it would ever happen again. She didn't know if she would come to her senses. She should… Go now. She should come to her senses and put a stop to all of this. But she really didn't want to.

No. She wanted to savor it. To live in it.

And so she would. Now. Because now they were past the point of no return. Now there was no going back.

It didn't matter what anyone would think. Because it was only the two of them, here in the fairy grove, here in this place that was the closest she had ever gotten to showing any other person the deepest part of her heart.

She wondered if he realized. She wondered if he knew.

She watched as her fingertips skimmed over his ab muscles, over the ridges and dips and hollows in those beautiful, corded muscles.

He was hard. Solid from all the work that he did. And she loved the contrast between their bodies.

Loved that he was masculine to her feminine. And she couldn't recall ever having luxuriated in that before.

She didn't think about her femininity much. It didn't matter to her.

He deepened the kiss, pulling her up against him, and she parted her thighs, wrapping them around his waist and moving her hips restlessly against him, trying to do something to soothe the ache there.

"Be patient," he said, nipping her lip.

"No," she said. "I'm not patient. I want you."

"Say my name."

And she realized that if there was ever a taboo fantasy, for her, this was it. It had been.

"I want you, Chance Carson."

It couldn't be any more blatant if she had asked him to take her on their disputed property.

He shifted their positions, and she felt the blunt head of his arousal pressing up against the entrance to her body. Then he surged inside of her, bare and hot, and she could tell even there in the water like this. She gasped. And his eyes met hers, intense and beautiful. And it terrified her then, how well she knew that face. How close it was to hers, and how much she wanted it to stay that way.

She wasn't really in conflict with herself, not anymore. And she had spent a whole lot of time wanting to see him only so they could fight, while the underlying issue was that she wanted to see him.

But she wasn't lying to herself. Not now. She just wanted to be close to him.

He began to move, his movements hard and intense, his mouth set into a firm line as he began to push them both closer and closer to paradise.

She gripped his shoulders, digging her fingernails into his skin, digging her heels into his thighs as she was pressed firmly against the rock wall of the pool while he took her.

She put her hands on his face and his jaw went slack, his thrusts getting harder, more intense. And all she could do was cling to him. This man. Her storm, her porch, and how could one person be both? It didn't make any sense. And she wished for a moment that she could be the one with amnesia. That she could just forget absolutely everything and have this moment. But he was Chance, and it was complicated. And there was never a scenario where it wouldn't be.

And it was just… It was too much. It was all too much.

And still, her climax rose inside of her. Threatening like an impending storm.

And she knew that if it broke open, it would drown her completely. But she didn't have the strength to deny him. Didn't have the strength to turn back now.

Then he kissed her and began to whisper against her mouth. Dirty promises that shocked her, that amped up her arousal. That made her slicker still and created a delicious friction between their bodies.

She met his every thrust, and when they went over the edge, it was together. And he spilled inside of her on a growl, the unbearable intimacy of the moment creating aftershocks within her.

And he didn't draw away from her when he was finished. Rather, he stayed like that, looking at her, stroking her hair back away from her face.

"I promise I really did mean to give you work to do today."

"Well, now I can't work," she mumbled, resting her forehead on his shoulder. "I don't think I can walk."

He chuckled. "It's touch and go for me too."

Then they both turned their heads at the same moment, looking at the horses, who were standing there placidly. "I can honestly say I haven't performed a live sex show for a pair of horses before," he said.

She laughed. "That kind of surprises me, given that you are a rodeo cowboy. I would've thought there was ample opportunity for you to be playing around with women in various paddocks."

"Hell, no," he said. "I'm a grown-ass adult past the age

of having to have sex in strange places. I have a house, I have a bed, I have money for hotel rooms."

"That's awfully mature of you."

"Apparently, I'm not all that mature with you."

"Well, we've known that."

"I guess so." He sighed heavily. "What are we going to do about this?"

She lifted a shoulder. "Burn it out."

"Makes as much sense as anything."

And maybe on the other side of that, none of this would be there. Not the simmering anger or the burning desire. She could handle that. Lord knew she would actually be much happier.

She moved away from him, swimming to the shore and going to gather her clothes.

It was harder this time. Without the cloak of anger to do away with the tender feelings left behind by the connection created during sex.

Not that she'd ever been superaware of it before. It was worse, she decided—or better, she supposed, depending on how you wanted to look at it, but worse was the best descriptor for when it was with Chance—when it felt amazing. When you had an orgasm together. Because she felt somehow united with him in his pleasure, rather than an observer of his superior, easy-seeming male pleasure, which was how it had always been in the past. She was a participant. And he didn't go to where he couldn't bring her along.

A strange thing that it was with Chance she had found that.

"We ought to maybe go repair a fence or something," he said.

She laughed hollowly, tugging her shirt back over her head and then deciding to go hunt around for her shoes.

He was halfway dressed, and by the time she found her shoes, he had completed the job.

"Yeah. I guess that would be the responsible thing to do. If your version of revenge is just give me multiple orgasms, I have to say, it's not very good revenge."

"My bad," he said.

"Did you just say *my bad*? What year is it, and how old are you?"

He grinned. "Sorry."

She didn't know what to do with him when he was like this either. Good-humored and light and in general enjoyable rather than a big pain in her ass.

It was making compartmentalization nearly impossible. Because he wasn't just a little bit different when they were in the throes of passion.

He was a little bit different all around. Like they were finally able to drop some kind of guard they normally had up when they were with each other. And it made her wonder if he saw her as different too.

"I suppose we should go back and work on the fence now," he said.

"That would have been easier before you killed me," she said.

"Sorry," he responded, grinning. He did not look sorry.

She narrowed her eyes, but she couldn't really be mad. Mostly because the sex had been so good.

"I don't know very much about you," he said.

"You've known me forever."

"Yeah, I guess. But I don't really know much about you."

She realized the same was true of him.

"I don't know. I had a pretty normal childhood."

"Except people were gross to you at school sometimes."

"Yeah. But I don't really know any different than that.

I'm tough, I was raised to be tough. We both were. I have both my parents, and I have my grandparents. We have it pretty good."

"But that's not the extent of it, is it? That's just surface stuff."

"It's all I really know about you."

"I want to know about the men in your life," he said.

She frowned. "There aren't any notable men in my life."

"Good," he said, his gaze assessing.

"What do you care?"

"I don't know. But I do."

"What about you? What about the women in your life?"

"I've never been serious about anyone. On purpose. I'm a ho."

"Well, points for honesty," she said, laughing.

"I never wanted anything permanent." He shook his head. "My parents do all right, especially with their lifestyle. Living out of an RV for part of the year while my dad travels around for the rodeo. But we've made it into our thing. Something we can rally around. I'm like you. I have both my parents... I guess in the end that makes me pretty lucky."

"Who was the little girl?" She shouldn't be asking this, because he had told her when he didn't remember anything, and it didn't really feel fair to fling this at him now.

"Yeah. So we came to that part. I'd rather we talk about how I'm probably the best sex you've ever had?"

She rolled her eyes. "Settle down, boy, you're all right."

"Why haven't you found anyone?"

"I told you already."

"That feels like an excuse."

"It's not an excuse. It's my life. What I want and what I dream of doing isn't an incidental. It's everything."

He nodded slowly. "My sister Sophie," he said. "We were close to the same age. She was always very sick. We loved her. I mean, we just doted on her. It was really something. The only girl among all those boys. We couldn't play with her, not the way that we could play with each other, because we had to be really careful with her. But it was all right. Nobody minded. Boone used to carry her around on his shoulders. Buck and Kit made a little cart just for her. With a princess canopy on it. She was in and out of the hospital all the time. And one time… She went and she never came back. And I remember… I remember standing in front of the hospital, in front of the doors, and my dad was grabbing my jacket sleeve and telling me to go inside, telling me to go visit. I couldn't. I couldn't go in. I just was frozen. Was some kind of terror that I couldn't quite sort out. But it was real, and it had me completely shaken. So I waited in the car, and then my sister died. She never came out of that hospital, and I wasn't brave enough to go in."

She hadn't expected that. She would've thought that anything that serious she would know about. She would've thought that it would've been something that people spoke of.

"Callie came along sometime after. And at first I was afraid. Afraid of what might happen to her. But she was this rowdy, rambunctious delight."

"But you can't replace somebody that you've lost. Not like a straight-out trade."

He shook his head. "No. It couldn't be clearer that they weren't the same person. It's funny, it's been so long. But I remember her on her birthday, and I remember how old she would've been. And you know Callie… She's great. My mother wanted that little girlie girl, though. And Callie isn't that. She ran roughshod with us over everything."

"I'm so sorry," Juniper said, feeling everything inside of her twist and turn onto its head.

She really didn't know him. She had never allowed him to be a full person. Not ever. She had always just seen him as her sworn enemy.

"It's all right. It's been a long time, like I said."

She thought of Shelby, and Chuck. "All time does is change wounds," she said. "Makes them into something different. It doesn't take them away, or turn you back into the person you were before. I know it isn't the same, but my brother-in-law was a lot like a brother to me. He and Shelby were together from the time I was fifteen. And he was always around. I can't remember my life without him. And then he was gone. She's devastated by it. She'll never be the person she was before. He was her other half. And then... I don't know. There's my grief. Which is real, but it isn't hers."

He hung his head. "Sharing grief can be a good thing," he said. "But there is something about it. When someone else feels it also much more than you. When someone else has a claim to the greater grief in the moment. But it doesn't make yours any smaller. It just means you're afraid of hurting them with yours."

"It must've been hard to watch your parents go through that."

"Yeah," he said. "It was. And my brothers. And it's been hard to watch Callie too in some ways. I envy her. Because she was never touched by the grief of it, not personally. But some of it... Did a decent enough job of messing her up. Because you know... You can't replace what you've lost."

She felt bruised for him. Cracked open inside.

"I'm sorry, I really didn't know."

He looked into the distance. Like he might find an-

swers there, or at least find some break in the intensity
between them. "It happened before we came here."

"Well, how inconvenient that you're a human being."
She tried to say it with a laugh but she couldn't.

He aimed a lopsided grin at her. "I hate to be an in-
convenience."

They got back on their horses and began to go back
to the ranch. They found that fence line and set about to
repairing it. "You're the best I've ever had," she said, because it felt a fair trade after he'd shared this.

"Tell me more," he said.

"I dunno. I thought sex was all right, but not worth jumping up and down over. I haven't always been able to…"

"You mean to tell me you were sleeping with guys
who couldn't make you come?"

"Yeah, but I figured women don't really expect to
come every time."

"Honey, I expect a woman with me to come every
time. More than once."

"Well, so far, promise fulfilled. So, thank you for that."

"You're welcome."

She looked up and smiled at him, and her stomach
went a little bit tight. And she didn't even feel like fighting it, or telling herself it shouldn't be like this. That it
shouldn't be so easy to like him, or work his dadblasted
Carson land.

She liked being beside him.

And she let it be.

When they finished the fence, it was dinnertime, and
her hopes of sneaking away were dashed.

Because all of his brothers were sitting outside at a
table in front of the barn, with a big dinner spread in
front of them.

"What's this?"

"We had dinner sent up from the fancy hotel."

She blinked. She forgot sometimes that the Carsons were rich. Rich enough to cater a random dinner.

"Hey," one of them said. "Come join us."

She looked at Chance. He shrugged. "You're hungry?"

"Obviously."

And her stomach fluttered, because of course she was obviously hungry because they had burned so many calories not just fixing the fence, but with the activities from the swimming hole.

"Well, sit down and eat."

"Did you really order food from a fancy hotel just for a random dinner?"

"Yeah," Boone said. "I'm starving. And pot roast, mashed potatoes and dinner rolls sounded like the ticket to me."

"I guess with this many of you to feed..."

"Oh, my mom gave up being the person that tried that a long time ago. When we were high schoolers she resorted to basically throwing bologna our direction and running the other way."

"That's a lie," Kit said. "She threw bologna packages our direction and said make it your damn self."

Her stomach growled, and she took her seat at the table, Chance seated alongside her, his thigh touching hers.

The brothers were loud and boisterous, and she hadn't actually spent time with them in a group since school. Even then, it had been more being adjacent to them than actually being in the middle of them.

They were a lot. A lot of personality, a lot of tall, handsome cowboy.

And she couldn't pretend anymore that she was immune.

She looked over at Kit. Kit, who she knew Shelby was

attracted to. And she couldn't blame her. He was a handsome man, though he didn't do for her what Chance did. That was the thing. Objectively, every single one of the Carson men was stunningly attractive, with mixed and matched features from each other, hair ranging from dark brown to near blond. Brown eyes, hazel eyes, charming smiles, large hands.

But it was more than just finding him handsome. It was... Some kind of chemistry that seemed to defy everything else.

"I don't think I have ever seen you when you weren't scowling," Flint said.

"Well, normally I have something to scowl about if I'm around this many Carsons. But you're feeding me. So I'm not going to be a bitch."

Flint laughed and tossed another dinner roll her way. She caught it and started to slather it with butter.

And when she was done, she realized that she was smiling, and laughing, and eating seconds of berry pie while Jace encouraged her to put all the whipped cream that was left in the can over the top of it.

It was weird to recognize that they were a family. Like hers. That she had more in common with them than not. It had been so easy to make them enemies. To paint them something other, something less, than her own family. But here they were, sitting together, eating together, being immature at each other. It was just so shockingly normal. When they got up from the table, Chance put his hand on her lower back, and she stiffened. He dropped his hand, as if he had sensed the reaction.

They got closer to her truck, and he looked at her. "You want to spend the night?"

She laughed. She couldn't help it.

"What?"

"I haven't been asked for a sleepover in quite some time."

"Do you need to get your mom's permission?"

"They wouldn't give it."

"Then it's best if we don't ask."

"You are going to get me in a lot of trouble," she said.

"You started the trouble."

"Maybe we need to make sure your head injury didn't dramatically change your personality."

"No. Sleeping with you might have done that."

She flushed. "I have to go home and grab some things. I won't be a minute."

"I know. We're neighbors, after all."

Yes. They were neighbors. Feuding ones at that. And she would do well to remember that. Because at the end of the day, no matter how much the Carsons were like the Sohappys, no matter how much she liked him, no matter how much fun it was to kiss him, no matter how exhilarating it was to have him inside of her, her grandfather would never get over the betrayal. And that was something that could simply never happen.

Nine

It had been two weeks of sneaking around with Juniper while she worked his land. And he really enjoyed it. He did.

But he'd been thinking. A lot. About the proposed endgame of all of this. He wasn't angry at her, not anymore. It was impossible to be. But what he wanted was to speak to her grandfather. He had decided that that was what he had to do.

What had become clear to him was that the biggest issue between him and Juniper was they could only see things one way. They saw the way their great-grandfathers had seen things, and had passed down that perception. And he was completely mired in that. He had to hear their side of the story. He needed to speak to her grandfather.

He could tell her, but…

He didn't want her to worry or have unnecessary anxiety about it, because he knew she was so protective of that relationship.

He'd be careful.

Because he was being careful with her.

He pulled up to the old farmhouse that was situated nearest the road on the ranch. There were two old cars in the driveway, and everything around the property was immaculate. No leaves, no debris. No nothing. The porch was spotless, with hanging plants all around.

Everything showed its age, but it also showed the incredible care that the owners put into it.

He parked, then walked up the steps, pausing for a moment before knocking firmly on the door.

He heard dogs barking, and then the shuffling of feet. The door opened to reveal a tiny gray-haired woman who was wearing a denim housedress and had her hair back in a low ponytail. "Yes?"

"Mrs. Sohappy," he said. "I was hoping I might be able to speak to Mr. Sohappy."

"Ron is sitting in his chair," she said. "What's your name?"

"I'm Chance Carson. I wanted to ask him a few questions."

The woman's eyes narrowed. "A Carson." Then the door slammed in his face, and he heard those same footsteps moving away from the door.

Well. Shit. Juniper hadn't been kidding. Her grandparents really did hate the Carsons, and he couldn't just show up and start talking to them, apparently.

He turned and started to walk down the steps, but then he heard the door open again. "Where you going?"

"I thought I wasn't welcome."

"I had to see if you were welcome," she said. "I wouldn't say *welcome*. But he will speak to you."

He nodded. "Thank you."

He walked back up the steps and followed the woman into the house. "I'm Anita," she said.

"It's nice to meet you, Anita," he said.

"We'll see if it's nice to meet you, Chance Carson."

He walked through a narrow hall and into a sitting room, where an old, gray-haired man was sitting in a mustard-yellow recliner. "What is it you want, Chance?" The man's voice was rough.

"I wanted to ask you some questions. About what you know about what happened between my great-great-grandfather and your grandfather."

The man looked at him then, his dark eyes serious. "You want to know what I think happened?"

"Yes."

"He wasn't of our blood. Our family. He married my grandmother. He was too fond of alcohol and card games. He lost a portion of the ranch playing cards with your great-great-grandfather. He was drunk and I think your great-great-grandfather was a cheat. There were witnesses that said he had an ace up his sleeve."

Chance nodded slowly. "And how is it… How is it you have the Sohappy name? If your grandfather wasn't part of the family."

The old man smiled. "I changed it back."

There was something in that simple statement that challenged a deeply held wall inside of Chance. Left it cracked.

That simple.

If something wasn't right, you changed it.

"Why are you asking now?" the old man asked, his eyes piercing. "Why now?"

"Because I realized just how wrong it is to hold on to your assumptions. When you could just ask. That's what we do, isn't it? We stay steeped in our own perspectives, and we never challenge them. We never looked to see what anyone went through. Juniper told me... She told me about something that happened at school. Someone who treated her badly because of her skin. I never saw anything like that. Not because it didn't happen, but because I wouldn't. Because people wouldn't do it in front of me, and they wouldn't do it to me. And you think then that that means things don't exist. Things you don't see. You think that your slice of the world is the whole thing, rather than just being a piece. I don't want to be like that anymore." He took a breath. "She has made me question a lot of things."

The old man's stare was sharp. "And now what will you do?"

"We need to redraw the boundary. We need to move the fence."

"Just like that?" he asked.

"Yes. Just like that."

"We should see if we can find proof."

He looked at the old man and saw pride radiating from him. And he knew he was never going to talk him out of that.

"All right. If that's what you want, then that's what we'll do."

He nodded.

"I had already agreed to see if my family had any records of what happened. I talked to Juniper about it."

"She's a good girl," her grandfather said. "She's going to make this place great."

"It looks to me like it's already pretty great. Because there's been a lot of great people here for a long time."

"It's family that helps make you who you are. But it

seems to me that your great-grandfather, your grandfather... They didn't have an influence with you."

"Family does make you who you are," Chance said. "And sometimes, when what it would make is a bad thing, you have to make a decision to change it. My dad did that. I'm grateful to him. You have to break cycles or they just carry on. We need to break this cycle. We are neighbors. We don't need to hate each other."

Then the old man stuck his hand out, and Chance took it. And they shook.

Ten

"I heard that Chance had a conversation with Grandpa," Shelby said.

"What?" Juniper popped around the rack in the clothing store she and her sister were in.

"Yeah. Apparently, he came to get his side of the story. He told Dad about it, and Dad was floored. He couldn't believe it. He said he didn't think one of those, and I quote, *arrogant sons of bitches* would ever do something quite that reasonable."

"I… I don't even know what to say."

"You must be good in bed," Shelby said. Then she grinned.

"Don't say that out loud, and don't ever say it so Mom and Dad can hear you. Or Grandpa."

"Well, Grandpa has new respect for at least him. So… Maybe things wouldn't be so bad if he found out."

"I have no desire for that to happen."

"Yeah. Fair. I mean, it would be somewhat horrifying."

"More than somewhat."

"So what exactly is going on with him? He must really like you to do that."

"I don't think so," Juniper said, suddenly feeling uncomfortable. "I think he's just… A lot nicer than I give him credit for. Or maybe *nice* is the wrong word. He's more reasonable. But there are things about him that I didn't know and…"

"Such as?"

"He… He had a sister that died. When she was really little. And he was just a kid and… I don't know. There's just more to him. There's sadness in him. And hearing him talk about his family, about the way that he loved her, it just made me feel…" She felt almost guilty telling Shelby about his pain, but…

If anyone understood loss, it was Shelby.

"Are you falling in love with him?"

She jerked up. "No. That would be impossible. Completely and utterly impossible. How would that even work?"

"I don't know. You seem to like him, plus you enjoy sleeping with him…"

"And that is not love," Juniper said.

"It's pretty close," Shelby responded. "Trust me."

"Surely there's more to it than that."

"Marriage is long. You have to find the person that you like to be around most in the world. Who you most like to see naked."

Her sister smiled for a second, and then her smile dimmed. "Of course, marriage is long unless it isn't. I so forget sometimes."

"I'm sorry," Juniper said.

"Hey," Shelby said. "It's not your fault. And you don't need to keep yourself from being happy because of me."

Juniper laughed. "I'm not that benevolent."

"You actually are much more benevolent than you need to be. I mean, why are you in a feud with him to begin with? Why are you doing any of this?"

"What do you mean?"

"I'm just curious. What would you be doing if you didn't feel obligated to Grandpa?"

"I don't feel obligated," she said. "I agree with him about what's important. I care about it. I want to do the same things, because it matters to me."

"All right, I believe you. But I do wonder…"

"What do you wonder?"

"Are you keeping yourself from being really happy?"

Juniper frowned. "I don't understand."

"It's something I've been thinking a lot about," Shelby said. She got a faraway look in her eye.

"What?"

"How many things I do just because I'm already here. Just because I started doing something, and I don't know what else to do."

"I want to establish an equestrian program here at the ranch. It's what I want to do, it's what I care about."

"But do you really care about border disputes and all of that, or is that just something that you're holding to because Grandpa was mad about it?"

"Those things matter. I'm not letting it go."

"At this point, what I wonder is if you're not letting it go because you feel more comfortable having that line drawn between yourself and Chance."

"I don't have any issues with Chance. Obviously."

"You lied to the man and kept him stowed away in your cabin when he got a head injury. And I feel like you do have some issues. With him, and maybe with relationships in general."

"I don't have issues with relationships."

"You're so dedicated to the land, Juniper. But why? At the exclusion of everything else? You wanted to do other things at one time…"

"But I realized I couldn't and still stay here and give it my all, and I needed to."

"Why is that? Is it because of Grandpa? Is it because you don't think Mom and Dad take his concern seriously enough? I know you love him, I know you have a really particular relationship with him. But it's not up to you to dedicate your whole life to this place. You can have the equestrian stuff without sacrificing everything else."

"I don't know how to do it. Anyway, I'm not in love with him, so it isn't an issue."

"Okay."

"Are you thinking about leaving?"

Shelby shook her head. "No. I'm not going to leave. But I'm thinking of going back to school. My life just isn't any of the things that I thought it would be. We were supposed to have kids, you know? And then that never happened, and I wish I would've done something, but we were just in a hurry to get married, and all I wanted was for us to have a family. Now he's gone too. That's the thing. He's gone too. And whatever I thought… It's not what I'm getting. It's not what I had. So, I need to figure out how to make something new. And thinking about that got me thinking about you. I don't know how you imagined your life at this point…"

"I didn't, really," she said. "I have the ranch. And that's what I care about."

"But you also have Chance."

"Stop saying that. I don't really have Chance. He's

not… He's not a factor. He's just a dude. And he's not worth upending my life over. Good sex is hardly something to go crazy over."

"It's not nothing. Take it from someone who's been without for a good long while."

"Well. I appreciate the fact that you dreamed of that. Of the family and all of that. I just… I never did."

"Why not, Juniper?" she asked.

"Because you can't have everything, can you? You have to choose. You have to decide what manner of life you're going to make. And for me, the ranch is my primary baby."

"And who will you pass it on to?"

She looked at her sister, and she realized that right now… They were the last of the generation. The last of all the generations.

"I don't know. It doesn't matter. We'll be dead. So I won't care."

"It doesn't work like that. You don't care about generational legacy and then magically not care when you're old."

"Future Juniper's problem. I'll fuss about it when I'm a hundred."

"Well, I think you should worry about yourself a little bit now."

"Thank you for your feedback. I'll be sure to take that on board."

Shelby rolled her eyes and made a scoffing noise.

"What?"

"What is the point of even being your sister? You don't listen."

"You're the baby. It won't work. At least you tried."

"I did," Shelby said. She shook her head. "It wouldn't hurt you to try, you know?"

"I guess not."

Juniper grinned and went back to browsing.

The thing was, she heard what Shelby was saying. That Shelby didn't understand. She didn't want to do all this with the property. She didn't want to make the ranch her life. So, they were just different. They wanted different things.

And that was okay.

Juniper couldn't imagine a scenario wherein she could make room in her life for a relationship that superseded the ranch. Shelby couldn't imagine a life where enjoying some hot sex with a good-looking man wouldn't end in love and marriage. That was fine. It was just the differences between the two of them. That was all.

There was nothing wrong with Juniper.

Nothing at all.

Eleven

He hadn't had dinner with his whole family for quite some time. But Callie was visiting from Gold Valley, and they had determined to have a dinner with all the siblings—except Buck—and their parents.

Dinner was loud and boisterous, as it always was when their family got together; it was just how they were.

"We need to talk for a second," he said, once everybody had dessert in front of them.

"What about?"

"I had a talk with Ron Sohappy," Chance said.

His dad scowled. "You mean he yelled at you and threatened to unleash his dogs on you?"

"No. I had a talk with him. About what happened initially with the ranch."

"And you think that he's going to tell you the truth?"

"I think he did, and I told him we'd try to find some sort of proof."

"How are we going to do that? Look for the smoking ace?"

Chance shook his head. "I've decided I don't want that. Why can't we share water rights? Why can't we work together? This feud has gone on long enough, and it's pointless. I want to be in a situation where I'm not fighting with my neighbor."

"That's noble of you, son," his dad said, "but I wonder what brought about the change of heart."

"It just seems like the right thing, Dad," Chance said. "And I care about it. I want us to do better than the generations that came before us, and I think we have. You know Grandpa was an asshole. Why are we on his side? Why do we listen to that story of how this ranch came to be, and how everything just is? I don't really understand. We have a chance to be better than those that came before us, and I believe that we need to do it. Because it's just right. Because it's fair."

"Hey, whatever you say, Chance, but I doubt you're ever going to join the two families together or anything like that," his dad said. "Some things are just too ingrained."

He nodded slowly. "I get that you feel that way. Because that's just how it's been. But I don't see why we gotta keep doing things one way just because it's how they've been."

"Well. If you say so."

"I do. Actually, I want to have them over for a barbecue."

"Damn," his dad said. "You really are trying to break ground."

His sister, Callie, smiled. "I like it, Chance," she said. "As you know, I'm all for shaking things up."

Being that she was responsible for the movement of

women breaking into new events in the rodeo right now, he absolutely knew she'd understand.

"You're a good one, Callie," he said.

"I agree," said her husband, Jake.

"Well, I'll get planning," he said.

Of course, he was going to have to get Juniper to agree.

He wanted to make it right. He needed to. The journey they'd been on…

He felt suddenly like he was standing in front of old, familiar doors that were too forbidding to ever walk through.

They couldn't go on like this.

But he'd made his mind up.

And he could give her this.

"How good of a mood are you in?" he asked when she came through the door of his cabin that night.

She was no longer working at Evergreen Ranch; there was no need to keep up the pretense anymore. The fact of the matter was, he just wanted to spend time with her, and anyway, they just did when they wanted that.

"I don't understand how to answer that question," she said.

"Should I get you naked before I start asking you for things or…"

"Well, I'm always for being naked with you." She smiled.

It was the easy camaraderie between them that never failed to surprise him.

Because it was just there, and they didn't have to try, after all that time of sniping at each other for so long… This was just there.

They had way more in common than they had different. They both loved this place equally, and they were both willing to work to make it better.

They were both absolutely and completely stubborn, hardheaded pains in the ass. But they appreciated it about each other. So there was that.

"You better go ahead and pitch it now," she said, sighing heavily.

"I want to have a barbecue," he said. "With both of our families."

"What the hell?"

"I want to make some things clear. I don't want to fight with your family anymore. I want to fix it."

"Why?"

"Because it makes no earthly sense. All this bullshit. All this hanging on to things in the past. It doesn't make any sense."

"That's…" She sighed. "I mean, I guess you're right. Honestly, I can't pretend that you're wrong. It's been a long time with all this stuff, and… I don't know that it benefits anyone."

"It doesn't. Your closest neighbors, and we should be allies, not enemies. We need to share the water rights."

"That's… I mean, it would definitely help."

"It would help us both. And I get that…that might seem like a bullshit thing to offer if your family was cheated." And he realized then, no matter what, there was only one real way this could go. "I want to sign the land back over to the Sohappy family. If you'll allow us water access, great. But it needs to go back to you. It's your land. Your blood."

Her eyes went glossy and he felt something terrible and fierce tighten his chest.

"I trust you," she said. "You don't need to sign the land over to us."

He felt like those words had cost her.

"You really are something," he said.

"Well, so are you. Something kind of undeniable, whether I want that to be true or not."

"It should be yours," he said, speaking of the land again.

She nodded. "Okay."

"So let's have a family barbecue. And let's put the bullshit feud to rest."

"I'd like that."

"I would like to get you naked also," he said, lowering his voice and moving toward her. And he kissed her, and it was like taking a full breath for the first time all day.

Because she was wonderful, brilliant. Amazing. Because she was everything that he had ever wanted.

Those words came out of nowhere and struck him like a thunderclap, and he chose not to pay them much mind. He chose not to think about them at all.

Instead, he just focused on her. On the way she looked, the way she tasted. He let the desire between them carry him somewhere else.

And it was like having amnesia again. Like being free of all the shit that weighed him down day in and day out. When they were together, it was like they both forgot.

And it was a gift. A blessing.

And he didn't normally use words like that or even think he needed them. But right now he would take them. Right now he would feel them.

But when she ran her hands over his skin, he tried to keep himself from feeling it too deeply.

When it was done, she curled up against him. "So when is this barbecue going to be?"

"I'd like to have it before my sister and her husband go back to Gold Valley. So as soon as possible."

"Well, my dad is retired, as he likes to remind me, so that means he's probably available whenever. Though, it'll be interesting to see if he will willingly sit in the same room as your dad. He doesn't feel the same way about the ranch that my grandpa does, but he's not neutral on the subject of the Carsons."

"We're going to do our best to change that. I don't want them to be neutral. I want him to actually have some nice feelings for us. Let's be neighborly."

"You and I might be someplace past neighborly," she said.

"Yeah, maybe." He moved over top of her and kissed her. "Spend the night with me."

She nodded. "Okay."

But for the rest of the night there was no need for talking.

It hadn't been easy to convince her family to come to a barbecue hosted by the Carsons. And, of course, her grandmother had refused to go empty-handed, so that meant a rally to make mass amounts of fry bread.

And keeping it hot on the drive over was everyone's burden.

Juniper, Shelby, their mother and father and their grandparents all drove separate trucks over to the ranch. And when they pulled up to the grand main house at Evergreen Ranch, Juniper knew a moment of disquiet.

The Carsons were something else. They were wealthy, they were extravagant with it even, and her family had a much more modest existence.

But when Chance broke away from his brothers and his parents to come and greet them, she felt some of her disquiet dissipate. She just hoped that her family didn't see the connection between the two of them. Because that was something she didn't want to have to explain on top of everything else.

But he was so… Oh, he was wonderful and she couldn't keep the smile off her face. The way he spoke to her parents, her grandfather and grandmother. The respect and manners, and she really didn't know that would make her swoon, but it did.

Her family mattered.

And he was treating them exactly as she wanted them to be treated.

"Thank you for coming," he said. "We really appreciate it." He shook her grandfather's hand first. Then went to her grandmother.

After that, he greeted her parents.

Then he moved to Shelby, who treated him to a sly look. "You must be Shelby," he said. "Haven't seen you in a while."

"No. Neither. Except I did see you from a distance a few weeks ago."

"I see."

"Yeah," she said.

Juniper elbowed her.

"What?" she asked.

The brothers all took their turns making introductions, and then they all got to setting out food.

Her grandfather, who wasn't shy at all, immediately engaged the senior Carson.

"Your son is a good man," he said.

Abe Carson nodded. "He is."

They talked about cows, they talked about water, they talked about the rodeo.

Once the rodeo stories started, they didn't stop.

At the big table, which was laden down with meat,

and her grandmother's fry bread, she was seated next to Callie, Chance's sister.

"Hi," she said. "I know who you are, but I don't think we've ever really met."

Callie was bright and chipper, and she made Juniper feel old. But then, she had to be somewhere around five years older than her.

"Yeah. It's good to see you."

"I think it's great what Chance is doing. That he cares about getting everybody together, and making sure they're getting along."

"Yeah. I never would've thought it about him, but he seems invested in it."

"He seems to like you," she said.

And Juniper stiffened. She wasn't sure how anyone could get that from their interactions.

"Does he?"

She shrugged. "Just a feeling I get. When he looks at you."

"Oh. Well. He's a good guy. He really is."

"I think so."

At some point, half the people bundled up and went to target practice, and everybody ended up out by the gravel pit on the property, sitting in lawn chairs and drinking beers and shooting rifles.

And there was a time when she would've worried about her grandfather having a rifle around the Carsons, but things seemed to be just… Different now. Was it all because of the way that Chance had gone to talk to Grandpa?

Had it really been enough to change the tone of the relationship between their families?

Maybe respect was the first, most important step. And then listening.

It forced her to see him differently, watching this interaction with his family.

Yet again.

And what she couldn't quite believe was the way that things had changed between them in these past weeks. The way that her ideas had been challenged.

When she went back home, her dad commented how they were actually such a nice family.

And she didn't… She didn't know what to do about that.

All of a sudden this barrier had been lifted, one that had once existed between herself and Chance. And yes, it could be argued that that had been dispensed with the minute they started sleeping together, but that had been something else. And this was… This was something emotional, and she didn't quite know what to do with it.

"Thank you," her grandfather said. "Your commitment to the ranch is truly commendable. I feel like you must've done something to make him change the way that he saw things."

Oh, that made her feel terrible.

Because it had been so momentous for her to be given the chance to run the ranch, and it meant the world to her to do right by her opportunity.

But what would they think if they found out that a huge reason Chance had changed his mind about everything was because she'd slept with him? Even if that was a simplified version of events, it was how it would look. Like she'd bought the land back with her body. By sleeping with the enemy.

"I just care about the ranch," she said. "It's my life, Grandpa, you know that."

He nodded his head. "I know."

"I'll honor it."

"I know," he said again. He patted her hand. "You're a good girl."

There. She was a good girl.

That was everything she had ever wanted to be. And now that she had it, she didn't know quite what to make of it.

Except… She really had no reason to continue on being with Chance.

And it wasn't sad or anything like that. There was no reason for it to be. They were at a conclusion. She was actually really happy. It might've all happened in a strange roundabout way, but she had accomplished something. She had changed some things. For the better. And she was just so grateful for that. Because they didn't need each other anymore.

And they didn't hate each other. And surely that was progress. Surely.

"Good night," she said, giving her grandpa a half wave.

"Good night."

And then she went back to her cabin and went to bed alone, and tried to tell herself that it was just fine.

Twelve

Juniper went down to the First Bank of Lone Rock the very next day. She was ready to try to get her loan to get the barn built.

A newer barn. A bigger one.

Yes, she would continue to work on restoring the one that she and Chance had worked on together, but she wanted something state-of-the-art, cutting-edge. She had her money saved up for the first of her horses, and this, she would be getting some help on.

Her plan was also to rent out space for people to board their horses, helping turn more of a profit at the ranch.

So a state-of-the-art facility was important.

And she finally had all of the years at her job required to go for a loan this size.

It was a big deal. Because this was debt. Real debt. Attached to her name. This was all the real stuff, as real as it got, in fact. This was her marriage. Her dream.

She laughed hollowly.

Then she walked into the banker's office, and two hours later, she was fully approved for the loan.

Now she would just need to line up construction workers and all of that. She had her plans, which she had needed before she could present them to the bank.

It felt big. And the first thing she wanted to do was... Call Chance.

She didn't need to. He wasn't a key part of this enterprise or anything like that. He wasn't even a factor.

She could call Shelby, and she did want to talk to Shelby about it. But she found she wanted to share the triumph with him, and she didn't quite know what to do with that.

They didn't talk on the phone, not very often. Mostly it was just texts back and forth. And then they were together. To hook up, not anything else. They'd never been on a date. Of course, when you had held a man captive while he had amnesia, she supposed you didn't really need to go on a date.

That was just kind of silly.

"Stupid," she muttered, and took her phone out, and found Chance's name in her messages.

"Hey," he said. "Everything okay?"

"Everything is wonderful," she said. "I got a loan. I'm building a new equestrian facility."

"That's... That's good. You want to do that, right?"

"Yes," she said. "I do. I really do. Chance, this is the biggest... It's the biggest thing. Nothing else has ever been this big."

"We should go out and celebrate," he said.

And her heart swooped inside of her chest. "Really?"

"Yes. We should. We should go out and celebrate that you're amazing."

"I… Okay."

And that was how she found herself at Shelby's. "He wants to go out," she said.

"You've been sleeping with the guy for like a month."

She nodded. And she didn't tell Shelby that she had just been thinking about how she needed to end things with him. About how she needed the two of them to get back to some semblance of sanity.

Because all that they were was a little bit intense.

Because there was no point. Because they had that whole reconciliation with the family, and her whole goal of having him see her and her family as people had been realized.

"And you need a dress," Shelby said.

"It's dumb, right? That I would want to wear a dress for a man?"

"It's not dumb," Shelby said. "It's normal. I know you don't have a lot of experience with this…"

"Well. It's because I… I've been trying so hard to live up to the fact that I'm the first girl to get this opportunity."

"Juniper," Shelby said. "That's ridiculous. Grandpa doesn't care that you're not a boy."

"No. And he totally thinks I can do anything that a boy could do. That isn't what I mean, it's just… I'm the first. And our great-great-grandpa who lost the ranch was the first to not be part of the family by blood and make a mistake and…and then it was why Grandpa didn't want Chuck to have the ranch. Why he wanted it in the family. So I can assume if I screw up…"

"First of all," Shelby said, "you'll be in charge. So you'll get to decide who carries it all on. Second, he wouldn't have given it to Chuck. Not ever. He'd have always trusted you with it, no matter the family history."

"But…"

"And if you have to love this land more than everything else, who will you pass it to?"

"I was counting on you reproducing."

Shelby laughed. "Well, that's blown to hell, isn't it? You might have to make your own life." Her tone softened. "You have to do what you want, you can't just be the fulfillment of Grandpa's dreams. He isn't going to live that much longer, Juniper. He's ninety-four."

"He could live another ten years," Juniper said. And it made her feel panicky, because she really did love him more than just about anyone or anything else.

"I know that you love him," Shelby said. "And I know that all of this comes from how much you love him. But he wants you to be happy. You didn't ever have to be a boy. You didn't ever have to love nothing more than this ranch."

She did her best not to let her sister's words sink too deep. "I still don't own a dress. And I would like to wear one to go out with Chance."

"Well, I can accommodate you. Especially because my dresses don't get any use these days."

Her sister tried to smile, but it came out a little bit thin.

She grabbed a stack of dresses, and after she had tried on two, Juniper suddenly understood why women were often upset about the shapes of their bodies.

Some of them showed off too much of her hips, some of them were too low-cut. And some of them emphasized that she had a little bit of roundness to her stomach.

"These are instruments of torture. Mental torture," she said.

"It's fine," Shelby said. "Wear the red one. You look amazing in it."

"What if I'm wrong?" she said, staring at her reflection. "What if he just wants to go to a bar and have a beer? Like friends?"

"Well, you'll be the best-looking bitch in the bar."

"Oh no, I'll feel really stupid. What if I have all of this wrong?"

"I thought you didn't want it to turn into anything."

"I don't," she said, her heart pounding heavily. "I don't want it to be anything else. I want it to be… What it is. I actually wanted it to be over." She was always meaning to not tell her sister things, and then accidentally blurting them out.

"You wanted it to be over?" Shelby asked, her eyes wide.

"Yes. I just wanted things to get back to normal. Or, not normal, better. Because I did it, right? I mean, I showed Grandpa that the Carsons could be good people, and I showed Chance that we weren't wrong about the situation with the land and how it wasn't fair. I did that. So, the two of us don't need to be together anymore."

"Did you stop being attracted to him?"

"No. Not at all. He's gorgeous…"

"I know," she said. "I've seen him."

"He's gorgeous, and I like being around him… And don't say anything. It's not that, it's just that today when I got the loan I just wanted to talk to him."

"You care about him," Shelby said.

"I like him. And I don't know what to do with that. I've never split my focus from the ranch. I do the EMT thing because it's necessary, and it was… Look, it wasn't really being a doctor, but it helped with the ranch instead of taking from it. I needed it for the money. But I need to love the ranch more than I love anything else. It needs to be the thing that I focus on, it needs to be…"

"You're a human being," Shelby said. "And it doesn't

matter whether you were born you or born a man. You're just you. And you get to be a human being."

"I don't know how. I don't know how to have balance. I don't know how to have… Any of this. All I know is the ranch, all I know is obsession."

"Maybe this is a great opportunity to try and not just be obsessed. With him or the ranch."

"I guess. Do you have lipstick? Who am I?"

"You're my sister," Shelby said. "And will figure this out."

Thirteen

He pulled into Juniper's driveway at five, because while she had asked if they could meet in town, he had decided that was bullshit, and he needed to take her, since they were celebrating something, and… Hell. He just wanted to. He couldn't recall the last time he had felt compelled to take a woman out, and in fact, he wasn't sure he ever had.

Maybe this was the chance to…finish it.

Not that he was going to end things tonight, but it might be a good chance to draw a line under things.

The issues with the family were resolved.

Maybe this would tie up the unfinished business with them.

Maybe you just want to be with her…

He shrugged that off.

And then when she came out of the house, his stomach went tight. She was beautiful in a red dress that hugged her figure and stopped just above her knee. She had on red lipstick, her black hair loose and hanging around her shoulders.

He had never seen her look quite so… She was always beautiful. He didn't care what she wore. She was the damn sexiest woman he had ever seen. That was just a fact. But right now she was testing him. Testing the limits of his restraint.

He got out of the truck and rounded to her side, opening the door for her. She looked up at him, her dark eyes wide. "What…"

And then he leaned in and kissed her. Hard.

"You look beautiful."

Her face went scarlet. "Thank you."

"No problem."

It was a bit of a drive down into Lone Rock, and he had been thinking of taking her to the Thirsty Mule, but he was going to have to take her to the Horseshoe. The old saloon building was restored to its original glory, with luxurious private dining rooms, and all kinds of things that hearkened back to the Gold Rush era of Lone Rock.

It was a favorite of his family, and they ate there every Christmas Eve.

"You like the food here?"

"There aren't many options in town," she said.

It was true. Lone Rock was tiny, a little gold speck out in Eastern Oregon, with very little surrounding it. The main street of the town was all original buildings, restored over the years to keep the look of the late 1800s alive.

It was certainly never going to modernize.

"Well, it is the best food in town," he said. "But don't tell Cara I said that, or she'll start a riot."

"The food at the Mule's great," she said. "It's just that, you know, it's…"

"Bar food?"

"Yes."

"You've never really lived anywhere else, have you?" he asked.

"No," she said.

"I have," he said.

"Where all have you lived?"

"Well, if I'm honest, mostly in an RV in different locations." They got out of the truck and walked toward the restaurant. "You know, until we had to slow down for Sophie. The nearest hospital. We lived on the outskirts of Portland for quite a while. Sophie needed to be near Doernbecher so she could receive specialized care. The Children's Hospital there is one of the best in the country."

"Oh wow. That must've been very different."

"It was. But… We were willing to do anything for her health. And then after that… Well, my grandpa died, and Lone Rock seemed like the place to go. With Evergreen Ranch available, that was just where we went. It was the best thing. For all of us."

They walked inside the restaurant, and Janine, the hostess, who he'd known since he was a kid, greeted them.

"Your usual table?"

His family often rented private dining.

"It's just the two of us tonight," he said. "We can sit out in the main dining area."

The carpets were a rich cranberry color, with the original lights, covered in carnival glass, turned low to give the place a romantic ambience. The tables were covered in white tablecloths, the walls red brick.

"I've actually never eaten here," Juniper said when they took a seat.

"Never?"

"It's not really our…"

"Hey. I get it. We're from different experiences."

"Well, I appreciate that you understand that."

"I do. I more than understand it."

He decided to go for an expensive bottle of champagne, in spite of her protests, and encouraged her to order exactly what she wanted, no matter what the cost was. She gave him a slightly wicked look. "I have always wanted to pretend like ordering something expensive meant I was afraid I'd have to pay for it with my body."

"I am happy to accommodate that fantasy," he said, his voice getting gravelly.

She ordered the fillet.

He gave thanks.

He loved watching her eat. Loved watching her smile and sigh over every bite. And he encouraged her to order a couple of different desserts after they brought out the tray with all the examples of the evening's selections.

"You can take the extras home," he said. "But it really is the best."

After much pushing, she agreed.

When they were finally finished, he had several boxes for her to take back home with her.

And he liked that. He liked giving her things. He liked seeing her happy. And he couldn't remember the last time he'd ever felt like that. Like sharing in somebody else's enjoyment was as good as having his own.

"Why don't you come back to my place?" she asked.

And he wasn't going to argue.

Something felt different between them tonight, and she didn't know if it was the dress or the dinner. She just didn't know. She felt different.

And she was... Electrified with it.

All the way back to the tiny cabin, she let herself get more and more wound up. She wanted him so badly she could hardly stand it. Maybe it was the adrenaline rush of having him again when she had been determined to break it off and never experience the pleasure of his hands on her skin. Maybe it was that she wanted him in a way that made her entire body ache. In a way that made her feel like he had been worth the wait, even though she would've said that she wasn't waiting for him. And tonight she felt completely and utterly one with her womanhood, and that was another thing she had struggled with. Even with him. Even as he had made her feel like her curves were a good thing. Like her body was special. Wonderful. Valuable. She couldn't say that she had felt purely feminine, or purely comfortable with it. But something about the dress, that lipstick, the whole night, made her feel a connection with herself that she hadn't before.

They got out of the truck, and her hands were shaking as they went up the front steps into the house. Then she turned and launched herself into his arms. She kissed him like she was dying, parted her lips and let him consume her.

And he did.

"I hope you know you don't actually have to pay for the steak," he said.

She laughed. "Maybe I just like the fantasy?"

"Do you?"

"Because I never felt like I was one of the pretty girls. Because I never felt like I was allowed to be. Because I never... Because always for me it's been about being convenient, not caught up in passion."

"I want you," he said. "You. This has nothing to do with feuds or anything else. I just want you."

"Thank you," she breathed, and she kissed him again, pouring all of her desire, all of her passion, into it.

He moved his hand around her back and unzipped her dress, leaving her in the borrowed high heels she was wearing and her underwear, leaving her feeling more feminine than she ever had in her life.

She stood back, leaning against the wall and arching her hips forward. He growled, pressing his hand to the front of his jeans, to where he was already hard and in desperate need of her.

"You want this?"

She nodded.

Then she went over to him and put her hands on his chest, slid them down his body as she dropped to her knees.

She had never done this before. Because she had never been in a relationship long enough to think that the man merited this kind of special treatment, and she knew that some women treated it like a free and easy thing. A little bit of action without the commitment of full-on sex, but she had always felt like there was something a bit more intimate about it, and she had always hesitated to try it.

But not with him. Not with him at all.

She undid his belt buckle, undid the zipper on his jeans and freed him, wrapping her hand around his heavy arousal, looking up at him as she leaned in and stroked him from base to head with the tip of her tongue.

His breath hissed through his teeth, the glint of desire in his eyes nearly undoing her completely. She felt powerful. Female. Incredible.

She took him into her mouth, as deep as she could, and began to suck him like he was her favorite flavor of Popsicle. The taste of him was… Amazing. And she would never have thought that. But then, she thought he was singularly beautiful. She could write poetry about his anatomy, without ever having been all that impressed with the look of a naked man before this.

But she loved the look of him.

He was glorious. The most incredible man she had ever seen in her life. And she reveled in just what she was making him feel now. What she alone seemed to be able to make him feel. If there was anyone else, she didn't want to know about the bitch. She wanted to be the only one.

It made her feel desperately sad that she wasn't... That she couldn't be... That it couldn't be forever.

Why not?

Because it couldn't be. It couldn't be so easy.

And to just decide that you wanted forever when, before, you didn't think you did. To just decide that you loved a man when, before, he was your sworn enemy. To be able to love something more than her family land when she'd committed to not allowing herself that. Not ever.

It couldn't be that easy.

She shut her brain down and continued to lick, suck and stroke his masculine body.

She brought him to the brink, until his thigh muscles were shaking, and then he grabbed hold of her hair and moved her away from him, nearly lifting her up off the ground by her hair and bringing her in to kiss him. "I have to have you," he growled.

"No complaints from me," she said breathlessly. He lifted her against him and kissed her. Wildly. Recklessly. Then he carried her back into the bedroom, and she stopped him, pulling him up against her, pulling them both against the wall.

"Is that how you want it?" he growled.

"Yes," she whispered.

He pulled her panties aside, pushing his fingers between her legs, then dropping to his knees, taking her with his mouth, putting her thighs over his shoulders and eating her diligently as he pinned her body against the wall.

She arched against it, pushing her hips more firmly against his mouth as he continued to consume her.

She dug her fingers into his shoulders, tugged at his hair.

"Please," she begged. "Please."

"Not until you come for me," he said.

His words, electric, magic, set off a spark inside of her body that started deep within, shivering outward as it bloomed into a deep, endless climax that left her gasping. Left her breathless.

Then he rose up and, keeping her pinned against the wall, thrust into her, her hands pressed back against the drywall, held firmly in place by his ironclad grip, as he thrust, hard and fast, into her body. And it was a funny thing, because this was how she had always thought it would be between them. Desperate and needy, and not with the civility of a bed.

But their first time had been in a bed, and now here they were against that wall, when there was no more hate between them. When there was no more distrust.

But they had made it here. And somehow, something in her had always known they would.

She had always known that they would. And as her eyes met his, she knew why.

Because she loved him. She felt it clear and loud inside of her. She loved him.

She loved Chance Carson, and it didn't matter if it felt impossible. Because she would do whatever it took for the two of them to be together.

She wasn't only a rancher.

She didn't only love this ranch. She didn't only love her family name. She loved him. And it felt like a powerful realization. One that made her feel like she could scarcely breathe. Scarcely think.

He thrust into her, and her climax hit her like a wave, and then his own overtook him just a split second later, like a lightning bolt had gone through them both at once.

He held her while he shook, while he spent himself inside of her, and she clung to him. And she knew.

She knew. She had no idea what he would say. No idea what he would do. But it was the truth, and she could no more keep it in than she could ever keep in the animosity that she had once felt for him.

Because above all else, between herself and Chance Carson, there wasn't room for any more lying.

She had lied to him once already, and she would never do it again. "I'm sorry," she said, stroking his hair, and she hadn't meant to say that. Hadn't meant to say that she was sorry, but it had come out, and she realized once it did that it had been an important thing for her to say. "I should never have lied to you. When I found you. I should've taken you straight back to your family. I'm so sorry that I did that. It was selfish. I was blinded by the fact that the only thing that I thought mattered was the ranch, was getting even, was getting what I wanted. I wanted to force you to see something... And it was wrong of me. I swear I will never lie to you. Not again."

"It's okay," he said, looking slightly mystified by her intensity.

But he would understand. Eventually, he would understand.

"And the thing is," she said, touching his face, "I love you, Chance Carson. And I need you to believe me. I need you to trust me. I love you, Chance, and I would be willing to do anything, absolutely anything, to get you to love me back. Because I've never wanted anything but this ranch, and now that I've committed myself to it, now that I'm in debt for it, all of that… Now that I have that, what I want more is you. But it's a good thing. I want you. And I will split my time anywhere. And I said I'd never do that. But I would. For you. For you I would."

"Juniper," he said, his voice rough.

"You don't have to say anything," she said. "You don't have to say anything now. It's just… I'm kind of blown away by how strong I feel about this. By the fact that for the first time… For the first time I know what I want. Not what someone else wants for me. And not what I think I have to do. Just what I want. So. It's okay if you can't feel the same. It's okay if you can't answer me yet. I'm just glad that I know. I'm glad that I know." But her mouth was dry, and her whole body felt like it was poised on the edge of a knife, and it did matter. It did fucking matter what he said. What he wanted. It mattered because if he didn't want her… Well, if he didn't want her, then everything was just going to be kind of terrible.

"Juniper, I…"

"You're going to say something anyway. You hard-headed asshole."

"I'm not going to leave you thinking that I might be able to… That I might change my mind. That I might change who I am. I won't. I can't."

"You're right about one part. You won't."

"You don't understand…"

"I understand what it's like to live your whole life so afraid that you're going to do the wrong thing, and then the person that you love most in the world will tell you that you want what they wanted. I know that fear. But you know what, if that's how my grandfather feels, then that's how he feels. And if that's how you feel… That's the thing, I can't control what anyone else feels. I can't control what you say or do or want. I can only control myself. I love you." She swallowed hard, tears springing into her eyes, and normally, she would despise that weakness. But right now she couldn't. Right now she didn't.

Right now all that mattered was she knew how she felt. And she wasn't afraid. She felt more herself than she ever had. She felt like… She didn't need to perform. She didn't need to do anything but be. And this was who she was. She loved the ranch, and she wouldn't compromise. She loved Chance, and she wouldn't compromise there either.

This was the most vulnerable she'd ever been, but also the most certain. And as difficult as she could feel the coming moment would be, she didn't resent it. Because it had brought her to this place of being one with herself. Certain of herself.

"Juniper, this isn't what I want. I watched my parents' lives be torn apart by losing a child, and I… I lost my sister. And I can't… I can't."

It broke her. But she wasn't angry.

She had been angry with this man so many times over things that weren't justified, and she had a feeling she would be a little bit justified in being angry about this. But she wasn't. She just wasn't.

Because she could see that he believed it. Deep down in his soul, and she understood that. She knew what it was to believe something so deeply about yourself.

It was all fear. That was what it was. Fear of losing the thing that you had, all that you had managed to make for yourself, in exchange for something that felt uncertain. Something you had lived without all this time, so maybe you didn't even actually want it, maybe you didn't need it.

"I want you to remember something," she said. "That I loved you. Even when you said you couldn't. That I care about you. I want you to remember that."

"Juniper…"

"No. I don't want your apologies. I don't want your speeches. You know what you can and can't do. You know who you are. And if you don't, I hope you find out. And then I hope you come find me. But if not, I want you to know… I think we really could've been something. Something I didn't even think I believed in. But now here I am, asking for it. Demanding it."

"I can't."

"Then you have to let me go," she said.

And she looked at him, and realized his face had become the dearest thing in the world to her, and it hurt to walk away. It hurt worse than anything ever had. Than she'd imagined anything ever could.

But she would let him go anyway.

Because she wouldn't compromise. And she finally realized she didn't have to.

Because she didn't need to be in service to what her grandfather wanted in order to be loved. Any more than she needed to leave the ranch to love Chance. Any more than she needed to keep her feelings to herself, or to stand there and compromise.

She had meant it when she'd said she didn't need him to say anything now. It was true.

But if he insisted on ending this, she would accept it. And she felt… Impossibly brave making that choice. To speak her heart to the person she loved most in the world and risk losing him.

And he left.

And her home felt empty, and so did she.

She sat in her pain for a long time, tried to sleep and

failed. Marinated in her pain all day the next day until she finally drove from her cabin, to her grandfather's house. Her heart in pieces.

She walked up the steps and went inside, her heart thundering heavily. "Juniper," he said when he saw her. "What brings you here?"

"I have something to tell you."

"Yes?"

"I'm in love with a Carson. And I love the ranch. And I love you. I'm not a son, and I'm sorry. I'm a granddaughter. But I love this place, and I will take care of it. I'll take care of it even if I end up living at Evergreen Ranch. I'll take care of it if Chance doesn't love me back and rejects me. And I'll love you even if that makes you angry. But I need you to know. I need you to understand."

"Juniper," her grandfather said, his voice rough. "You thought that I wouldn't love you?"

"It isn't that. But I promised you I'd do this. Perfectly. And I was just so afraid… I was just so afraid. That I couldn't quite be what you wanted. That I wasn't quite what you needed. And I wanted to prove myself. I gave up on my dreams of medical school. Of being a doctor. I threw myself into everything I could do here. All this time. And the problem is I liked Chance, from the first moment I saw him, and I wanted to hate him with the fire of a thousand suns, so I did everything I could to make that happen. But I didn't. I've always wanted him."

"I never wanted you to not be true to yourself," her grandfather said. "Not ever. I love you, and I want you to be happy. I'm sorry if an old grudge made you feel that you had to do anything differently."

Juniper laughed, but she wasn't mad. She wasn't. The risk had been hers to take all along, to be honest about herself and who she was, and she hadn't taken it.

And now she had taken the risk, she had spoken her truth. She had faced down her fears, with Chance, and now with her grandfather. And she might've lost Chance for now, but her grandfather was looking at her with love, and she knew that she'd made the right choice. She knew that things would be okay. They would be.

"Juniper," her grandmother said. "Will you stay for dinner?"

She could wait to dissolve. She would dissolve. Because she wanted Chance, and right now, he didn't want her. Or at least, he didn't think he could.

"Yes," she said. "I will."

Because there would always be time for her to dissolve. Because the grief would be waiting for her when she got up from this table.

But right now she had her grandparents. She had her family. And she had herself. And she would take a moment to celebrate that.

Fourteen

He couldn't sleep. Or worse, he could. And when he did, he dreamed. And he was back there. Standing in front of the hospital, unable to go through the doors.

Because whatever was behind there was so terrible he couldn't face it.

He couldn't bring himself to stand. Couldn't bring himself to move over there. He was completely blocked. Bound by an invisible force that he couldn't see. That made it impossible to breathe.

Grief. His body whispered the truth of it even as his brain resisted giving it a name. Grief.

So much grief, and his feet felt like they were encased in cement. And he couldn't take a single step. His breathing was labored, and when he did finally wake up, he was in a cold sweat.

Grief. This unending grief.

But it wasn't Sophie he was thinking of. It was Juniper.

He had really told her that he couldn't do it. That he couldn't love her.

You already do.

Maybe that was true. But how? He didn't understand.

He felt like she was there, just on the other side of that door, but for some reason, for some damned reason, he couldn't get there. He didn't understand it. He didn't know how the hell to make sense of it. He wished that there was someone he could talk to, but he found he only wanted to talk to Juniper.

And he had sent her away, so, that was going to work out real well for him.

He loved her. It was the reason he had been motivated to talk to her grandfather. The reason he'd wanted to bring the families together for a barbecue. And he knew that he did. He knew that rejecting her was cowardice.

But what had he been thinking? That she wouldn't want it to be love? That it wouldn't come down to this? Of course it had. It was inevitable. It had always been fucking inevitable between the two of them. There had never been any other option. And yet he was running scared of it. Running scared of it like a child, not acting at all like a man.

Why can't you go through the damned hospital doors? And it took a while to realize he'd said it out loud. Why couldn't he go?

He had regretted it. All of this time he had regretted it, and here he was, doing it to himself again. Ruining things for himself again.

You will regret it always if you don't do it. That's all you have to do. Just have the balls to move forward.

It was the hardest thing. But this was different than having his sister behind those doors, dying, with no chance of survival.

This was an unknown. And maybe on the other side there would be joy. Maybe there would be struggle. Maybe there would be pain. But it would be worth it. It would be worth it.

For her. And suddenly that made all the difference. Imagining her walking forward with him. Imagining her there, taking his hand and leading him through.

And yeah, all the bullshit he'd ever had to deal with was right there still. Behind those doors.

But so was the potential for everything else. For joy, for love, for happiness. The kind that he had let himself believe he didn't want, let alone need.

But he did.

And most of all, he needed her.

Walking with him.

But he had to take that first step on his own.

He got out of bed, and then Chance Carson took a step forward.

Juniper was out working when Chance showed up.

She recognized the sound of his truck now. Recognized him.

Just the feel of him.

It was because she was different now. Because they were different.

She dropped the stack of wood she was holding and stood there, watching as he crossed the space and made his way to her.

"What are you doing here?"

"I walked through the door," he said. "And I'm ready. For whatever's on the other side of it. I'm ready. I recognize that it's been what's holding me back. I punished myself for all those years, for not being able to go and see my sister one last time. And I felt like it meant I wasn't going to be able to go any kind of distance for anyone. I felt like I deserved to sit in that same loneliness she might've felt because I wasn't there. But you know what, that's self-protective bullshit. It was never about me. That's the thing. It never was. It's always just been about love. I loved her, and I was a kid, and it kept me frozen. Loving you kept me frozen too. But I remember what it was like to forget. To forget that I'd ever been hurt, to look at you without any of that weighing me down, and it made me want to change."

His breath was unsteady and it made her heart seize up, but he kept on talking. "It makes me want to reach out. Makes me want to walk through the door. Because there I was, when you walked away, standing on the outside just like I was then. I don't want that. I don't want to stand on the outside anymore. I don't just want to be looking in. I want to be with you. Even if it hurts. I want to be with you no matter what's on the road ahead of us. For a while I got to forget. And that was a powerful thing. But it's so much more powerful to stand here remembering all of it. Every fight we've had, every shitty thing I've been through, and want to be with you anyway. Because I do. Please believe that. It just took me a long while to realize.

"Juniper, I know how much it hurts to lose somebody. I've held it close for all these years. But I almost chose to lose you, and I can't accept that. I can't accept that choice I nearly made. Because it isn't living. When I have all this, when I have you, standing there wanting me, how can I choose any different? How can I choose not to love you when I already do? How can I choose to walk away like it would be the best thing? It wouldn't be. It wouldn't be living. Yes, I'm living with grief, but I'm still living. And so many people are, so many people do, every day, and they still choose to love. My parents chose to keep on loving. They had another child, even after all that. It's the lesson I missed. That love is worth it. Every time. No matter what. Love is always worth it."

"I love you," she said, flinging her arms around his neck, her heart pounding heavily.

"I love you too," he whispered, his breath hot against her ear.

And she wept. She thought maybe he did too. "We can live here," he said, his voice rough. "Whatever you want."

"Really?"

"Yes. We can live here. We can live in Evergreen Ranch. Hell, we can live at both. Or away. You could go to medical school. Be a doctor like you wanted. Stay here, make the equestrian thing happen. Do both. Do everything. Do nothing. Just be with me, and I'll be with you."

He was so earnest, so…him. The man she'd rescued, who had no memory. The man who'd had it all come blazing back. He was both.

And he was willing to give up the thing that stood between them: the land.

And she realized in that moment she was too.

"You would live here, in my tiny little house?" she asked.

"Home is wherever you are. Love is where you are. I… I only just realized… I didn't need to be in the hospital. Because my love was there already. Love goes before you. And it always goes with you. It's not a place. And for me, it's you."

"For me, it's you."

"You said you couldn't compromise."

"Well, that was back when I would've told you I couldn't have loved a Carson."

"And when was that?"

She smiled. "You know what, I can't remember. Maybe I have amnesia."

"As long as you never forget how much you love me."

"Oh, Chance, I could never forget that."

"Do you still want me to be your ranch hand?"

"I wouldn't say no."

"What if I was just your husband?"

"I can't imagine what our grandfathers would say about a Carson and a Sohappy getting married."

"It doesn't matter what they would say," Chance said, grinning.

And she smiled, because it was true. "You know, all that really matters is that we want it."

"And I do."

"I do too."

She kissed him, and she could only ever marvel about the fact that she loved him now far more than she had ever hated him. And one thing she knew for sure, it wasn't his ranch or hers that would be their greatest legacy.

It was love.

It was the only thing that had ever made their land worth anything. Love.

And it was the thing that made life worth living.

Always and forever.

* * * * *

FROM FEUDING
TO FALLING

JULES BENNETT

To all of the loyal readers who anxiously await my stories. Thank you for letting me fulfill a childhood dream and enjoy a career of making up stories.

One

"How's the new title, Mr. President?"

"Presidency looks damn good on me."

Carson Wentworth adjusted his tie in the mirror of his new plush office in the Texas Cattleman's Club clubhouse. His seventeen-year-old stepbrother, Tate, had called to check in as he usually did most mornings. They had a close bond and Carson knew Tate was proud of this accomplishment.

Tate had stood by his side the entire time from the start of the campaign. Their father had been around as well, but nobody supported Carson like his little brother.

"Do you often talk to yourself in the mirror?"

Carson jerked his attention away from the mirror and his cell on the table, focusing on his unexpected guest.

His rival, his enemy and the woman he couldn't get out of his damn fantasies. The very shapely, very intriguing Lana Langley was standing there giving him a once-over.

And it was that hoity-toity stare of hers that had him wanting to see if he could pull some kind of emotion out of her. He wondered if he peeled her from those body-hugging dresses and suits she wore, if she'd show him anything other than disdain.

"I'll call you later, Tate."

Carson tapped the cell to end the call without moving his gaze from Lana. The Langleys might be the sworn enemies of the Wentworths, but that memo had never quite reached his hormones.

Their families had started fighting a century ago, and from generation to generation, that animosity had been instilled in the children. But Carson's frustration with Lana had nothing to do with their families' past and everything to do with the fact she always seemed to be in his way.

She was too bold, too over-the-top. She had a take-charge attitude and he could appreciate that in some aspects of life, but they continually butted heads over what was best for the club.

Over the years, even a casual conversation would turn into something heated.

The damn woman was infuriating most days, but those curves begged for a visual lick and he was all too willing to sample.

She had to know she drove men out of their minds with the way she dressed—like she'd just stepped off a magazine shoot for sexiest woman alive. Lana had a confidence and an audacious attitude that most found intimidating, but Carson saw her as a challenge…and he never backed down from a challenge.

"Giving yourself a little ego boost?" she asked, crossing her arms over her chest. "Staring at your reflection is a tad cocky, don't you think?"

"Confidence is an attractive trait," he retorted.

Her red lips spread into a slow smile. "Then you must think I'm sexy as hell."

Confident and sexy—yes. Those two terms definitely applied to Lana, but she wasn't just a family enemy, she'd also been his opponent in the TCC presidential race. She'd been quite a formidable opponent to beat, what with her being the chair of the Cattleman's Club Women's Association and all. Carson had defeated her by a good margin and come out on top, despite her having the backing of every female rancher around.

"Did you come to see my new office or did you need to discuss club business?" he asked, turning fully to face her. "I have a meeting in a few minutes, but I can spare a moment for you."

"Well, aren't I the lucky one," she muttered.

Her dry comment had him chuckling. Lana was known for her quick wit, her independence, and for getting what she wanted…mostly. No doubt the recent loss still left a sting, but someone had to come in second and Carson never allowed himself to be vulnerable enough for anything less than number one.

"So what brings you here?" he asked.

Lana slowly crossed the open office area, her high heels echoing off the new hardwood floors. Carson watched as she examined the space, taking in the rustic decor of the sconces on the walls, which held photos of prior TCC presidents. Then she stopped when she got to his oversize mahogany desk. It was a piece he had brought in himself. He liked a large work space and wanted something of his own in this new role he'd taken on.

The silence made him twitchy...or perhaps those twitches came from watching her body shift beneath that sexy pencil dress in siren red. He couldn't tell if she'd come here to make him suffer or if she was taking in all she'd lost.

Perhaps a fair bit of both.

Finally, she turned to face him and laced her fingers in front of her body. The woman put up a good front of not giving a damn. She had her business face on and everything in Carson wanted to peel back that layer and see exactly what was beneath that steely exterior.

Passion...no doubt. A woman didn't dress with the confidence and sex appeal of Lana Langley and not have a burning passion beneath.

"Listen, Twenty-Two. My first order as club president was going to be focused on a new area exclusively for women," she began. "The good ol' boys ran this space for so long, and since women were allowed to become members ten years ago, we haven't our own designated space. That's too damn long to have to wait while we watch everything else get a face-lift around here. Everything in this building screams masculine and rustic, nothing is feminine. The ladies need something posh, something where we can unwind for a fun girls' night out."

Carson listened to her argument for changes at the club and realized she'd stopped. He'd heard it all before during the campaign and he didn't discredit her wants and needs. They just weren't going to be a priority on his current agenda, since he had a budget to stick to.

Silence continued to weigh heavy between them and her wide eyes were still locked solely on him. Clearly, she was waiting on his reply. He really didn't want to get into all of this when he was waiting on another woman to come through that door.

"Are you asking me a question or just telling me about your dashed dreams?" he queried.

Those bright blue eyes narrowed. "My dreams are far from dashed, Carson. I've given you time to settle in. Now I'm here as the chair of the women's association to make sure our needs are being met and we are getting what is fair and right. Just because I didn't win, doesn't mean I can't still fight for what we deserve."

Were they really going to have a showdown this early? He'd only had one cup of coffee and skipped breakfast. He needed more caffeine to deal with any type of altercation with Lana Langley. The woman was the most challenging person he'd ever dealt with. He could admit now that there had been a moment during the campaign he'd been worried she was going to win. She was damn good…but it wasn't something he'd admit to her.

The club meant too much to him, to his family. No matter the ties Lana had to the place, and hers were deep as well, but Carson had poured his entire heart into winning.

Carson actually did have a job to do within his family's ranching and oil business. The club was his escape, his joy. This was where he came to decompress…not negotiate with his sexy rival. The campaign had worn him out. He'd never worked harder in his life. Lana had challenged him at every turn and managed snappy, efficient comebacks when he would address a topic. If he hadn't been running, he would have voted for her. Again, not something he was about to admit to her.

Dealing with Lana was a necessity—Carson knew that. With their powerful positions here at the club, dealing with one another was inevitable. That didn't stop him from wishing they could just do phone calls or something else, rather than face-to-face meeting, where he had to take in the entire delectable package.

"While I appreciate your stance, what you're proposing sounds costly and there's no reason to—"

"There is every reason, Twenty-Two."

Carson shook his head. "Why do you keep calling me that?"

"If you'd done your homework on the club, you would know you're the twenty-second president."

"I'm well aware of the number I am." Carson sighed, really wishing he'd grabbed a second cup of coffee before that call with Tate. Maybe adding a little whiskey would've been a good idea as well. "Listen, I have an appointment any minute, so you're going to have to harass me another day."

That low, sultry laughter of hers filled the room, wrapping him in something too akin to arousal and he didn't like it. Not one bit. She made him so irritable and turned on, he'd instantly transformed into some kind of jerk with his words. He didn't mean to come across as condescending, but he'd opened his mouth and there it was.

Why this woman? Why couldn't someone, not a Langley, have him in knots? The media and locals had all been on the edge of their seats seeing how the feuding families would act during the campaign. Carson half wondered if they were waiting for the two of them to exchange punches or something. But there had been an agreement between the two of them going in. They weren't going to discuss their families' pasts because they each wanted to focus on the club and the future.

So at least that had been off the table.

"I've drawn up a proposal for the new women's area, along with a budget and bids from local contractors," she went on as if he hadn't said a word. "I actually emailed the options in very detailed spreadsheets to you this morning, so they will be in your inbox now. Once you go over that, we can discuss moving forward."

Wow. She really was something. The way she attempted to steamroll right over him took guts, but he wasn't having it. The rivalry between the Wentworths and the Langleys went back a century and didn't appear to be ending anytime soon.

Carson could see that if he didn't nip this in the bud now, she would become an issue now that he was president, and she'd try to see just how far she could push her own authority.

Perhaps her loss had damaged her pride more than he thought, or maybe she was one of those people who refused to admit defeat. Either way, he was in charge of the club, including any renovations and budget, and she needed to recognize that.

While Carson admired and even found Lana's determination attractive, he also knew if she even thought for a second that she could wrap him around her finger…she damn well would.

"There will be no moving forward," he informed her, taking a step closer. "I have other projects that need my immediate attention and building on an entire new wing isn't in the funds right now. I will take a look at this project for the future, but it certainly isn't on the top of my list right now."

Those blue eyes turned icy as she continued to hold his gaze. The woman was relentless, not backing down from something she wanted. Good for her. He admired her tenacity, but that didn't mean he'd give in, nor did he want to. Maybe it was about time Lana learned the word *no*.

"You'll see it is in the budget when you look at the proposals I sent over," she stated through gritted teeth. "I'm not sure why you aren't even up to discussing this unless you're afraid of—"

"I'm not afraid of anything where you're concerned."

Except this growing, unwanted, unnecessary attraction. Those damn curves got him. He loved nothing more than running his hands over the slopes and silky skin of a shapely woman. And, damn it, Lana was lusciously shaped in exactly all of his favorite spots. Too bad she was a Langley.

"Excuse me?"

Carson turned toward his open doorway to see Sierra Morgan standing there with a smile on her face.

The investigative journalist who had come to town a few months ago to do a piece on the Texas Cattleman's Club's tenth anniversary of admitting women members had ended up staying longer, as she'd decided to write a book on the subject and then stumbled upon even bigger stories.

Now, freelancing for the *Royal Gazette*, she not only was investigating a historical feud involving club members that would connect to her book, but she was also writing stories about an abandoned baby found in the hospital parking lot back in October…and the continuing search for the baby's father, who was supposedly a TCC member. Sierra had found herself caught up in all the scandals and secrets Royal, Texas, had to offer.

Now she wanted to interview Carson about his new position as president, though he had a strong feeling this session would turn into a grilling about his great-grandfather. Harmon Wentworth thought he was near death, and he was determined to discover who his birth mother was before he passed on. In whatever spare time she had, Sierra seemed to be helping Harmon, using a diary filled with clues.

Carson resisted the urge to rake a hand over his head because he seriously needed to get that second cup of coffee before tackling this interview. There was too much drama, too many secrets floating around this town, and he didn't want any of that to overshadow one of the biggest accomplishments of his life.

"Is this a bad time?" Sierra asked.

"Yes," Lana replied.

"No," Carson said at the same time.

Sierra's smile faltered as her eyes darted between

the two. "I can come back," she suggested as she started to turn back around.

"Not at all."

Carson refused to let Lana have any control, especially where club business was concerned. Again, the woman needed to learn who was in charge.

"We have an appointment and Lana was just leaving."

He focused his attention back on her and raised his eyebrows.

"I was?" she asked with a wide smile and a little lilt in her tone. "I thought we were just getting started on negotiations."

"Actually, since you're both here, maybe I could interview you, too, Lana?" Sierra asked.

Now Carson did rake a hand over the back of his neck and sighed. Great. Just what he wanted. He'd lost control to his enemy and a nosy reporter. So much for being president.

Damn it.

Things could only get better from here...right?

From Carson's tight lips and stiff posture, it seemed Mr. President wasn't thrilled one bit with the idea of her sticking around for this impromptu dual interview.

Lana couldn't help but smile, knowing full well she was getting under Carson's skin. Well, that was just too bad because he'd been under hers for too damn long.

Aside from the presidential race, where her loss left her ego too bruised for comfort, she found him far too attractive.

And why was that? The man was arrogant and egotistical, not to mention he was a Wentworth. Might as well be a spawn of the devil himself because the Wentworths and the Langleys meshed about as well as fire and ice, all because one hundred years ago there had been a lover's tryst and hidden secrets. None of that had anything to do with any of them today, but for whatever reasons, people just couldn't let the war die off.

Settling into the leather club chair across from Carson's oversize desk, Lana crossed her legs and flashed her smile to Carson as he took a seat and shot her a glare.

Poor baby. He was getting steamrolled by two powerful women. Must be hell on his overinflated ego.

He'd gotten a cup of coffee from the coffee bar in the corner after Sierra and Lana had both declined a cup. Now he looked like he wanted something a bit stronger in that mug.

"This is just great," Sierra said as she pulled her notebook and pen from her bag. She shifted her focus to Carson. "Before we get to how the new presidency is going and the future of the club, I'd love to get your take on your great-grandfather searching for information on his birth mother."

Lana perked up at that statement as she watched Carson's reaction. His eyebrows drew together and he eased forward in his seat, but before he could respond, Sierra went on.

"As you know, in addition to researching the Texas Cattleman's Club, I've been doing some articles on the abandoned baby, Micah. Just to catch you up... After finding his deceased mom's diary, we were able to connect Micah with his aunt Eve. Eve Martin had been heading to the hospital to look into DNA testing for Micah when she suddenly fell ill from a heart condition—the same genetic condition that killed her sister, Micah's mother, Arielle. Eve barely made it to the lobby before passing out. Now we know she left her nephew in his carrier on the trunk of a car—a car that belonged to your cousin, Cammie Wentworth. Cammie, along with her fiancé, Drake, are serving as the baby's foster parents until Eve can recover enough to resume custody.

"But the unknown father remains a mystery. And there were rumors all over town as to who he could be. I'm using Arielle's diary to find any suspects. The diary says he's a club member—I'm still working on that—but the diary also has some interesting information in there about your great-grandfather Harmon and his search for his birth mother.

"Arielle was helping him with research before she died. I've decided to take over where she left off. Another mystery to solve," Sierra stated, pulling in a deep breath. "And there's also mention that Harmon wants the Wentworth-Langley feud to come to an end. He wants peace restored to the families in his lifetime, but no one knows what started the feud a century ago."

Lana marveled at how Sierra knew all of this, but the woman was a top investigative reporter, so she had her ways. She had come to town to do a piece on the history of the Texas Cattleman's Club, which had become a book project. Her timing couldn't have been better. She'd stumbled onto several town mysteries.

Now Sierra found herself all tangled up in the intricate weave of the web known as Royal, Texas.

Every single day seemed to bring some new nugget

of information and Lana figured Sierra was having the most exciting career moment of her life.

"I've been following your stories about Micah. You're a good writer. But I'm not really at liberty to discuss my great-grandfather," Carson stated, clasping his hands together on his desk. "Our family issues are between us and certainly nothing I want in your reporting, since we all have mixed views on the quarreling between the Wentworths and the Langleys."

"Well, I do have the diary right now." She pulled the item from her purse and placed it on Carson's desk. "It was rather enlightening, but there are still chunks missing and that's what I need to find. I don't like missing puzzle pieces."

Sierra pursed her lips before turning to Lana. "And what about you? Do you have any input on this feud?"

Lana had always wondered what on earth could have been so bad that the hatred of two families could last for generations. What would be so terrible and unforgivable that it had to trickle down the lineage?

Lana had heard rumors of relationships gone wrong, but she really never asked questions. She'd been too busy living her own life in the here and now to worry about something petty that happened a century ago.

Still, just because she wanted to ignore it, didn't mean it didn't exist. But, because of the wedge between the families, Lana had never even tried to be chummy with Carson...and because of that arrogant personality of his, she was just fine with that.

"I can't give you any information on the family feud,"

Lana replied, honestly. "But I wouldn't mind visiting Harmon and finding out what he knows firsthand."

"Like hell."

Carson's outburst had both women jerking their attention toward him.

"And why is that?" Lana asked, straightening her spine. "Aren't you interested?"

"Ancient history is irrelevant to my life now," Carson stated.

"Actually, I've been wondering if Harmon's birth mother is what started this feud between the Langleys and the Wentworths." Sierra pursed her lips and tapped the tip of the pen against her notebook. "And a source told me Harmon said he wasn't going to release his fortune to the Texas Cattleman's Club upon his death if the two families are still at odds with each other."

Lana couldn't tear her gaze away from Carson. Clearly some of what Sierra had just shared wasn't news to him, but he seemed surprised that she had that information.

This town was riddled with secrets and it was giving Lana a headache. Lana really just wanted to focus on her own goals, which she'd set while she'd been campaigning. She'd wanted to continue the hard work her sister-in-law, Abby, had started ten years ago. Abby had fought to make the clubhouse coed and had been the first female club member. Abby had been Lana's biggest cheerleader and confidante during the presidential campaign. No doubt this loss had torn at Abby's heart just as much as Lana's.

But just because Lana had lost didn't mean she couldn't fulfill a need where she saw fit. The women of the club still needed an area they could call their own, something luxurious and extravagant that didn't scream of male ruggedness.

One thing at a time, though. Right now, she had to deal with Sierra, Carson, and the idea of seeing Harmon.

Making sure to keep her own questions to herself, Lana took in a good breath of self-control and waited on Carson to say something regarding Harmon.

"Whatever my great-grandfather has going on with his past or his fortune really isn't fodder for the press," Carson added. "But, if you want to talk about my new title here at the club, I would be more than happy to get into that conversation."

"I mean no disrespect," Sierra scoffed. "I'm simply an investigative journalist doing my job. Maybe Lana has an opinion on Harmon and these rumors."

Oh, Lana had opinions for sure, but she was smart enough to hold her thoughts inside…for now.

"Do you want to know what started this battle between the families?" Sierra urged.

"It's certainly something I've thought about over the years," Lana admitted. "But this has gone on for so long and really doesn't have anything to do with me, exactly. Generations are just trained from the start to know who they are at odds with. Sounds like Harmon is tired of the pettiness and wants to resolve things while he's still alive."

Lana pursed her lips, then spoke before she could think twice. "I'd love to pay Harmon a visit. I mean, I'm a Langley and if he really wants to put an end to this feud, perhaps we can work something out."

"Hell no."

This was the second time an outburst from Carson surprised her. She'd known he had a defiant opinion and could be outspoken, that much had been obvious during their election campaign, but she'd never seen him this defensive. Lana couldn't help but wonder what he was so worried about.

"And why is that?" Lana asked. "Maybe we can put this to rest once and for all, plus get those funds for the club. You already made a comment about my ideas and the budget. There's no reason I can't pay him a visit."

"Then I'm coming, too."

Judging from his wide eyes and slight intake of breath, apparently Carson was just as surprised by his abrupt statement as Lana.

"Fine. I'll be back this afternoon and we can head over." She got to her feet and glanced to Sierra. "I do apologize, but I have to run. Maybe we can do lunch or coffee sometime and you can interview me."

Sierra nodded with a bright smile. "I'd love that."

Lana didn't bother saying goodbye to Carson as she made her way out of his office. She had a few errands to run and she wanted to change her clothes. She'd put on a killer outfit for this morning's verbal sparring session with Carson, but to pay a visit to Harmon in the assisted-living facility, she wanted to be a little more comfortable and conservative.

That's not to say she still couldn't have a killer outfit, though. She had curves—curves that she actually loved accentuating and showing off. And it wasn't lost on her that Carson seemed to appreciate a shapely woman as well. For years she'd been aware of him visually sampling her, and though he might despise her, simply for her name if no other reason, she knew that he found her attractive. She'd have to be completely oblivious to not notice...and Lana was quite aware of everything about Carson Wentworth. From his sexy Southern drawl to his broad, muscular frame.

Too bad he was a Wentworth and she was a Langley.

Two

As if her body-hugging dress from this morning wasn't enough, now Lana was wearing ass-hugging jeans, a red sweater, and cowgirl boots. Carson stood at her front door taking in the total package and wishing he would have really thought this through. He needed to keep his distance, but since she'd insisted on seeing Harmon, Carson would damn well be going with her.

Lana looked totally different than she had earlier in his office. She'd pulled up her long, dark hair into a high ponytail and looked too damn adorable, like the girl next door…but he knew the vixen that she truly was.

Lana could go from CEO style to country girl in a snap and both looks were hell on Carson's system. He shouldn't want to find her attractive, but damn it.

She'd been a stunner all through school, and the older they got, the sexier she became. That body nearly had him forgetting he'd been conditioned his entire life to despise her and anyone else with that dreaded last name.

The shape of Lana Langley could make any man forget everything else, except the hope of exploring…

Stop. Just stop. Carson had to get control over his thoughts or he'd look like a damn fool. She knew what she looked like and that was likely why she purposely tried to drive him out of his ever-loving mind with want and need. She was aiming to get those wily claws in him and if he didn't focus on his own life and his own goals, he'd fall prey to her.

Now that the election was over, Carson needed to shift back to finding the social life that he'd put on hold for so long. Go on a date, get laid, anything to exorcise Lana from his mind.

Getting entangled with a Langley wouldn't bode well for either of them. Not when the feud was front and center now, with Harmon's will conditions and that diary with his thoughts floating around. Thankfully, though, Sierra had gotten Eve's permission to lend him Arielle's diary to see if he could spot any clues Sierra had missed. Carson wished the family war had never started, then maybe he and Lana wouldn't already have this rift between them. He wouldn't mind exploring his attraction to her, if that was the case.

But that wasn't the reality he lived in—not only did the war exist, but the two of them had also thrust it into the limelight with their campaign, as the Wentworths and Langleys went at it again.

"What are you doing here?" she demanded, holding on to her front door.

Carson was starting to question that himself. Clearly he was a masochist, but he preferred to cling to the fact he would try to have the upper hand wherever and whenever possible. He hadn't gotten this far in his life by letting others get the edge over him.

"I'm here to take you to see my great-grandfather."

Lana rolled her eyes. "I told you we'd meet at your office, and I'm more than capable of driving myself."

"It's a free service from your new club president."

Now those piercing eyes narrowed. "I like the amenities the way they are, Twenty-Two."

"Quit calling me that," he commanded.

"It's a free service," she retorted.

Why? Why had he thought coming here and taking her was the smartest move he could make? Because clearly he should have met her at the office and merely monitored her there.

But he wanted to talk to her before they went in to see Harmon, and now he realized texting or a simple old-school phone call would have proved just as efficient. Yet, here he was on her porch, and leaving now would only make him look weak, which was the last thing he could afford around Lana.

"If we're riding together, I'm driving," she commented with a smirk. "I only relinquish control when absolutely necessary."

That naughty grin, combined with the bold statement, had him visualizing Lana spread out on his bed beneath him, thoroughly enjoying everything he gave…and not one bit in control, as she came utterly undone beneath his touch.

In that instant he knew he was in for trouble—just how much was the scariest part. And he also had to assume that whole control comment of hers was also a warning.

Their verbal sparring matches were continually on-going. Different day, same banter laced with sexual tension. At some point, one of them was going to snap.

"Fine," he conceded. "I don't have trouble giving up control."

Lana stared into his eyes, then her gaze dropped to his mouth before she looked directly at him once again. "I do find that difficult to believe. Someone like you would never give up control."

Carson took a step forward before he even realized he'd moved. Suddenly, he was within an inch of her face and her swift intake of breath seemed to wrap around him. So, like the masochist he was, Carson took this a step further.

"A powerful, confident man knows when to let the lady take charge," he murmured, pleased when her eyes widened and that dainty pink tongue moistened her red lips. "There are many circumstances when I'm more than happy to let my woman dominate me."

Shut up. Shut up. Why the hell was he doing this? Why couldn't he get that image of Lana and her sweet curves wrapped in his sheets out of his mind? And why was he playing the mental game of foreplay? None of this made sense, but he couldn't stop himself. It was as if his mind had two completely different compartments and they were battling against each other: common sense versus aching desire.

Lana took a step back and tipped her chin. "Good thing I'm not your woman," she replied. "I'm positive you and I would never get along, no matter how sexy those seductive words and mental images are."

Carson said nothing, but remained in her doorway holding her gaze.

"You *were* trying to seduce me with your words, were you not?" she asked, quirking one dark, perfectly arched eyebrow.

Carson couldn't help but smile. "Are you looking to be seduced, Lana?"

Those striking blue eyes darted to his mouth once more and hovered there a fraction longer than he was comfortable with.

Carson stepped onto the threshold and her focus came back up to his eyes. She said nothing, and he wondered if she wasn't a Langley and he wasn't a Wentworth what would happen if he closed that door behind him and flicked the lock. Would she welcome him in? Would she make good on the promise that stare had been offering up?

Mercy, they'd tear each other up in the bedroom. If he thought their encounters were heated now, he couldn't even imagine what might happen when he got her into his bed.

When? No, that couldn't be…could it? Why did he automatically assume they'd be intimate?

They were the modern-day Montagues and Capulets, and sex, no matter how amazing it would be, wouldn't change their names or circumstances. And, damn it, he knew they'd be combustible and it would likely be the greatest affair he'd ever enter into.

Carson nearly cursed himself. They hadn't entered into any agreement, sexual or otherwise, and he'd already somewhat dubbed her the best he'd ever had?

Clearly, he needed to call one of his lady friends and remove Lana from the forefront of his mind.

"We need to leave." Her voice cracked a little, then she cleared her throat and reached for her purse, which was hanging by the door. "Step aside."

Carson stepped back outside, onto the porch and off to the side so she could come out. He needed to remember that command of staying out of her way because now that the election was over, there really was no need for them to worry about seeing each other as often. There were no debates, no TCC rallies or meet-and-greets. They'd run into each other at the clubhouse and maybe an occasional society affair, but nothing more than that.

Which might help him tamp down his attraction and ease his mental state. He'd likely go mad if he had to keep in too much contact with the intriguing, lush Lana Langley.

All of those verbal matches over the last few months had only made the great divide even larger... unfortunately, it had also made him realize just how sexy and powerful she truly was.

Lana walked beside Carson as they entered the assisted-living facility. On the ride over Carson had attempted to lecture her in the dos and don'ts of her visit with Harmon, but she'd completely tuned him out.

Honestly, how did he expect her to even form a coherent thought, let alone try to hold a conversation? She'd stared out the window for fear that her entire face, neck, and upper chest was flushed because of the way Carson had lowered his voice and made his Southern drawl all the more arousing.

And why was that? She'd grown up in Royal, so that sexy twang was all she'd heard her entire life. Why did this man and his toe-curling tone have to get to her?

At first, she'd only assumed because he was off-limits, but now…she honestly didn't know. During the debates, he'd gotten under her skin in all sorts of ways. He'd been demanding and cocky, and she'd found that both annoying and sexy as hell.

"Remember what I told you," Carson said as he turned to her.

Remember? If she'd heard the first time maybe that would be an option.

Lana pasted on a smile and nodded because she just wanted to get into this room to see what Harmon Wentworth would share about the epic family feud. At one hundred, the man certainly wasn't getting any younger and she really didn't want the secrets dying with him.

"Believe it or not, I don't make a habit of badgering the elderly. I save that for my opponents."

Lana patted his cheek, shocked when that coarse scruff on his jawline raked against her palm. Her entire body zinged from just that one, simple act and she couldn't help but wonder how that facial hair would feel against her bare skin in more…delectable areas.

Carson reached up and grabbed her hand before she could remove it. The muscle beneath her palm clenched and she couldn't tear her eyes away from his for anything. She should, though. She should jerk her hand away, turn and waltz into Harmon's room, yet she stood here staring at those captivating green eyes, wishing they were somewhere else more private.

No. She couldn't wish such naive things. Carson didn't like her any more than she liked him. Even in school they'd hung out with opposite crowds and kept their distance just because of the simple fact that she'd always been told to avoid the Wentworths. All those years of having that drilled into her head went right along with the opinion she'd formed on her own, that he was an arrogant man.

She could find Carson attractive, but there was no way in hell she could act on unwanted desire. He was just getting under her skin, that's all.

Before she could speak or move her hand away, the door was flung open. Carson jerked in surprise and Lana removed her hand from his face...but not before she caught the smile from the nurse and the curious look of Harmon, who was seated and had clearly seen the near embrace.

"So sorry," the nurse said as she stepped back. "Please, come on in. I was just passing Mr. Wentworth his afternoon medications."

Lana moved into the room and was surprised how spacious and homey the private suite appeared. For assisted living, this was rather nice. Though Harmon certainly had the money and wouldn't pay to just be anywhere. This room was likely the nicest in the entire place and seemed more of a posh hotel rather than a home for seniors who needed assistance.

Carson returned the smile to the nurse before heading in. Once the nurse stepped out, he closed the door behind him before turning back to his great-grand-father.

"Well, this is a nice surprise," Harmon stated.

The elderly man's wide grin sent deep wrinkles

scrunching around his eyes and hairline. His silver hair had been combed neatly away from his face and he was wearing a button-up shirt and dress pants. He had on slippers and there wasn't a doubt in Lana's mind the man would much rather have on his cowboy boots.

Harmon Wentworth had been a staple in Royal for decades. The man could always be seen in the bar at the clubhouse and he'd been known for ruthless business transactions. He had been quite the mogul in his day.

But those days of farming and ranching and running his empire were over for Harmon. That was the brutal reality of life. Everything came to an end at some point whether you were ready or not.

"And who do you have here?" Harmon asked, using the arms of the chair to ease himself up.

He pasted on a smile and extended his hand like the Southern gentleman he'd been raised to be. Lana crossed the room and immediately took his hand.

"I'm Lana Langley, Mr. Wentworth. It's so nice to meet you."

His grip was firm, but he quickly released her hand. Those white, bushy eyebrows rose as Harmon's attention shifted to Carson. Behind her, Carson moved toward them.

"Langley?" Harmon asked, clearly surprised. "Carson, I didn't certainly expect something this fantastic."

Lana watched as a slow smile turned into a low laugh and Harmon pulled Carson into an embrace before releasing him and reaching for her.

"This is wonderful news," he declared. "Simply wonderful. I never thought I'd see the day, but I'm so glad I'm still on this earth for this moment. I can honestly say, I don't know that I've had a happier moment in the last several years than this right here."

Lana nearly stumbled as he ended the hug, but she pulled herself together with a deep breath. What was he talking about?

Harmon gestured to the sofa across from his sitting chair. "Please, sit. Why didn't I hear about this relationship before now? Finally, a Langley-Wentworth union. I never thought I'd see the day."

"Sir—"

"So, how long have you two been together?" Harmon asked, cutting off Lana as she took a seat next to Carson. "I hope this isn't just something temporary. A long-term commitment would simply be… Well, life-changing."

"A serious relationship with Lana," Carson chuckled. "Grandfather, she and I—"

"Are hopefully heading down the aisle soon," he said with a grin as he eased back into his chair. "This is absolutely epic, Carson. I wanted the families to bury the hatchet, so to speak, but I never thought an engagement would come from my warnings. No matter if this makes the family angry or not, it's time for this to end. I meant it when I said I would be withholding my funds from the clubhouse upon my death if there isn't some unification or rebuilding of the relationships between the Langleys and the Wentworths. But an engagement… I hope I'm not getting carried away. From what I saw in the doorway, you two are in a committed relationship, right?"

"Engaged?" Lana whispered, her gaze darting to Carson as her heart clenched in her chest.

In a moment that shocked her even more than opening her door to see Carson standing on the other side earlier, he reached for her hand and gave a squeeze. She didn't like that silent gesture and dread settled deep as she feared she'd just stepped into an impossible situation.

Absolutely not. This was not happening.

"We wanted to come here and tell you first," Carson said in a voice far too calm under these absurd circumstances. "I knew you would be happy with the news."

Lana kept her focus on Carson, silently willing him to glance her way so he could see what she was sure was her best death glare.

What the hell kind of game was this? Had this been a setup on his part? Is that why he'd insisted on accompanying her?

Well, she couldn't let this go on for one more minute. Faking an engagement or any other type of union with Carson was wrong. Not only was it wrong, but it was also never going to become a reality.

Lana started to step forward, but Carson's grip tightened for a fraction of a second. His eyes held hers now and she saw it—pleading. Never in her life had she seen such a gesture from Carson. If this had been some type of setup, he had a reason. And they were going to have one hell of a talk once they left because she deserved an explanation.

"So, when is the big day?" Harmon asked, his thick eyebrows raised and his dark eyes wide. Clearly, the man was eager for details.

Carson held her gaze another second before turning his attention back to his great-grandfather.

"Everything is still so new, we haven't made any arrangements," Carson replied.

Harmon nodded. "I suppose with the club presidential race and all of that, you two haven't had a chance to do much else."

"We haven't," Carson acknowledged. "We actually both had an interview this morning with Sierra Morgan. She's digging around into your past and the feud. That diary of Arielle Martin's has really piqued everyone's interest."

"That's one of the reasons I wanted to come see you, Mr. Wentworth," Lana chimed in, really needing to take back some semblance of control.

"Call me Harmon. You're joining the family."

Like hell.

"Can you tell us anything about why this feud started and why it's still going on?" Lana asked.

Harmon glanced out the window next to his chair and seemed to be contemplating how to answer, or even if he was going to give her a response. Lana slipped a side glance to Carson, whose eyes remained on his great-grandfather.

Coward. She never took Carson for a coward, but the man wasn't able to look at her. Well, he couldn't hide forever and he would certainly be getting an earful the moment they got to the parking lot.

Another bubble of fury started within her when she thought back to Carson at her home. He'd been flirty, almost too much. Was this why? Damn it. He had a plan and he hadn't wanted to tell her?

Did he think she'd actually go along with this preposterous scheme? He might have won the TCC presidency over her, but there was no way he was taking

charge here and forcing her hand into some engagement. Even if she was looking for a husband, Carson
Wentworth would be the last one on the list.

No, he wouldn't even *be* on the list.

"I think the feud started with my birth, but I don't
know anything else," he answered. "Now I want to
find who my birth mother was before I die and I
wanted this feud settled, so I guess I'm halfway there."

Harmon now seemed to believe that the families
were merging together, and he was sitting there looking back at her with such happiness, she would only
be a jerk if she called out Carson on his lie now.

"I'm not sure when we'll actually…marry." Lana
couldn't believe she was even speaking these words.
"We're both pretty busy people."

Harmon nodded. "I understand, Lana. No rush on
the wedding. But what do you all say you have an engagement party at the club at the end of the month?
We can celebrate your union and the end of the family
feud. You can then make an announcement that I will
be donating an exorbitant sum to the club for any renovations or new amenities you both deem necessary.
You won't have to wait until I die to get the money."

Was she seriously considering this farce?

Yes, she was. Because if lying for a short time
would finally end this century-old battle, then she
didn't mind doing her part.

But, an entire month? That seemed so long. Weeks
worth of pretending to be in love with Carson? What
would that entail? Scenarios bounced around her
mind, from holding hands to kissing to…

No. There could be nothing else. If they had to

fake anything, it would all be in public for show.
Nothing more.

Once this was all said and done, Lana would have
the funds she'd wanted for the women's lounge. Abby
would be proud that Lana was continuing the hard
work she'd started a decade ago.

"How are you settling into your new role?" Harmon asked Carson.

Well, obviously the man had spoken and assumed
they would just fall in line with his demands. How in
the hell had her impromptu idea to visit only hours
ago suddenly lock her into a month-long engagement
to a man she hated…yet desired so much more than
she should have? She didn't want to hurt Harmon, despite him being a Wentworth. The man had done nothing personal to her—he seemed genuine, and he just
wanted to make peace. How could she go against that?

"I'm excited to get started on the new plans and the
next chapter," Carson replied as if his life hadn't just
taken a drastic turn in the last five minutes.

Lana listened as Harmon and Carson discussed
club business, clearly having moved beyond the engagement chat or anything regarding the diary.

And Carson still had a hold of her hand. Oh, she
could pull away, but then what would that look like?
Maybe there was some reason Carson wanted to enter
into this absurdity. Maybe he wanted this so Harmon
would give the club the donation. She couldn't deny
that she wanted those funds, too, and clearly this was
the price she'd have to pay.

Lana had so many questions and concerns assault-
ing her from all directions, and she didn't want to sit
around here making small talk. She wanted to get back

out into the privacy of her vehicle and make Carson explain himself.

The conversation between the two men seemed to go on and on. Lana tried to focus on what they were talking about, but nothing of any importance was said about the diary or the fighting that dated back a century. That had been the sole purpose of Lana's visit. Never in her life had she expected to be trapped in such a circumstance, where she saw no immediate way out.

And the longer she sat here, pretending like nothing was wrong, like her life hadn't just come to a halt, the angrier she became.

She'd grown up surrounded by lies and deceit. Her mother had put up with that for far too long and Lana vowed never to be weak or a pushover when it came to men. Her father had been so dishonest about every aspect of his life and Lana's mother had simply gone right along with it, never questioning.

Lana found out years later about the affairs and the financial troubles her parents were having. While her mother continued to always put up a perfect front, Lana's father continued to live his filthy, lying life of infidelity.

Finally, Lana got to her feet and smiled at Harmon. "You'll have to excuse us, Mr. Wentworth."

"Harmon, remember?" he reminded her. "We're going to be family."

Lana nodded her head and offered, "Harmon. I'm sorry, but I do have an appointment with my sister-in-law shortly and we'll have to be going."

"Oh, I'm terribly sorry for droning on and on," he stated, as he slowly pushed to his feet and steadied himself on the arms of the chair. "Keep me updated on the engagement party and the wedding date. It was wonderful to see you, Carson."

Harmon turned to Lana and extended his hand once again. "And you, too, young lady. I look forward to hearing more about this union."

That made two of them, because this was just as new to her as it was to him.

"Nothing will bring me greater joy than seeing this feud finally put to rest." Harmon smiled and shook his head. "I never dreamed a wedding would turn these families around. Once and for all we will be joined in love instead of divided by hate."

Lana saw her opening and dove in headfirst.

"I hope I'm not overstepping here, but since I will be—" she swallowed the lump "—joining the Wentworth family, what started all of this fighting?"

"I don't remember. It was so long ago…" Harmon's eyes seemed to dim as his lids lowered. "Along with the feud, my birth mother is still a mystery. I'd do anything to have that truth uncovered. When Arielle came through doing research, I told her everything I know."

Lana felt for him. She really did. His time on this earth was running out and he just wanted answers. He not only wanted answers, but he also wanted all of this hatred put to rest once and for all.

But this trouble that started so long ago wasn't her fault, had nothing to do with her whatsoever, actually. So she shouldn't have to be punished…should she?

"I'll come by later in the week to see you," Carson promised.

The two men embraced and something flipped in Lana's chest. She hadn't imagined Carson as much of a family man. She knew he was close to his step-brother, Tate, but other than that, she didn't bother herself thinking of anything else regarding his personal life.

She'd known him since grade school, but he'd been an arrogant brat back then, playing all the sports, being the jock, and dating all the "perfect" girls with their teased hair and itty-bitty figures.

Her opinion of him hadn't changed much over the years. He still came off as an arrogant jerk...like when she'd found him admiring himself in the mirror earlier while on speakerphone.

But there was something about seeing him softer with Harmon that made her wonder if there was another side to Carson and why he never let the public see that one. Why was he always so harsh, so controlled, and powerful? Maybe he did have actual human feelings beneath that steely exterior.

Not that she wanted to see him in any other manner. She needed that arrogance, that stiff upper lip he had, because if he rid himself of either of those qualities, she'd be in trouble. That sex appeal could only be ignored for so long and she'd done a damn good job in her all of her thirty-two years.

But she wasn't about to let this little stunt go.

As she marched ahead of him to the car, Lana already had her virtual bullet-point presentation in her head regarding all the questions she needed answers to.

Sexy or not, there was no way in hell she was going to pretend to be okay being engaged—fake or otherwise—to Carson Wentworth.

Three

He'd barely gotten his door closed before Lana laid into him. She'd tossed him her keys in the parking lot, a definite warning she was pissed.

"You are out of your ever-lovin' mind if you think I'm going to act like the doting fiancée."

The fact that she gave up the driver's seat for the ride back was not a good sign.

He raked a hand down his face and blew out a sigh before shifting in his seat and turning to focus on her. Oh, she was angry. Those expressive eyes were wide, unblinking, and her lips had thinned. He didn't have to know her strong personality to figure out she'd not been too thrilled inside at the bomb that had been dropped between them.

"Trust me," he assured her. "I don't want to be tied to you any more than you want to be tied to me."

"Always the charmer," she murmured as she glanced out the windshield.

Carson studied her profile. Her beauty couldn't be denied, and neither could the punch of lust to his gut. Attraction wasn't the issue. Carson found many women attractive, but none got under his skin like Lana Langley. Perhaps it was because she not only had the looks, but she also had that independence and drive. She'd gone toe-to-toe with him for the club presidency and he could admit now that they were on the other side, that he'd been worried that she might win. She had the backing of all of the women, considering her position as the chair of the Cattleman's Club Women's Association.

"Did you do this on purpose?" she asked.

Carson jerked back. "What?"

"Did you know what he would think when you decided to come with me?"

Her accusation took a moment to register and Carson couldn't help but laugh. "You think I volunteered to come with you, a visit that was your idea, by the way, all to trap you into an engagement? Honey, don't embarrass yourself."

"Then what do you expect to come from all of this nonsense?" Lana turned toward him once again. "Do you expect me to marry you? Do you expect us to just pretend? How long will that have to go on?"

Lana let out a rich burst of laughter that did nothing to squelch the desire churning in his gut. Even angry and frustrated, she was still damn enticing— not enough that he wanted to be engaged, but here they were.

"Who on earth would believe us in love enough

to become engaged?" she added, still laughing. "We were at each other's throats during the campaign, and that's without the infamous family feud."

Carson shook his head. "I have no idea how to pull this off, but did you see his face? I haven't seen him that excited, that surprised and happy, in years. And to know that I was the one who created that joy for him..."

Damn it. He refused to lose it in front of Lana...in front of anyone, really. He couldn't mentally afford to come undone. With his powerful family name and his newly appointed position with the TCC, Carson had to be in control of his emotions at all times.

The last person who could see him as weak was the one person he couldn't get away from.

Lana waited as Carson trailed off and glanced out the side window for a moment. No doubt trying to compose himself.

When he turned back, Carson held her gaze with a fierceness she hadn't seen from him.

"I will do anything for that man," he went on. "Anything. If that means faking this engagement for the next month, then so be it. We pretend to be in love, we go to a party, the money gets donated to the club, and everyone is happy."

Lana laughed. "We'll both be miserable and I don't think you could handle me for that long."

"You think I can't handle you?"

When he reached his arm out to stretch across the back of her seat as he leaned in, Lana's breath caught in her throat. That unwavering dark gaze of his seemed to penetrate through the wall of defense she'd kept up. She had to have that wall, that barrier, between this strong, sexy man and her firm vow to herself that she'd never let another man control her. Not physically or emotionally.

Agreeing to this engagement would be just that. The circumstances would be out of her control...but only temporarily.

"I see your mind working," Carson murmured. "One month, Lana. That's all we need to make this ruse work for everyone."

Why did that husky, gravelly tone make her nerve endings stand at attention? And why did she suddenly have the urge to see if those lips were as soft as they looked?

Finding Carson Wentworth sexy was one thing, and something she could live with and ignore, but fantasizing about that mouth was a whole other territory she shouldn't venture into.

"And I will have no problem...handling you."

Had he eased closer? Was this space getting smaller? Good heavens, that woodsy cologne seemed to match perfectly with his cropped beard and those heavy lids. The man clearly was made for seduction, and perhaps using his charm was his key mechanism for gaining what he wanted.

But she had her own arsenal of tricks. She wasn't immune to how he looked at her, she wasn't immune to the crackling tension that had started during the campaign and seemed to be growing each day since.

Lana knew, though, that she did have the upper hand here. As much as she wanted those amenities for the women's group, she couldn't accomplish her goal without the new president on board, if she waited him out. But this would be the easiest way, and Carson was right in his assumption that everyone would benefit with a Langley-Wentworth union.

"One month," she agreed, then couldn't help herself and tapped his chin with her index finger. "Not a day more."

He snatched her hand and wrenched it aside as he leaned in closer. That heavy-lidded gaze dropped to her mouth a moment before he offered a naughty grin.

"Perhaps it will be you who's afraid to handle me," he whispered.

Then he turned her hand over until their palms were touching. She could pull back, she could ignore this insistent, invisible tug toward her enemy... but why, when it felt too damn good? When was the last time someone made her nerves tingle with excitement? When was the last time she enjoyed flirty banter?

It had been much too long. In fact, the last time was when she'd entered into what had ultimately become a serious relationship. Well, the joining had been serious on her end until she realized she wasn't being treated the way she deserved.

But that time in her life was over and she refused to allow the negativity to take up any headspace.

"Propose to me."

Carson blinked. "What?"

Lana smiled. "You want me to be your betrothed? Propose."

Carson laughed. "Betrothed? Let's not romanticize this."

"We're in the middle of a family feud and we've

made ourselves the sacrifice. Give me some romance, Twenty-Two."

"Is that the type of woman you are?" he asked, taking her hand and examining her fingers one by one. "You said you were the type of woman who wanted to be in charge in a relationship?"

Lana eased back slightly. This was too much. The way he'd manipulated her, this situation...not to mention the manner in which her body kept responding to Carson.

"Oh, I remain in charge, but that doesn't mean I don't want my man to put forth some effort."

"Are you going to be high-maintenance during this engagement?" he asked.

Lana laughed. "I plan on being myself. You still think you can handle me?"

In a swift move she never saw coming, Carson tugged her just close enough that the minuscule space between them was a mere whisper.

"Car—"

His lips closed over hers, not in a forceful, commanding way, but something... Hell, she had no clue how to explain such an unexpected response. New? Curious?

He explored her mouth as if getting to know her, as if taking his time would give him insight to something.

Lana had never been kissed this way before and she'd been convinced that Carson would be a domineering kisser... Yes, she'd thought about it, but she'd never, ever thought he would be so...thorough.

He released her hand as he framed her face, tipping her head just so, right where he wanted it, as he released her for a fraction of a second and then dove back in at a new angle.

She should stop this. Kissing Carson Wentworth was absolute madness. No good could come from acting on the chemistry and attraction. A faux engagement was enough to have her head spinning.

Carson eased back, his hands still secure on her face as his piercing green gaze met hers.

"What was that for?"

Did her voice sound as shaky as she felt? Because somehow the oxygen in the vehicle had all been sucked out and she was having a difficult time breathing.

"This needs to be believable, Lana. If my great-grandfather wants this century-old ax buried, you and I are going to be the ones to bury it."

"We don't even know what battle we're fighting and I never thought I'd team up with you for anything."

Carson dropped his hands, leaving her cool to the touch, which was positively absurd. She didn't crave his touch, nor did she want. She didn't. She just needed to find a date and kiss another man to prove Carson didn't affect her.

But apparently she would have to wait several weeks before that much-needed said date with another man.

"I think this is something we can both agree on," Carson stated. "If that kiss is any indictor, I'd say we can get along for a few weeks in order for the club to receive a very generous sum and to make an old man's dying wish."

Yeah, that last part was actually more important than the money. Lana might have been brought up to hate the Wentworths, but in all honesty, they had done nothing personally to her. Well, Carson was a jerk at times, but that was just his personality.

Harmon was one hundred years old and could die at any time. If his wish was to see this feud cease, then why wouldn't she want to help with that? Other than the fact that everything was a lie.

"This feels wrong," she murmured. "I've never lied in my life."

Carson's eyebrows rose as he eased back a little more. "Never? Not even as a teen?"

Lana curled back. "Never. First of all, I'm a terrible liar. I never saw a reason to back myself into a corner like that and I really don't want to ruin my excellent track record."

Carson nodded. "I get that, and I hate lying to my great-grandfather. But this is something he wants before he dies and we are the only ones who can fulfill that wish. I need your help."

Well, that final statement was sure as hell telling. She'd never known Carson to beg or plead before in her life. Typically, he flashed a smile or tossed money to get what he desired.

"How much did that cost for you to say that?" she joked.

"You have no idea the pain I'm going through knowing I need you in my corner."

Oh, she had a pretty good idea. Realizing she held the upper hand here really did amazing things for her self-esteem…which she appreciated since that dramatic loss by a landslide for the presidency.

"I'll agree to pose as your fiancée if you will immediately start on the women's wing at the clubhouse."

Carson nodded. "Done."

All of this seemed too easy. What was the real hang-up? Posing as a faux engaged couple wouldn't be too difficult. The hardest part would be convincing other people she and Carson were actually in love. But, for that expansion, Lana would do nearly anything. Women deserved just as much private space as the men and there were more female members now than ever before, thanks to her sister-in-law, Abby Langley, who'd opened that door years ago.

Lana fully intended on carrying out what Abby had started and if that meant playing nice with Carson, then so be it. Maybe he'd offer up more of those toe-curling kisses. At least that was something to look forward to, right?

"I'm still waiting on that proposal." Lana reached for her seat belt, silently hinting for him to get going. "People will want to know and I can't make up something like that."

Carson shifted in his seat and started the engine. "I knew this would be a high-maintenance relationship," he murmured.

"Anything worth having is going to take work." Lana reached over and patted his cheek. "If you want me to be your wife, I'm going to need you to give all you've got, Twenty-Two."

He grumbled something else beneath his breath as he pulled out of the parking lot and Lana just smiled as she stared out her window. She had no clue what this next month would bring, but she did know these next few weeks wouldn't be boring.

Four

What the hell had he been thinking kissing her like that? Now that's all he could think of because the damn image wouldn't get out of his head. Lana had always been too sexy for her own good, but he sure as hell hadn't expected her to taste or feel like all of his fantasies rolled into one.

Carson blew out a sigh and headed to the Colt Room for a drink. He'd sent several emails and made some calls regarding contractors for the new women's area. He planned on making good on his promise to Lana, because in turn that would make Harmon happy, and at the end of the day, that's all that mattered.

After that last phone call and then the visitor he'd had, Carson needed a stiff drink. He'd started off his day with an unwanted interview with Sierra, then had a bomb dropped in his life with that fake engagement to Lana, and now…hell. That ring box was way too damn heavy in his pocket.

As he entered the Colt Room, the instant smell of cigars and bourbon hit him and he felt like he was home. The atmosphere in here just appealed to him more than going home to have a drink.

With the rich wood and the dark steel, the Colt Room definitely lent itself to more of a masculine crowd. Carson could see why Lana wanted to push for the women to have something to call their own.

Perhaps that would be the best way to announce their engagement? Make a huge deal about the addition, as well as their joining the families together.

Carson couldn't think about all of this right now. He just wanted to take a minute to decompress before he moved on to the next stressful portion of his evening.

"Hey, Carson."

Blinking, Carson spotted his cousin Rafael and Rafe's dad, Tobias, at the end of the bar. Had Carson been focused when he walked in, he would have seen them. Granted, the Wentworths were a huge family and there were tons of members in their clan. Carson was glad Rafe and Tobias were finally coming together and getting along after years of being estranged.

He headed toward the end of the glossy mahogany bar and took a seat next to Rafael. Some considered him the black sheep of the family because Rafael had disappeared and done his own thing for years. Going against the family—against Tobias—had never been accepted. The Wentworths were a dynasty of moguls and barons, and breaking from tradition had stunned everyone. Being a world-renowned playboy hadn't helped, either, but now he was back and at the top of the list for the possible father of the abandoned baby found months ago.

Rumors about baby Micah were floating around town as to who could be the biological father, and Sierra was actively trying to identify Micah's dad. The only thing that was certain was that the mystery man was a Cattleman's Club member. That didn't necessarily narrow down the list, considering how many men in Royal, Texas, belonged to the elite establishment.

"How's the new president?" Tobias asked with a wide grin, the gesture creasing the corner of his eyes.

Aside from the fact that he had an unplanned engagement and a lie weighing heavy on his shoulders, things couldn't be better.

"I can't complain," Carson replied. "What are we drinking?"

"Bourbon." Rafael swirled the contents around in his glass. "Let me buy you a drink."

"I wouldn't turn that down."

The bartender came over and Carson chose a top-shelf bourbon before turning back to the guys.

"So what brought both of you out to the club on a Monday evening?"

Tobias adjusted his Stetson and shrugged. "We decided to meet here for a drink to unwind from the day. We'll probably end up eating dinner here."

The usually confident Tobias looked at Rafe. Obviously, they were still unsure of where they stood with each other and whether dinner together might be pushing it.

When Rafael nodded, Tobias turned back to Carson and said, "You're more than welcome to join us."

Carson would much rather have dinner with them as opposed to what he actually needed to do. That damn box in his pocket mocked him and he really had nobody to blame but himself. Had he just let Lana go visit Harmon on her own, there would have been no misunderstanding.

But there wasn't much he could do now to untangle the web of lies he'd started.

"Thanks, but I can only stay for a drink."

The bartender set his tumbler on the bar and moved back down to the group of men who'd just entered. Before Carson could take his first sip, Rafael jerked up from his stool and grabbed his cell off the bar.

"Excuse me. I've been waiting on this call."

Whatever it was, it must be something big, Carson mused. Rafe stepped off into the corner and raked a hand through his hair. Carson tried not to pay too much attention as he took a sip of his bourbon, but Tobias couldn't peel his eyes away.

After a moment, Rafael came back and slapped his hand on the bar top with a soft chuckle. "The next round is on me, guys."

"Good news?" Carson asked.

"You could say that. The DNA tests results are finally in and, as I've been saying, I'm not the father of Micah."

"I never thought you were the father," Tobias stated. "But I'm glad you have the proof. So who does that leave for them to look at next?"

Rafael shrugged as he took a seat back on the leather stool. "I have no clue, and now that Micah's mom, Arielle, is gone, there's no one to tell the truth. But whoever he is, I'm afraid he'll get raked over the coals from the people in this town for abandoning a pregnant woman and then not coming forward."

"Maybe he never knew she was pregnant," Carson added.

"That has to be the reason," Tobias agreed. "Regardless of who it is, someone's life is about to change dramatically."

Carson had his own issues to deal with and an infant was not one of them. The baby was in good hands, and right now, that's the best anyone could hope for.

"So what are your plans?" he asked Rafael. "Are you planning on leaving town or sticking around for a while?"

Rafael gripped his glass and shifted in his seat to face Carson. "Actually, I'm looking to open a luxe guest ranch as an investment property. I think something like that would really bring more people to Royal and produce a nice profit."

Carson nodded. "That sounds like a great plan. Certainly something the town could use."

"Nothing is official yet, I'm still just in the planning stages," Rafael added. "Hopefully this won't be long to turn into a reality."

Carson picked up his tumbler and tossed back the rest of his bourbon, welcoming the familiar burn. He needed a little courage right now. Which was ridiculous. He wasn't afraid of Lana…but he was afraid of the emotions she pulled from him.

The unwanted, disturbing, terrifying emotions. He wanted her. Plain and simple—or maybe not so plain and simple. Perhaps this was all complex and disorderly for all he knew. They'd just started on this path together and they still had the entire month left to go.

"I appreciate the drink." Carson got to his feet and tossed a couple bucks on the bar for the bartender. "I have to meet someone in a bit. It was good to see you both."

Tobias tipped his hat and Rafael nodded with a smile. Carson made his way out of the Colt Room and out of the clubhouse. The lot was full, which was the norm. At nearly any time of the day or evening, the Cattleman's Club was hopping. With all the amenities, the restaurant and the bar, there was something for everyone.

And there would be even more for the ladies once he and Lana went forward with their engagement…or at least pretended to. She'd make that ladies' lounge top priority the moment that money changed hands and was passed over to the club.

Why was he so nervous to head to Lana's house? He didn't plan on doing anything other than handing her the ring and leaving. That's all. Just to make everything look official before they went public with this farce.

The sun had already set and Carson turned off the main street through Royal, heading toward Lana's home on the edge of town.

Obviously, over the next several weeks they would both be venturing into new territory and spending more time together.

Their ruse had to look legit. Lying to his great-grandfather already had a heavy stone of guilt resting in his gut—the last thing he needed was to be caught in the lie.

For the second time today, Carson pulled into Lana's circle drive and killed the engine. He stared at the stone-and-wood home with the tall peak over the wide porch. A light inside the front door shone bright and another light at the end of the house was also on. She was awake. Maybe he should have called or texted. Hell, something to warn her he was coming.

He muttered a curse beneath his breath as he stepped from his SUV. He was dropping off a damn ring. That was all.

But mercy, what would she be wearing? Because she continually killed him with those damn body-hugging outfits. Those curves she had made him want to forget there'd ever been any feud, or that they now had a fake engagement. One night. That's all he wanted and then maybe he'd get Lana Langley out of his system.

Carson reached the porch and her front door swung open. Lana was standing there wearing a short robe and a crooked smile with one eyebrow raised.

Hell. He definitely should've called. This was a bad, bad idea.

Carson headed onto the porch, anyway, adrenaline and arousal pumping through him...totally ignoring the warning bells.

Five

Lana's driveway alarm had chimed through her house and echoed onto her patio just as she'd stepped from the hot tub and tied her robe. She'd dried off her feet and padded through the open area toward her front door. A quick peek through the etched glass and she knew who that strong build belonged to. She shouldn't have been surprised to see Carson on her doorstep, but she was.

Lana flicked her locks, opened the door wide, and gripped the edge of the wood as she stared at her unexpected guest.

The shadowy darkness combined with the slash of brightness from her porch light made him appear even more intriguing, sexy, and much too attractive for her to be noticing…especially half-dressed.

"Did I catch you at a bad time?" he asked.

"I just stepped out of the hot tub."

His shoulder relaxed as he took another step toward her. "For a second I thought I got you out of the shower and you had nothing on beneath that robe."

Lana laughed and propped one hand on her hip and one hand on the door. "I don't have anything on under the robe," she replied. "I live alone out in the country and have a private patio."

Carson's eyes widened a fraction, then they raked down her body. Maybe she should have kept that kernel of information to herself. The words had just escaped, and now with the way Carson's hungry gaze was traveling all over her body, she wondered what she had done. Like she needed more of a reason to be attracted to her temporary, fake fiancé.

"What are you doing here?" she asked, hoping to circle back to his reason for dropping by.

He continued to stare at her and Lana dropped her arms to her sides. Carson took another step closer, now coming fully into the light. Maybe he should've stayed in the partial shadow because now she could see every chiseled feature, the square jaw covered in stubble, the heavy-lidded stare, those piercing green eyes.

There was an intensity to him she'd never seen before. This wasn't oil-tycoon Carson or new-club-president Carson…this was Carson, the man who clearly couldn't hide his desire.

"Do you always answer your door nearly naked?" he asked, his voice husky.

That low tone sent shivers through her and made her think of a darkened room and rumpled sheets.

But she shouldn't be thinking of any such fantasy… at least not with Carson Wentworth.

"I'm not at all naked," she countered. "And believe it or not, I'm not naive. I looked out before opening the door. I didn't think you were here to rob me."

Carson closed the final few inches between them, causing Lana to tip back her head to hold his stare. She wasn't sure if he was trying to intimidate her, turn her on, or throw his masculine weight around. No matter what, Lana had to remain on her toes and in control…because she was about one more sexy statement away from ripping the tie from her robe and begging.

"What did you think I was here for?" he asked.

Lana licked her lips, another mistake. His eyes darted to her mouth and she honestly had not meant to do anything to draw his attention to any other parts of her body. It's just that her mouth had gone dry.

"I don't want to play games, Carson."

His lips quirked. "You said my name."

Confused, she jerked slightly, then remembered she'd been calling him by that silly nickname. Perhaps she should have stuck with that, but his name just slid through her lips.

"Why do you have to drive me crazy?"

She shifted her attention to the muttered statement he'd just made.

"What?" she asked.

Carson shook his head and raked a hand over the back of his neck. "You drive me crazy, okay? You have to know that."

"That's nothing new," she retorted. "We've driven each other crazy for—"

The man moved fast…too fast. One second he was

staring at her and the next one he had his hands on her face and was backing her into her house, with his mouth on hers. Lana gripped his shoulders—to prevent herself from stumbling or to get closer, she wasn't sure.

Damn, but he could kiss. He towered over her, he consumed her, he made her feel so feminine. She shouldn't find his commanding approach so attractive, but she couldn't help herself.

Carson pulled away just as abruptly as he'd come on to her. He cursed beneath his breath and turned away, staring back out the open front door. Was he ready to run? Was he having regrets?

Lana waited for him to finish whatever internal battle he seemed to be having with himself. She needed a minute herself to figure out why she craved Carson's kisses like those of no other man she'd ever been with.

"I didn't come here for this."

He took a step, closed the door, and then turned back to face her. That hunger in his eyes hadn't disappeared—if anything, the fire seemed to have flared even higher.

"I tried to talk myself out of any contact with you tonight and just having you come to my office tomorrow. Then I had a drink in the Colt Room and ultimately decided to do this now, when I knew we'd be alone."

He cocked his head to the side in that adorable way that she found much too sexy.

"Being alone isn't the best idea, though," he added.

"Why is that?"

"Is that a rhetorical question?"

No, but she wanted him to say it. She wanted to force him to say what he was thinking, what he was feeling.

"There's too much between us," he murmured. "The history, the engagement, the tension."

She took a step toward him. "Yet you showed up at my house at night without a warning. Makes me wonder if you were curious what would happen."

A muscle in his jaw clenched as his lips thinned and his nostrils flared. Oh, the man was tempted and furious about it. Well, that made two of them. She couldn't deny her attraction—what would be the point? Ignoring something wouldn't make it go away… If anything, she would just be even more agitated and aroused than usual.

Even during the debates and electoral process, she found Carson infuriating, yet sexy and powerful. Of course, she never admitted that to anyone, really not even to herself, but again, she couldn't ignore the glaring facts.

In a move she didn't expect or see coming, Carson reached out and snaked an arm around her waist. Lana tumbled right against his chest and flattened her palms against him to hold on.

"What if I did wonder?" he muttered as his gaze dropped to her mouth. "What if I need to get you out of my system?"

Lana slid her hands along his shoulders and around his neck, threading her fingers through his hair. She tipped up her head as her entire body ached for him to rip away these barriers between them—the clothes and the rivalry. Just for one night. Would that be too much to ask?

"Be sure," she told him. "Because I'm about a second away from tearing this robe off and showing you exactly what you want."

Carson's lids lowered as he rested his forehead against hers. "Your confidence is the sexiest thing about you, right next to this damn body I need to get my hands on."

Well, say no more. Finally, something truly raw and honest from his mouth.

Lana took a step back and slid the knot loose on her robe, all the while keeping her eyes locked on his. She wanted to see his face—she needed to see his face as she undressed before him.

And he was right. She was confident and loved her body, and she couldn't wait for him to show her just how much he'd been wanting her. They'd been doing the visual foreplay dance for months now and there was no reason they couldn't just take what they wanted. Why should either of them let a century-old feud rob them of a night of passion?

As the robe slid silently to puddle at her feet, Carson's eyes seemed to rake all over her and Lana's entire body heated with arousal.

"Just for tonight." He took a step closer, then another, until there was nothing between them. "You're mine for tonight."

Without a word, she started working on the buttons of his shirt, until one proved to be difficult, so she yanked the material, sending the troublesome button flinging to the other side of the room.

"You're killing me," he growled.

Carson took over, and within seconds, he stood before her wearing nothing but a hungry gaze. He gripped her waist, lifted her, and carried her toward the living area. Lana wrapped her legs and arms around him, turned on even more by his strength and dominance.

She'd envisioned this moment way too many times. A fantasy with Carson as the star had consumed her thoughts much more than she should have ever allowed.

But she wasn't sorry this was happening and she didn't give a damn about the red flags waving around in her mind.

Would this complicate their fake engagement? Doubtful. It's not like they'd vowed any solid, long-term promises to each other.

"I haven't exactly been immune to you, either," she retorted. "But I'm done talking."

She cupped the back of his neck and pulled his mouth down to hers, then found herself tipping backward until her back hit the cushy sofa. Carson's weight came on top of hers, pressing her deeper into the couch, and she'd never imagined how glorious this would feel. Well, she'd imagined, but nothing could have prepared her for exactly how amazing this was.

And she couldn't help but have a bit of a thrill knowing this entire charade was a secret between them. Nobody had to know their relationship was fake, but their one-night stand was oh, so very real.

Carson's mouth slid from her lips, along her jawline, and down the column of her neck. Lana arched back to allow him better access. No way was she denying those talented lips. She'd waited too long to have them roaming over her body.

When the stubble of his beard raked over her nipple, Lana shivered and clutched his shoulders. Gracious sakes, this man was hitting all of her delicious spots and they'd barely gotten started.

"Wait," she panted.

Carson lifted his head. Those full, damp lips were too damn tempting, but she wasn't one to rush into anything…save for this moment. But, she still had to be smart.

"I don't have any protection," she told him. "I'm on birth control and I've never gone without, but…"

There were a whole host of other things they could do, but she'd been wanting the real deal.

"I have something."

Carson eased from her body and crossed the room to where he'd left his pants by the door. He pulled out his wallet and grabbed the protection.

Lana couldn't tear her eyes away from that fine form of muscle tone and lean man. Carson made his suits look good. He made a pair of jeans and cowboy boots look sexy. But seeing him in her own living room wearing nothing but a bedroom stare was flat-out toe-curling and panty-melting…well, if she had any panties on.

As he crossed back to her, completely ready now, Lana got to her feet and gestured toward the sofa.

"Sit," she commanded.

Carson's dark eyebrows rose as he quirked those lips into a grin. "That bossy attitude is much sexier here than during the debates."

He stood in front of her and she placed her hands on his chest and eased him down until he sat. Those hungry eyes kept her attention as she settled her knees on either side of his waist, braced her hands on his shoulders, and hovered just over where she ached most to be.

"Not bossy," she corrected. "Determined."

Without another word, she joined their bodies and stilled. Carson's hands gripped her waist as he let out a low groan. Lana just needed a moment to adjust to this amazing sensation. She'd wanted to take control, but that grasp was slowly slipping away.

When his hips jerked beneath hers, Lana shifted, working into a rhythm that couldn't be contained or controlled. She'd wanted to go slow, to savor this come-to-life fantasy. But she needed him too bad and she wasn't going to deny herself any longer.

Carson's hands traveled from her waist up to her chest. The second he palmed her in each hand, Lana arched her back, seeking his touch. When his mouth replaced his hands, Lana cried out and shifted her gaze to watch him. She framed the side of his face, holding him exactly where she needed. To feel Carson all around her, to be consumed by this man, was more than she could bear.

Every euphoric sensation bubbled up and overcame her. She curled her fingers into that taut skin over his shoulders and quickened her pace. She needed more, craved more.

Carson released her breasts and framed her face, pulling her in for a kiss. He covered her mouth with his as she went over the edge. That was it. That was what she needed. Just that basic connection of a passionate kiss from the man she'd been dreaming about.

Carson's body tightened beneath hers and Lana poured herself into the kiss, drawing out his own pleasure. She wanted him to feel just as much as she did...

and part of her admitted she didn't want this night to end. He broke from the kiss and tipped his back head, giving her the most spectacular view of his undoing. The man was positively gorgeous when he became vulnerable.

When Carson stilled beneath her, Lana eased off his lap, but he grabbed hold of her hips. In a swift, clever move, she found herself on her back with him hovering over her. That naughty grin only had another stirring of arousal curling through her.

"Where are you going?" he asked.

"I thought—"

"We said one night." He grazed his lips across hers. "And the night just got started."

Six

Lana rolled over in her bed, not surprised to find it empty. Still, that didn't stop the disappointment from hitting her. They had agreed on one night, but part of her just assumed he'd at least hang around for coffee, or at the very least a simple goodbye.

But she wasn't going to dwell on what didn't happen because she was still feeling all sorts of amazing from what *did* happen.

Lana reached for her phone, but remembered she had other things on her mind and she hadn't brought it to bed. Carson had carried her in here with ease and his strength was just another major turn-on. How could she not thrive in the fact a man could handle her physically and mentally?

Stretching her arms over her head, Lana swung her legs over the side of the bed and pushed aside last night. She'd given herself that one pleasurable time and now she needed to move on and shift her focus to the women's area that Carson promised to build with the funds from Harmon.

Which reminded her, they also needed to plan the engagement party. Well, she would plan it because she had control issues and she wanted everything to be perfect. Not to mention the fact that the party was the place they were going to announce the new expansion for the women's facilities. She couldn't wait to tell Abby about this.

Even though Lana's brother, Richard, had passed away, Lana had gained a true sister when Abby had married him. Lana shared everything with her sister-in-law, even though she was now remarried and so happy and in love. Lana was thrilled that she'd found her second chance.

Abby had been the pioneer of getting women into the club in the first place, so Lana was beyond anxious to fill in Abby on the plans. Should those plans also mention the fake engagement?

As much as she wanted to spill all to Abby, Lana figured it was best that this secret stayed between her and Carson. If word leaked at all and somehow got back to Harmon, the funds would be gone and the dying wish of a man would be destroyed.

Lana reached for her robe on the antique trunk at the end of her bed. Good thing she had a few robes because her other one was still in a silky puddle at her front door.

As she padded through the living room, heading for the kitchen and much-needed coffee, she couldn't ignore the flood of memories from last night…or the sight. There was the robe just like she recalled. The couch cushions were a little askew and she couldn't help but stare, her body heating up all over again.

The things they'd done on that couch had been nothing compared to what had happened when Carson took over in the bedroom. How could she not want a replay of all of that?

She could want, but she couldn't have. They'd made an agreement, right?

When she turned back toward the kitchen she spied her cell on the island and a small blue box next to it. Confused, Lana crossed the space and picked up the box. The second she lifted the lid, she gasped.

The most incredible diamond-and-pearl ring stared back at her and she had no clue what it was doing here…but she had an idea who had left it.

Lana picked up her cell and noticed a missed text from Carson. When she opened it, her heart clenched a bit…and not in the sweet, romantic way.

Your engagement ring I meant to give you last night, but got sidetracked. We need to focus and keep the goal in mind.

She glanced back to the ring once again and suddenly the beauty of it seemed almost tarnished. Even though they had agreed on the one heated night, that didn't mean she wanted a cold, lonely morning.

She closed the lid on the box and didn't bother replying to the message. As much as she wanted to slide that beauty on her hand, she wasn't quite feeling this proposal. Granted it was fake, but he could have at least…

Hell, she didn't know. What did she want him to do? Get down on one knee with a candlelight dinner and then whisk her off to bed? What was the protocol for a proposal for a fake engagement?

She knew this wasn't reality, but couldn't he have put forth a little effort to pretend she wasn't just some one-night stand? All of this was such new territory for both of them, but she still had feelings and as much as she hated to admit it, she did want romance...even if that had to be a show as well.

Lana tried to ignore that pang of frustration as she got ready for the day. She opted to spend a little extra time on her makeup and hair, and she chose a killer black suit with a jacket that nipped at her waist and had matching pencil pants. Solid red pumps completed her look and she felt much more like herself than she had just an hour ago.

Getting ready was more for herself and the tempo-rary fiancé she'd be seeing today. She never dressed for anyone else other than herself and sometimes her wounded pride needed to step it up a notch.

Lana grabbed her favorite handbag and gave that box another glare. She slid her cell into her bag and tossed the ring box in, too. Maybe a meeting with her "betrothed" would be best before she let her emotions swelter and she exploded. Because the more she thought about it, the angrier she became that he'd just left this ring like some parting gift after their night together.

Once she was in her car, she started rehearsing just what she'd say to her beloved fiancé.

"Sure, Dad. Sounds good."

Carson leaned back in his leather office chair and

turned to stare out the wide window that offered him
a view of the grounds behind the clubhouse, where
the stables were located. He'd barely gotten in the office before his father, Hank, had called to invite him
for dinner tomorrow night.

"Will you be bringing a date?" his dad asked.

Carson nearly cringed. Should he bring Lana? They
were going to have to announce this engagement soon,
but he was going to have to text Lana before he committed to anything with his family.

"Not sure about that," Carson replied. "You know
I'm not one to bring my dates around the family."

"I heard you were engaged."

That unexpected punch to his gut came out of nowhere, but Carson couldn't let his dad know he'd
caught him off guard.

"I see you've talked to Harmon."

"I stopped by last night and he informed me you
have a very interesting story, which is why I called
you about dinner."

Of course. So asking about the date had been a
leading question. He was going to have to tell Lana it
was game on from this point forward and they needed
to get their stories matching, because there would sure
as hell be questions as to how a Wentworth and a
Langley had managed to "fall in love."

"I'll save the story for dinner entertainment," Carson promised.

No way would he say anything without talking to
Lana first.

"I better see Ms. Langley at my doorstep with you
tomorrow," his father warned. "I had no idea you two

were even talking friendly toward each other, let alone ready to spend your life with her."

Movement from the corner of his eye caught his attention. Carson spun his chair and spotted his fiancée...who didn't seem as happy to see him as she had last night, when she'd stripped out of her robe. Hadn't she seen the gorgeous ring he'd left for her? How could anyone be upset with that?

"I'll see you tomorrow, Dad." Carson got to his feet. "Someone just came into my office."

"Bring Ms. Langley."

Carson didn't reply as he ended the call and slid the cell onto his desktop. His eyes met Lana's and he offered a smile.

"Morning." His focus shifted to her hand...and bare finger. "Didn't you see the ring?"

Lana laughed, but there was no humor and suddenly he had a gut feeling she wasn't too happy with him.

"Oh, I saw it." She sat her handbag in the leather chair across from his desk and pulled out the ring box. "Here it is. And, while it's lovely, your proposal sucks."

Confused, Carson leaned back in his chair and continued to stare across to Lana's fiery gaze. He much preferred her heated look from last night as opposed to this one. Clearly something about the ring had set her off. And the proposal... What the hell?

"You are aware this is a fake engagement, right?"

"You are aware I told you I needed a real proposal because I'm a terrible liar." She opened the lid on the ring box, yanked out the ring and circled his desk.

"People will want to know our story and we have to get this together."

Agreed, but damn it. What had she done to her hair and makeup? There was something sultry...something sexier, like she'd just gotten out of her lover's bed.

Oh, wait...

And that curve-hugging suit made him want to lock his office door and familiarize himself all over again with all of that smooth, silky skin beneath his touch.

Lana dropped to one knee. "Will you marry me?"

Carson stared down at her and way too many fantasies came to mind with her looking like a vixen in that position. But they'd agreed on one night and they'd gotten that out of their systems. Right?

He had to keep his eye on the goal of the funds from Harmon that would benefit the entire club.

"Are you asking me?"

Lana nodded. "Someone needs to do the asking. Now, put the ring on my finger."

Carson reached for the ring, keeping his eyes locked on hers the entire time. He slid the ring on, then got to his feet, tugging her up with him. Clutching her hand between the two of them, he cupped the side of her face with his free hand.

"Lana, let's put this century-old feud to rest. Will you help me build a dynasty that only we could and help our families move on once and for all?"

Her eyes widened and he wondered if he'd gone too far. He wondered, after last night, if Lana's feelings for him had changed. He couldn't afford for hearts to get involved here—*they* couldn't afford it. Two headstrong people actually trying to have a relationship? They'd never make it—not when both needed full control.

"If you don't say yes, I will."

Carson jerked his attention to the doorway, where Sierra was standing with a bright smile on her face, her eyes darting between Carson and Lana.

Lana eased her hand from between them and met his gaze for a brief second before she pasted a smile on her face and turned toward their unexpected guest.

"You caught us," Lana stated with a soft laugh. "We were trying to keep it a secret for a little while, but I guess that would be difficult to do."

Sierra stepped into the office, her eyes wide as she shook her head. "I just can't believe this. I mean, you two were so opposite during the debates. But I saw that spark every time you were together. Did you guys have a secret fling going on during that time?"

Oh, no. All of that frustration and their rivalry had been one-hundred-percent real...just like the battle between their families.

"That's when we realized we were perfect for each other," Carson replied. "We figured this wedge between our families could end with us, and despite both wanting the presidency of the club, we have quite a bit in common."

Lana glanced to him, eyebrows quirked, as if silently asking him what exactly they had in common. Well, there was their shared fiery passion, but probably best not to mention that to Sierra. Who knew what would end up printed or online?

"This is absolutely wonderful news," Sierra gushed. "Can I get an exclusive or do you have something planned for a big announcement?"

Carson glanced to Lana. Even though this entire charade was a farce, he didn't want to disrespect Lana or do anything that would harm the deal they'd made. She gave him a slight nod before turning her attention back to Sierra.

"We wouldn't mind an exclusive with you," Lana told her. "We haven't really told our families yet, but we can schedule something."

"Tomorrow morning?" Sierra asked, hope lacing her tone as her eyes darted between them. "I can meet you here around ten and we could do a short interview, but I'd love to get some pictures."

"I'm fine with that," Lana told her.

Carson nodded. "Sounds good. What did you need today?"

Sierra blinked. "What? Oh, right. I forgot when I saw that touching engagement. You two must really be in love."

So far, so good. Getting their families to believe this crazy scheme was one thing, but having a busybody reporter running a story was actually going to be a big deal. With Sierra already convinced, there was no doubt she'd come up with a gushing write-up for them tomorrow, and once the people of Royal caught wind of the engagement, there would be absolutely no turning back.

Not that he was going to, anyway, but this was getting even more serious and those nerves in his gut were becoming damn uncomfortable. Lying to his great-grandfather, lying to his father, now lying to the town he loved and the people who trusted him. He'd built a solid reputation, which was how he'd secured the club presidency, and now he was lying to everyone…except the woman who should be his enemy, yet had turned into his lover.

How the hell had this gotten so skewed?

"I came by to see if you cared if I went to visit Harmon," Sierra continued. "I promise to be gentle with my questions, but after reading Arielle's diary and talking to most of the people of Royal, I wouldn't be a very good investigative reporter if I didn't interview him personally. I'm hoping Arielle told him something about Micah's father."

"Why didn't you just call?" he asked.

"I'm actually meeting someone for a horse-riding lesson in the stables shortly, so I thought I'd just swing by and ask in person."

Carson mulled over the idea and he completely understood why she'd want to see Harmon. Even though his great-grandfather was still in his right mind, he was one hundred years old and his time was limited. But he liked Sierra. He had no reason to believe she wasn't trying to find out the entire story, and show Royal and the entire town in the best light.

Carson had always been a good judge of character, so he trusted Sierra, and he didn't trust just anybody. For example, he wasn't sure he trusted the woman wearing his ring whom he'd spent the night with…but that was a whole other issue he didn't want to think about right now.

"I believe you have baby Micah and Harmon's best interests at heart," Carson stated. "The way you keep working every angle makes me see you actually want to uncover the truth. I don't mind if you interview him. I'll call to let them know you're coming."

Sierra beamed. "Thank you, thank you. I'll see you

both in the morning, and congrats on the engagement. This is so exciting."

She spun on her booted heel and swept out of the office, leaving Carson and Lana alone once again. Perhaps alone wasn't the best place for them to be, not with the images and the emotions running high from last night.

He'd thought that being intimate with her would have satisfied his wants and he could have moved on, but those wants had only grown into a fierce, aching need. That's why he'd left so early, without a word. He'd left the ring and sent a text because if he'd stayed at her place and waited for her to open those gorgeous eyes, he would have had to have had her all over again. And that wasn't in their business arrangement.

Seven

The ring on her finger seemed so foreign, so wrong. That twinge of pain she'd felt this morning upon seeing it seemed to grow. She'd been so focused on her duties as chair of the Cattleman's Club Women's Association for so many years, she just hadn't had time to date much. But she did want a husband and a family. She'd dreamed of having a sprawling ranch and a sexy, Southern gentleman who could match her wits and strength.

And while Carson certainly fit that criteria, this life wasn't real. The ring meant nothing in the grand scheme of things.

"We're having dinner with my father tomorrow evening at the ranch."

Carson's words pulled her from her thoughts and

she turned to focus on the man who'd turned her world, and emotions, upside down.

"Was that a question or a demand?" she asked.

"It was a fact," he informed her. "I'm not thrilled with taking you to dinner, either, but this is the role we both have to play."

Lana rolled her eyes and stepped around his desk, putting distance between them again. "I'm feeling so welcome already."

Carson blew out a sigh as he unbuttoned the sleeves of his black dress shirt and rolled up the cuffs. When he glanced back her way, he caught her staring at his bare forearms.

Why did she have to find everything sexy about him now? He'd been sexy yesterday morning, too, but after last night, well…

She was in serious trouble here.

"This isn't about our feelings or our comfort zone," he reminded her. "We're doing this for Harmon as a dying wish, not to mention the club and all of the funds that will be coming in. This will help my reputation as president and get you what you want with the women's portion of the club, so you'll maintain good standings with our female ranchers. It's all business, Lana."

Business, yes. She knew that. She did…but that didn't stop her from wanting him again. Last night hadn't been enough and she'd been a fool for thinking one night would get someone like Carson Wentworth out of her system. The man exuded everything she found sexy: confidence, power, wit, and he was beyond attractive…and now she could add "amazing lover" to the ever-growing list of gold-star qualities.

They weren't meant to be and she was letting naive thoughts override common sense here. A hot body, a powerful man, and great sex did not make the foundation of a solid relationship. Well, those certainly helped, but trust was certainly a main factor and she couldn't really trust a Wentworth. She'd been brought up hearing "those damn Wentworths" at her kitchen table for the past thirty plus years.

Her parents were simply going to be in utter shock when she broke the news to them, which was something she needed to do before speaking with Sierra in the morning.

"I'm all for getting what we both want," she told Carson. "And I think now that Sierra saw my proposal to you, that will help start that rumor mill."

"I proposed to you," he corrected.

Lana laughed. "I didn't see you getting down on one knee."

"I left the ring and a text."

"And people wonder why you were still single," she muttered. "Anyway, I'm meeting with one more local contractor this afternoon to go over my ideas. I'll get his quote and then discuss everything that was in my original email with you, hopefully by the end of the week."

Carson's dark eyebrows rose. "You move fast."

"Considering yesterday morning you were my enemy, last night you were my lover, and this morning you're my fiancé, I'd say that's the theme as of late."

Carson laughed and raked a hand down the stubble along his jawline. That bristling sound against his palm had shivers racing through her body. She knew exactly how that coarse hair felt against her bare skin and, honestly, she wasn't opposed to asking him for a replay of the night before.

Right now, though, they needed to focus on business and kicking off the announcement of their engagement. Sex could wait—not for long, but it could wait until she was sure her head was on straight and no more emotions other than physical attraction would get in the way.

"We also need to discuss the engagement party at the end of the month," she told him. "Let's have a dance. I've put together a spreadsheet of all the necessary contacts and what I would need from each one."

"When did you have time to do that?" he asked.

"Before you came over and ended up in my bed."

Carson's lids lowered, his lips thinned, and that muscle in his jaw clenched. Perfect. Good to know he wasn't immune to what happened. Likely he was sorting out his own feelings, which was why she was giving him some time before she invited him back for round two.

"I'm too busy to plan a dance, so I'll trust you on that," he told her. "Just tell me the date and I'll make sure the ballroom is cleared for the day."

"I already cleared it," she told him. "And I'll take care of everything. Just wondering if you had any special requests. Your favorite song, a party food you'd love, a color dress I should wear?"

"Green," he said without hesitation. "My favorite color is green. I don't care what else you do."

She should've known the color of money was his favorite color, but if he wanted green, then she'd find a killer dress in a beautiful shade. This might be a fake relationship, but that didn't mean she couldn't look like the stylish queen she prided herself on being.

Lana would have to put in a call to her favorite designer as soon as she left the office. This was going to be her engagement party, after all.

"I'll see you tomorrow morning, then."

Lana grabbed her bag from the chair, turned on her heel, and headed toward the door.

"Wait."

Carson's command stopped her before she could make her exit. She glanced over her shoulder and met his heavy-lidded gaze across the room. With those dark jeans that hugged his narrow hips and that dress shirt with the sleeves rolled up, he looked more like a Royal rancher than the Cattleman's Club president. Both sides of him were starting to appeal to her way too much.

"About last night…"

Lana used every ounce of her willpower to keep her thoughts and words inside while she waited on him to finish his thought.

"I lied," he told her. "Once wasn't enough."

Lana smiled. "No. It wasn't. I'll see you tonight."

Eight

"I can honestly say I never thought this day would come."

Lana cringed at Hank Wentworth's statement the moment he swung open the front door of the family ranch.

"You thought I'd never want to settle down?" Carson asked.

"Never," his father said with a shake of his head. "And to a Langley, of all things. I can't wait to hear how all of this came about. Come on in."

Carson slid his hand over the small of Lana's back and escorted her inside. She had every desire to turn around and wait in the car. Clearly, Hank was going to be a tough nut to crack. But Lana felt solid in their scheme.

After their passionate night back at her house and

their interview with Sierra this morning, Lana was ready for the real test—convincing Hank Wentworth that she was madly in love with his son and they were going to forge the families together for life.

A burning of guilt gnawed at her. She hadn't been joking when she said she was a terrible liar. She was so bad at it because she loathed lying and couldn't pull it off.

She didn't want to get into the reasons with Carson, or anyone else for that matter, as to why she couldn't tolerate anything less than honesty.

Yet here she was in this web of deceit because sex and money had lured her in. Part of her knew she was doing this to better the clubhouse and get everything she'd promised her female ranchers, but another part felt she was no different than her father.

When this month was over, Lana vowed to never lie again, and she truly hoped Carson did most of the speaking during this family dinner. She didn't know him well enough to know if he was skilled at stretching the truth, or if such things even bothered him.

"Whatever you have cooking smells amazing," Carson stated as they made their way through the grand foyer and toward the back of the house.

"I had the chef prepare all of your favorites." Hank glanced over his shoulder and smiled. "Alli and Tate are here, too. Alli is ready to discuss wedding plans, so don't disappoint her. But first, I want to hear all about how this crazy engagement came to be."

Carson tensed beside her and Lana wished they had both come up with some excuse as to why they couldn't attend tonight's dinner…or at least a reason why she couldn't.

She could only assume Hank didn't care what impression he made on her in a more personal setting. She'd only encountered him on occasion at the club, or during the presidential race. But this was the first time she'd ever been in the Wentworth estate and she might as well have been walking into a waiting room full of people waiting on a colonoscopy.

"Oh, my word. You're here."

Alli Wentworth came around the large kitchen island with her arms extended and heading straight for Lana. Suddenly she found herself pulled into an embrace, something she wasn't used to by near strangers and definitely not something she expected from Hank's wife.

"We are so excited for you guys," Alli exclaimed as she eased back. "You are just so stunning. Carson is one lucky man."

"Yes, he is," Lana agreed easily. "It's good to remind him of that."

"Where's Tate?" Carson asked, clearly not wanting to discuss just how lucky he was for having Lana as his fiancée.

"He's out back on the phone with his girlfriend." Alli gestured toward another room. "Let's head into the dining room. He'll come in when they're done arguing. It's that crazy teenage love right now."

Lana remembered her teen boyfriend and the petty arguments they would have. She remembered that sense of freedom when she broke up with him, too.

Carson guided her into the dining room, and that hand on the small of her back did nothing to stop the nerves from swirling around in her belly. Which was so ridiculous, really. The things they'd done in that hot tub of hers last night alone would be enough to make anyone blush. Yet the simple gesture of the way that he was firmly escorting her had those giddy schoolgirl feelings bubbling to the surface.

"Have a seat anywhere you like," Alli told them.

Lana glanced at the spread and couldn't believe all the food. Steaks, mashed potatoes, grilled asparagus wrapped in bacon, a nice big bowl of fresh salad, homemade bread, and a plate of cheeses and fruits.

Lana was glad she'd skipped lunch today, but she'd only done so because she was nervous about coming here. Another thing that was completely ridiculous. She never got nervous about anything, not since she realized her worth and her value at a young age. But this whole charade had her on edge…or maybe it was the good sex that had her out of sorts.

Either way, all of it would come to an end in one short month.

"So let's hear how you both went from being at each other's throats to planning to spend your lives together."

Hank's judgmental tone had Lana straightening her spine. She didn't care to answer his questions, but she was certainly going to let Carson have the first shot at any. Lana had dealt with high-and-mighty men before—some women, too—so this was nothing new. She just had to put on her proverbial suit of armor and prepare herself for a verbal battle.

"We just realized that we did have quite a bit in common, but we simply had different ways of saying it or going about our goals," Carson began. "It's no secret I've always found Lana beautiful, but the more I got to know her mind, the more I fell in love with that strength and determination. I found that she matched me in too many ways to ignore."

Lana tried to block out what he'd said, seeing as it was all part of a hoax, but ignoring his convincing statement was damn difficult. Aside from what Carson had said, the man was also sitting so close that his thigh was resting against hers beneath the table…

He certainly had a way of making her feel like she was the one. If she didn't know this was fake, she'd start believing Carson really did have a thing for her. He was putting on a great show here already and the two nights they'd spent together had quickly solidified him as the best lover she'd ever had.

"So just a few months of running for club president and you've already put a ring on her finger?" Hank asked.

Alli started around the table filling everyone's plates. Clearly Hank's second wife loved entertaining and she was the quintessential Southern-hospitality hostess.

"As I said, we have quite a bit in common and I can't help who I fall in love with." Carson eased over to let Alli reach through. "Marriages have been based on less than what Lana and I have already. We're both determined and stubborn enough to make this work. Neither one of us want to fail at anything, let alone a marriage."

Damn. He was good. Did lying come that easily to him? One right after another just rolled off his tongue and there was no way in hell Lana could fall for someone who could fabricate such a convincing story with ease. Her father had been the same and her mother had been a fool, or naive, or simply didn't care. Lana vowed to never turn a blind eye, as her mother had.

"Is this some publicity stunt?" Hank asked.

"Oh, really," Alli scolded. "Leave them alone. They want to get married, just be happy for them."

"Are we already arguing?"

Lana turned her attention toward the dining room opening, where Tate Wentworth came strutting through. The boy might be young, but Lana thought he looked just like his big half-brother. Carson did have a special relationship with Tate. During their debates and the campaign, Tate seemed to be his biggest supporter.

"We are done arguing," Carson stated. "Have a seat. We're just getting started."

Tate took a seat across from them and Alli finished filling all the plates before she took a seat at the opposite end of the table from Hank.

"Our families have fought for a century," Hank went on. "How the hell do you think this is going to look to the rest of the Wentworths?"

Carson shook his head as he reached for his steak knife and fork. "I think it's going to look like Lana and I don't care about a feud that has nothing to do with us or our future. It's going to look like our love will bridge the families together and anyone that doesn't want to get on board with that is too busy living in the past. And that's not my problem."

Lana swallowed the lump in her throat. How did Carson do this? How did he just spout off exactly what needed to be said, and at precisely the right time? Perhaps that's how he'd defeated her for the presidency.

"Harmon wants this feud to die down, so this is

serendipitous," Alli stated. "Let's focus on the happy and that these two are ready to start their lives together without the black cloud of a family war hanging over their heads. So tell me what your plans are so far for the wedding?"

Lana glanced down the table at Alli's questioning, eager gaze. "Well, I don't have anything finalized quite yet. This is all so new."

"I'm sure you have something in mind," Alli replied. "Most women have an idea of a dream wedding. A favorite color or a favorite flower. What about the ring?"

Lana held up her hand and flashed the still foreign object.

"Oh, Carson," Alli gasped. "You did good. I love it."

"She deserves something just as striking and bold as she is," he told his stepmother.

Lana placed her hand back in her lap and stared at her plate of food. There was no way she could eat all of this…not with all the nerves in her belly.

"Do you want outside or in?" Alli asked. "Hank and I had an outdoor fall wedding and it was absolutely beautiful."

Of course, Lana had given her real wedding some thoughts. She just hated sharing them now because she didn't want to share her personal, intimate ideas in a fake setting.

But, since she was a terrible liar, she had to stick with the truth and what she knew.

"I've always loved the idea of an outdoor wedding. Something small and intimate," she told them. "Something with just a few friends. My favorite color is blue and my favorite flower is a lily. I guess I could incorporate those things."

"You don't want a large wedding?" Hank asked.

Lana turned her attention to him and shook her head. "I'm not one to be flashy with my personal life. I know I can be over-the-top with so many other things, but something like a wedding, I'd be fine with just my fiancé and the minister, and of course a few close friends."

Hanks silver eyebrows drew together. "The Wentworths are a vast family. I'm sure there are many Langleys who would want to attend. The fact that these two families are finally coming together will bring the entire town of Royal."

Yeah, that's another reason she was so glad this was fake. The idea of all those people watching her marry made her twitchy. She did value a private life, especially one with the man she intended to spend every day with.

An intimate wedding with a grand party afterward would be just fine. Something like merging these two families would be worthy of a town celebration.

Too bad that wouldn't come to fruition.

"We can discuss the guest list later," Carson stated, coming to her rescue. "I didn't know your favorite color or favorite flower, though."

Lana smiled as she reached for her glass of wine, but Hank, of course, had to chime in.

"That's because you two are rushing into this marriage without thinking."

Oh, Lana had thought…she'd done little else since Harmon assumed they were together. But there was no way she could actually start planning anything. She

wouldn't pull businesses or people in just to have to
cancel things in a few weeks. If she and Carson could
just keep feigning love for a month, attend the dance,
and make the big announcement about the women's
wing, then they could call off the engagement and
still remain friends.

There. The plan was all laid out and quite logical.
All of this would ultimately be for the greater good
and nobody would be hurt in the end—she hoped
that was her truth. The last thing she wanted was to
end up pleasing everyone else, only to end up with a
broken heart.

"We're not rushing," Carson argued. "And you
can't talk us out of this, so move on."

"I think it's cool," Tate chimed in as he shoved a
bite of steak in his mouth. "This family-fighting thing
sounds like stuff old people do. At least Lana and Carson are trying to make things right."

Lana bit the inside of her cheek to keep from smiling. She'd never really talked to Tate before. She'd
seen him plenty at Carson's side, but the young man
did have a valid point. Well, it would be valid if Lana
and Carson were actually going to go through with
the wedding.

Even though this was all for show, that didn't mean
they couldn't bridge the family gap. Why not? What
could be so bad that one hundred years later these
families were still at each other's throats? Whatever
happened in the past surely had nothing to do with
the people who were here today…save for Harmon.

"Carson, how is the club going?" Alli asked. "Any
new plans now that you're president?"

As much as she hated the reminder of her loss,

Lana would much rather this topic than trying to come up with wedding details she didn't have and didn't plan on having.

Lana ate as much as she could with her overactive nerves, and thankfully, when the dinner was over, Carson didn't want to stick around too long. He chatted a little with Tate and then he escorted Lana from the estate and back into his SUV.

Finally, she could breathe a sigh of relief. One major milestone down in their fake engagement... and too many more to go.

Nine

"Well, that went well."

Carson headed out of the long drive, away from the estate. Lana had been quiet through most of the dinner and she still sat quiet in the passenger seat as she stared out the window.

"Did it?" she asked softly. "Because it feels like your father hates me."

"Did you want him to like you? This isn't real, you know, and your last name is still Langley. He's not going to be ready to drop this feud as quick as my great-grandfather. Dad doesn't know any different but to despise any Langley."

Something about Lana's tone and her question had him wondering if she really did care about the impression she'd make. Something about this evening had upset Lana and suddenly Carson realized he never wanted to see her upset…or be the cause of her pain.

He'd thought this temporary plan would be easy and they'd get through it together, with no one the wiser. But Carson hadn't thought about how real emotions would come into play in a fake setting.

"Forget I said anything," she stated as she shifted to face him. "I'm just tired and I definitely haven't forgotten the situation I'm in. I guess I just didn't expect so much animosity."

Carson hadn't really, either, but he should have. Even on the phone before arriving, his father had been cranky and skeptical about the whole thing. But Carson at least thought his father would have manners… which clearly hadn't been the case.

"I apologize if he made you uncomfortable."

Lana sighed and straightened in her seat. "Not for you to apologize. You didn't do anything wrong."

"Didn't I?" Carson gripped the wheel even tighter. "I could have set Harmon straight when he assumed we were together. I could have just been up-front and honest, but the last month or so he's gotten slower and more tired. He's dying. And that damn diary…"

Lana's hand rested on his thigh. "We were both in that room and I went along with it as well. Though I thought for sure you had planned that little ambush."

"Ambush?" he asked. "I swear, I was just as caught off guard as you."

"I realize that now, but at the time I was tempted to walk out and let you deal with your great-grandfather on your own."

That hand on his leg was so simple, a gesture meant

to console, but all it did was get his blood pumping as he sped up just a little.

"I'm glad you didn't," he told her. "Now we're both getting what we wanted for the club and maybe with this engagement, this crazy rift will come to an end. Even when we call off the engagement, we'll have to make it seem like we realized we're better as friends, but that we're glad we could forge the families together."

There. That all sounded logical and like a simple plan that would work and everyone would still be happy in the end.

Carson drove along in silence, still very much aware that her hand was still on his thigh. Did she mean to leave it there? Did she want something more to come from this night?

A one-night stand was easy to do because there was the one night and then nothing. But now they had slept together the past two nights, so he had no clue as to the expectations on her end. Carson would gladly take another night with her, but he also didn't want to overstep or disrespect her, either.

"Tate seems like a nice young man."

Lana's statement pulled Carson from his thoughts.

"He is a great brother," he agreed. "I was a little stunned and embarrassed when Dad and Alli announced they were having a baby, but Tate has become like my best friend. We have just enough of an age gap between us that we're friends and I can give him adult advice without him feeling like I'm his dad."

"That's nice to have someone in your life like that. I don't know what I'd do without Abby. We've leaned on each other quite a bit over the years."

Carson knew Lana's brother had passed some time ago, but his widow, Abby, and Lana had remained the very best of friends. Two strong women like that were bound to create a solid bond. Abby had fought nearly ten years ago for women to be able to join the Cattleman's Club. Her hard work had tipped the hands of the board and women had been welcome members since.

Now Lana was carrying on what her sister-in-law had started and Carson couldn't fault her for fighting for those female ranchers she represented. She was the chairwoman of the TCC Women's Association. She wouldn't back down and those women were damn lucky to have someone so determined on their side.

Carson made a turn and Lana shifted, her hand suddenly sliding off his thigh.

"Where are we going?" she asked.

"I'm going to show you where I live."

"Did you want to ask me if I wanted to go?"

Carson shrugged. "Do you?"

"Depends on your intentions once you get me there."

Carson couldn't help but laugh as he gave a quick glance her way and found her smiling.

"I'd never take advantage," he assured her.

"What if I take advantage of you?"

Damn. His entire body heated with just that one question. Lana could make him want more than he ever had before. Desiring a woman was nothing new, but this aching, relentless need he had for her was becoming too all-consuming. There had never been a woman like this before. He had to chalk it up to a mind game. He knew he had to pretend to be with the public, so perhaps that's all it was. He just figured why not keep up the pretenses behind closed doors…minus the whole love part.

"Have you checked online to see if Sierra posted our story?" Lana asked.

Our story.

For the next month, everything he did would be joined with Lana. They were a team whether he wanted to be or not.

"I've been too busy," he replied. "I take it you haven't looked?"

Lana reached for her bag and pulled out her cell. The bright screen lit up the interior of his vehicle as he passed the motion sensor for his five-car garage. Up ahead, the door opened to his bay and he eased inside, amid his other rides. He had a car for each mood and occasion. These were just the everyday vehicles. Behind his home, there was another five-car garage with his antique collection and the cars that only came out for special occasions.

"Oh, wow."

Lana's gasp had him jerking toward her as he killed the engine. "What is it?" he asked. "Bad article?"

"I haven't even gotten to the article." She turned her cell to face him so he could see the photo of the two of them. "I can't get past this."

Carson stared at the image, then reached to take the phone from her hands.

TCC President and Soon-to-be First Lady in Love

If that catchy headline didn't grab a reader's attention, the romantic photograph sure as hell would. Sierra had told them she wanted pictures in his office. The photo had Lana in her killer red pencil dress hugging every damn curve as she sat on the edge of his desk with her legs crossed. Carson stood behind her, leaning forward with one hand flat on his desk next to her hip, the other on her shoulder, easing her hair away from her neck.

And the way they were staring into each other's eyes could damn near set the phone on fire. How the hell had he not noticed how she stared at him? How could he not hide his own desires?

There would be no denying their chemistry, not after everyone got wind of this. Sierra was a force and she would make sure the town knew to look at her new article…a side piece on what she was really doing here.

"Damn. We look good."

Lana laughed, just as he'd expected her to. Sex was one thing, but another tone seemed to take over this picture—there was something on display that suggested they were much more than lovers. Perhaps it was the afterglow of their evening before, but Carson was getting another tone.

Which was absurd. There was nothing more here than sex and a business agreement. He and Lana were both on the same page as far as this arrangement was concerned. They might be lying to the world, but they weren't lying to each other.

"We do," she finally agreed. "I'm turning myself on."

Now Carson laughed. She always managed to do that. Somehow she knew how to catch him off guard and say the unexpected—although by now he should realize Lana would always tell the truth and her words were always bold.

"I think that's my job." He handed her phone back to her, grazing her fingertips with his. "Let's go inside."

She cocked her head and quirked a perfectly arched eyebrow. "You mean you're not going to make out with me in the front seat of your car?"

"I'm humbled by the idea you think I'm that young, but when I have a woman, she'll be in my bed."

Lana eased back against the door. "So now I'm just any woman? You know how to make your fiancée feel special."

"You know what I mean, Lana. I'm not some innocent. You and I both had relationships before this and we'll have them after this engagement is over."

That sounded so odd, but truthful. He had to keep reminding himself of the facts or he'd get lost in this entire charade. Spending the nights with Lana could make any man lose track of the end goal. She was a powerful woman in more ways than one.

Carson exited the vehicle and went around to open her door. When he extended his hand, she peered up at him with those expressive eyes that held so many passionate promises. He'd already had her, yet he was just as anxious and revved up as their first time.

How long would it take to get her out of his system?

He'd better enjoy every minute now, because no matter what he wanted or craved, their time would be up in a month.

Lana placed her hand in his and slid out of the car, rising to lean against his body, trapping their hands between their chests.

"You talk too much," she told him. "And I don't

want to discuss our past or future bedmates. I believe I was promised a tour. Let's start with your bedroom."

Carson's body stirred as he took his free hand and palmed her rounded hip. "I won't make it that far."

He crushed his mouth to hers and urged her with him as he backed to the entryway into his house. When he reached the step, he eased back from her slightly so he could turn and open the door and disarm his security system.

But he froze.

Those moist lips and heavy-lidded eyes, coupled with the flushed look on her chest and cheeks, had him nearly going back on his vow not to take her in his car. She was too damn sexy and had managed to hold her own with his father…which was really saying something.

Everything about her pulled at him in ways he'd never imagined and they were only a few days into this farce.

He was in a hell of a predicament with this one… but Lana Langley was worth the trouble. He'd deal with the consequences later. Much later.

Ten

Lana didn't want to talk. Talking to Carson made her realize he wasn't an enemy. Talking made her realize they had more in common than she first thought. Talking made her want to uncover more about the man she should hate.

But, no, she didn't hate him. She was more fascinated than she cared to admit.

So no talking. Sex she could handle. She had to keep everything shallow and superficial so she could come out on the other side of this charade unscathed.

Great sex for a month? There was no reason to mess all of that up by getting mixed up in feelings.

But there was something on Carson's face, something she couldn't identify.

She reached around him and turned the knob, silently gesturing for him to move on in. She knew his mind was spinning and whatever his thoughts were, she didn't want to know. Anything he had to think on that long would not be good for their situation.

Passion was easy and passion was all she wanted.

Carson turned, stepped into the house, punched in a code, and reached for her hand to pull her on inside as well. Lana closed the door behind her and immediately reached for the zipper behind her back. When her pencil dress spread apart down her spine, she shrugged her arms until the material fell down to her waist.

There it was. Carson was back in the moment and out of his internal thoughts, which had pulled him away moments ago. His eyes widened as they landed on her bright blue demi bra. That look he gave her each time he saw her bare only boosted her confidence.

"When you look at me like that…"

She didn't mean to say anything, so she stopped. She didn't want to talk, right? No feelings. No emotions. There was no room for any of that here.

"What?" he asked. "What were you going to say?"

Lana shook her head, but Carson reached for her. He slid his thumbs in the dress and pushed the piece the rest of the way down to puddle at her feet.

"When I look at you I see beauty," he told her. "When I look at you I see a strong woman who challenges me and makes me realize this fake engagement isn't such a bad idea. I see a woman who is just as determined as I am and I see a woman I can't get enough of."

He saw too much. He used words that made her uncomfortable because she couldn't let this tempo-

rary situation get out of control. She had a goal—
they had a goal.

Lana stepped out of her pooled dress and did a seductive little spin to keep his mind on the sex and less
on their forced predicament.

He cursed beneath his breath, then reached for her.
She'd barely gotten back around before he gripped
her backside, pulled her against him, and lifted her
up. Lana locked her ankles behind his back, and her
heels clanked to the hardwood floor in the process.

"You're driving me out of my mind," he muttered
against her mouth as he carried her through the house.
"If I'd known what you were wearing beneath that
dress, we would have never made it to dinner."

"I would have been fine with that," she told him.
"I'd rather be alone."

He reached the base of a grand staircase that curved
toward a wide landing before going up to the second floor. She'd have to admire the rest of his house
later—she had a need for something other than im-
pressive interior design right now.

"Stay the night."

Lana eased back and stared into his dark eyes.

"Stay," he repeated. "I'll take you home tomorrow. I'm not looking for anything more than what we
agreed on. I just want you to myself all night."

He'd stayed at her house most of the night the last
two nights, but he'd been gone before morning on both
occasions. This was different. She was going into this
knowing she'd stay in his bed and they'd wake up in
the morning…like a real relationship.

"Carson—"

"Nothing more, Lana." He nipped at her lips and

started up the steps. "I want you in my bed and I'm not ready to let you go yet."

Yet. At least he knew he would be letting her go.

She rested her head against the crook in his shoulder. "I'll stay."

Maybe she was making a mistake, but she'd made them before. At least she knew what all of this was for—she knew exactly what she needed to do and not do. Her eyes were wide open here and she was in charge.

And right now, she was going to take what Carson was offering. A night of passion with a man who made her toes curl and pleasured her in ways she'd never known was an obvious yes.

Once they reached the landing, Carson continued carrying her until she found herself between the wall and his rock-hard body. She lifted her head to look into his eyes, only to find him using the wall to keep her held in place while he worked on his pants.

"Do you have protection?" she asked.

He froze. "Upstairs in my room."

That seemed so far away right now. The indescribable need had her speaking before really thinking.

"I'm on birth control and I'm clean," she told him. "It's your call."

That muscle in his jaw clenched as his lips thinned. "I'm clean, but are you sure?"

Lana nodded, realizing she was sure. This was all so rushed, so temporary, but she wanted to feel him with no boundaries. Maybe that was crossing the line she swore she wouldn't cross, but this wasn't emotional, right? This was still that raw, physical need. Her heart certainly wasn't involved in this moment.

"I'm sure," she told him.

Lana braced her hands on his shoulders and waited. Carson finished getting his pants out of the way before he met her gaze. That intense stare locked her in place, and when he joined their bodies, Lana couldn't help but close her eyes and let her head fall back as she arched into his touch...into the sensations that overcame her.

This was their third night together and Lana still had those giddy feelings just like the first.

Carson set a fast, frantic pace that had her body climbing higher and higher. She cried out his name and was near the point of begging when his mouth closed over the curve in her neck, which only sent her body over the edge. She rocked her hips against his, using the wall at her back as leverage to complete her satiating experience.

Carson pumped harder and trembled as his mouth traveled from her neck up to her lips. He kissed her with a fierce passion she'd only come to fully know from this man. Never before had someone thoroughly loved her like Carson.

But love wasn't involved here...not in the sex and not in the engagement.

Lana pulled in a deep breath as her body started to settle. Carson grazed his damp lips across hers then rested his forehead to hers. His warm breath fell on her heated skin and she closed her eyes, wondering if she'd be able to just walk away from this unscathed. She was only a few days in and she had way too many to go...which meant she'd better guard her heart, or she'd find herself falling for the enemy.

Eleven

Carson scrolled through the numerous spreadsheets Lana had sent him last week. Had that already been a week ago? His life had certainly taken quite the turn. He'd not only found himself "engaged," but he'd also found himself bed-hopping between Lana's place and his. There wasn't a night they hadn't spent together and there seemed to just be some unspoken agreement that they'd use each other as some physical outlet during this crazy time.

The numbers before him seemed to all blur and run together as his mind flooded with images of his new sexy lover. How the hell was he supposed to concentrate on anything during the day when he could only count down to the evenings?

A tap on his door had him shifting from his computer screen to the opening of his office door.

"Hey."

Tate came in and took a seat across from Carson. The solemn look on the boy's face had Carson immediately shifting from his own thoughts to what was bothering his brother.

"What's up?" Carson asked, resting his elbows on his desk.

"Just wanted to come by and see how things were going."

Carson shook his head. "I know you too well. What's really going on? Still girl trouble?"

Tate sighed and shrugged. "Why are they so complicated?"

Carson couldn't help but laugh. "It's not so much that they are complicated, you just have to figure out a way to make your complicated and their complicated work together...if that makes sense."

Tate's questioning gaze landed on Carson. "Is that what happened with you and Lana? Because you two were really at each other during the campaign. I never would have thought you two would have ended up together. And engaged? Dude, that was fast."

Yeah, Carson's head was still spinning, but he couldn't let anyone in on this secret...not even Tate.

"Sometimes things just click into place," he replied, which was the truth. "Lana is headstrong and determined, which are qualities I respect and definitely understand. We have the same drive for business and have similar life goals."

"She's pretty hot, too," Tate said with that teen smirk he had.

Carson nodded. "Any man would be blind not to notice how attractive she is. We definitely have our differences, no doubt about that, and our families have been at odds for decades, but sometimes you just have to power through and go after what you want."

That was all damn good advice. Maybe if he actually loved Lana, he could stand behind these words. Tate didn't need to know the predicament Carson had gotten himself into—the teen just needed basic advice.

"Do you really like this girl?" Carson asked. "Carly, right?"

Tate nodded. "I like her, but she doesn't get me. She's not into the ranch life and that's all I know and love."

"Have you invited her to the ranch?" Carson asked. "Maybe try to show her your life and then do something that she loves in return. Relationships aren't fifty-fifty. You really have to give one hundred percent of yourself and so does she."

Man, the more he talked, the better he was sounding. Truth was, he knew nothing of relationships. His friends Drake and Cammie were completely in love, as were Jackson and Haley, and Gabe and Ros. Actually, many of his friends and fellow TCC members had fallen in love and married recently. There was definitely something in the air around here, but nothing he wanted to be a part of.

"I had her at the house for dinner a couple times," Tate told him. "We've never taken any horses out into the fields or anything."

"Well, there you go." Carson smiled. "Invite her for a horseback ride, show her what you love about the ranch without arguing or seeing all your differences."

Tate nodded. "That's a good idea."

"I'm full of good ideas. All you have to do is listen."

Tate got to his feet, shoved his hands in his denim pockets and stared more intently than before.

"Think you and Lana will have kids?" Tate asked.

Carson's breath caught. Kids were certainly not something he'd given any thought to with Lana. Hell, they went from enemies to being engaged so damn fast, his head was still spinning.

"Let's just get down the aisle before you worry about us having kids," Carson joked as he got to his feet. "Why don't you call your girl and then let me know how your date goes? If you really want to be romantic, you can always have the chef prepare a nice picnic that you could take out by the pond."

"Thanks, man."

"Anytime."

Tate turned and started toward the door, but stopped and glanced over his shoulder. "Do you care that dad thinks this marriage is a bad idea?"

Even if his engagement to Lana had been authentic, he wouldn't care what his father thought. Yes, he'd want his dad on board with the next chapter in his life, but on the other hand a Langley-Wentworth union could actually solidify this generation and pave the way for the next and all of them thereafter.

"Dad will come around," Carson replied. "Don't worry about me."

Tate gave him that signature Wentworth cocky grin. "Does anything ever bother you?"

The woman who drove him crazy both in bed and out, and in totally opposite ways, but that tidbit wasn't something worth sharing with his teen brother.

"Plenty, but I can't let it bother me or get in the way of my goals. And that's advice for anything from your personal to your professional life. If you want something, don't let anything stand in your way."

Tate gave a final nod before he left the office, leaving Carson hoping he had given him the best advice possible. The silence surrounding him also left him wondering who the hell was going to give him advice, because he needed to know how to maneuver through this delicate situation with his new fiancée.

"Let me get all of this straight."

Lana didn't like that tone from Abby. Lana also didn't like lying to her best friend and sister-in-law, but right now she didn't have a choice.

"I'm still getting used to you being engaged to Carson Wentworth, and now you're wanting my help to throw your engagement party at the end of the month?"

Lana smiled as she crossed her legs on the sofa in her office at the clubhouse. No matter that her insides were swirling with nerves and anxiety—she couldn't let any of that show on the outside.

"Pretty much," Lana confirmed. "I can do a low-key wedding, but an engagement party should be extravagant and fun. Something over-the-top and not near as intimate as the actual wedding."

Abby laughed and tucked her vibrant red hair behind her ears. "Lana, this is insane. You hate Carson. You hate all the Wentworths, actually."

"I don't, though. I was just brought up to hate that family simply for their name," Lana explained, glad she could at least tell some truth here. "I never really dealt too much with Carson until the campaign and, of course, he wasn't my favorite because he was my opponent."

The still skeptical Abby narrowed her eyes and tipped her head. Lana knew that look—Abby wasn't buying this story, but Lana had to stay on the path she'd started. She still couldn't believe she'd forged such a secret bond with Carson, of all people in this world.

"I'm just trying to figure out where all of this came from and why it's moving so fast."

Fast? If only Abby knew. Every bit of Lana wanted to just spill every detail—get it off her chest and out in the open. Lana desperately wanted some sound advice from her very best friend.

"You, of all people, have to understand where I'm coming from. You fell for your opponent, too."

"Oh, I'm well aware," Abby agreed with a smile.

But that smile eased away and skepticism fell back into place as Abby continued to stare and wait for answers.

Lana knew that Abby would be a tough sell because nobody knew her like Abby. They were just as tight as biological sisters and shared everything. So during the campaign days, Abby had heard Lana's ranting and hatred for Carson on the daily.

And now Lana had to sell a marriage to the man.

Uneasy and anxious, Lana got to her feet and crossed to the little minibar area she kept on the wall behind her desk. She didn't have a big office, certainly nothing like the president, but she did have her own space, since she was the main woman to get things done for the female ranchers in the area.

Despite wanting a larger office, Lana had made

do with what she had and had accessorized the hell out of the space with a plush white love seat, blush throw pillows, a white desk with a white-and-gold accent chair, and the chandelier she'd had sent from an online boutique in LA. She might be a country girl at heart, but she had all the taste of the big-city bling.

"Chardonnay?" Lana asked, holding up a stemless wineglass.

"I'm going to need the entire bottle from the way this conversation is going."

Lana laughed as she poured two glasses and crossed back over the white faux-fur rug. She handed Abby her drink and then took a seat, once again crossing her legs and ready to tackle this topic.

"You've not only found love once, but twice," Lana began. "When it's real, there's not much you can do to stop it."

Ugh. She was lying—she wasn't doing the best job, but she was doing it. Abby knew her better than anyone, and if Lana could put this over on her, then there would be no problem posing as an imposter to the rest of the town.

"I just don't believe it." Abby took a sip of her drink and swirled the contents before taking another sip. "Don't get me wrong, Carson is a damn fine man to look at, but he's so arrogant."

Oh, there was no arguing that fact, but for reasons Lana couldn't explain, his arrogance seemed to be growing on her. In the bedroom, that arrogance turned into something downright sexy and irresistible.

"He's determined," Lana amended. "I believe that's one of the qualities you love about me, yes?"

Abby rolled her eyes. "I love you no matter what.

And I don't want to be a black cloud over your happiness. So if this is what you want, then I'm all for it. I just don't want you hurt."

Well, that made two of them, but so far, so good. Nights filled with passion and days filled with meetings and party planning weren't the worst ways to spend her time.

"So you'll help me plan the engagement party?" Lana asked.

"You know I will." Abby shifted on the sofa and rested her elbow on the back as a wide smile spread across her face. "What are you thinking? Do you want to keep the rustic vibe going, like the clubhouse? I mean, I assume you're holding the event here."

"I am, but I'm not sure about rustic. I want a good mix of both our tastes."

"So let's start with Carson, because I know you as well as I know myself. What are his tastes?"

"He loves the color green, he loves his family, he's a night owl, and he'd do anything to make me happy."

Lana couldn't help but smile as images of their nights together flooded her mind. Keeping her happy was definitely first and foremost in his mind when they were alone. She'd never had such a giving lover, or a man who knew exactly what to do without a single word.

Why did he have to be so perfectly imperfect for her?

"Well, that grin on your face is rather telling," Abby teased. "But I don't think those kind of details are the ones we can incorporate into the party."

Lana shifted her focus back to her drink and took

a sip. She hadn't even realized she'd been grinning while thoughts of Carson rolled through her mind.

Damn it. She was getting in far deeper than she'd ever intended or envisioned.

This party clearly had to be about the engagement and the big announcement regarding the funds from Harmon. She had to keep her mind and her focus on those goals, because her emotions, or any type of newfound feelings for Carson, had no place in this faux engagement.

And that funding part was a secret Lana was keeping from Abby as well. If Lana let that slip, Abby would know full well this engagement was not legit.

Too many lies. Too much like her father. For all these years, Lana had vowed not to be like her mother, but she'd gone and done the opposite.

"What about keeping things simple?" Abby suggested. "I know you are completely over-the-top with nearly everything from your clothes to your decor. But hear me out. What if you just had simple centerpieces? They can still make a statement, but in more of a fun way. I've seen people have mini-cakes on each table, a different flavor and style even would be interesting. Do you know a color scheme? Obviously green if that's what Carson likes."

"What about a classic green with a pale gold? Something to soften the shade?" Lana suggested.

"I love it." Abby set her glass on the table in front of the love seat and pulled her phone from her bag. "I'm taking notes now. This is so exciting. I love planning parties with other people's money."

"That's why you're perfect for this job, because I'm

working with Carson on renovation ideas for a whole new women's wing."

Abby's eyebrows rose. "Is that so?"

"It took some persuasion, but he's on board. I can't wait to make an official announcement, so don't say anything just yet."

Abby beamed. "I'm so proud of the hard work you're putting into the club. I never imagined it would grow like it has when I first petitioned for female members."

"You were definitely a pioneer," Lana acknowledged. "I'm just making sure we get our own designated space. I think something more feminine will be perfect. I imagine baby showers and bridal showers and maybe even monthly wine-and-dine events. Something just for us. I'll work out the details for all of that later, I'm just starting on the design and getting a contractor and budget finalized."

Abby reached over and squeezed Lana's hand. "This is so exciting. You seem so happy and I guess I have Carson to thank for that. I guess this will make you the first lady?"

The first lady? That wasn't the title she wanted. She'd wanted president, but that wasn't to be.

And as far as thanking Carson for her sudden happiness? Maybe he was partially responsible. He did make her smile, and he had become a delicious distraction, but all of this was temporary and nothing was real.

The fact that the only person she could be "real" with right now was the man she was in a fake-committed relationship with was so ironic and completely unfair. None of this made sense, but she only had three more weeks to go.

Now, if she could just keep her heart guarded that long, she'd come out on the other side unscathed.

Twelve

Carson watched Lana smooth her hair over one shoulder, then shift her stance. She blew out a breath, and then adjusted her hair once more.

"Stop fidgeting," Carson muttered. "You look as beautiful as ever."

She glanced over at him as they stood on the porch of Cammie and Drake's home. He hadn't even knocked yet, but something had Lana behaving like a ball of nerves.

"What's wrong?" he asked, turning to face her fully.

She closed her eyes and shook her head. "It's just so real, yet not, if that makes sense. We're lying to everyone around us and I'm actually planning an engagement party like this is going to happen. Will we just be hated when we call this off?"

Carson took her hands in his and offered what he hoped was a reassuring squeeze. That fierce look in her eyes hid the vulnerability, but he saw it there. Maybe some people wouldn't recognize her anxiety, but he'd come to know her pretty well in their last week and a half together. Intimacy really did pull out a whole other side to someone, and he'd not only gotten physically intimate with her, but they'd also connected on an intellectual level.

"Nobody will hate us," he assured her. "Don't lose sight as to why we started this. Harmon's dying wish and to have the funds for the club. We are doing good for so many people. I'm right here with you, Lana. I won't let you fall."

Her eyes softened as her shoulders relaxed. She gave a slight smile and leaned forward, pressing her lips to the corner of his mouth.

He wanted more. Every time he touched her, no matter how innocent, he wanted more.

But at the same time, he also wanted her to realize that she wasn't in this by herself. Hell, he was the one who'd gotten her in this mess, so if she fell, he'd certainly be there to catch her. No matter what happened at the end of all of this, he would do anything to prevent her from getting hurt.

In such a short time, Carson had come to care about Lana. Great sex aside, he did respect and value her as a confidante and a formidable adversary. Never in his life did he believe his closest friend and lover would be a Langley.

Yes, this was all temporary, he totally understood that. But there was no way once this engagement was over that they could—or would—go back to being enemies.

The door swung open, immediately followed by the sound of someone clapping.

"You two lovebirds are adorable."

Carson kept hold of Lana's hands as he shifted his attention to Cammie.

"I was just stealing a moment with my girl," he stated.

"Which is what makes you two so cute," Cammie added, her smile wide. "Come on in. I'm so thrilled to have you guys here. Drake is just getting Micah changed for the third time today. Diaper blowouts— you don't want any more information than that."

Carson laughed. "No, I don't."

He gestured for Lana to go in ahead of him. Once they were inside the spacious ranch home, Cammie closed the door behind them and a moment later Drake came down the hall with Micah in his arms.

"Hey, guys." Drake came over and kissed Lana on the cheek before turning to Carson and shaking his hand. "This is great that you two could come by. Cammie has been dying to know all the details of the engagement since she read about it."

Lana stiffened beside him, but he slid his thumb in an easy pattern over the back of her hand. He'd give her credit, though—she kept that megawatt smile in place.

"It was sort of a whirlwind," Carson admitted. "But definitely worth it."

"Love is worth everything," Cammie replied as she reached for Micah. "Come on into the dining room.

I just set everything up. I hope you all like Italian. I was craving some carbs."

"Italian and carbs are my love language," Lana chimed in. "Is there anything I can do to help you set up?"

Cammie started through the foyer and then into the dining area, cradling Micah with one arm.

"Nope. Just have a seat."

"Oh, I left the wine out in the car."

Lana started to turn, but Carson placed his hands on her shoulders. "I've got it. Go on ahead."

"You didn't need to bring wine."

He heard Cammie's statement as he stepped back onto the porch. The door closed behind him just as his cell vibrated in his pocket. He stopped and slid the phone out to check the screen and sighed.

Part of him wanted to let it go to voice mail, but the other part knew he had an obligation to his family. So he answered.

"Dad, what's up?"

"I'm visiting Granddad and I didn't know if you could come on over for a bit."

"Now isn't a good time." Carson headed toward his SUV and retrieved the bottle of cabernet. "Is something wrong?"

"No, no. Nothing like that. I was just having an interesting talk and Granddad mentioned a large sum of money going to the club."

"That's right, but people aren't supposed to know about that right now. We plan on making a surprise announcement at our engagement party at the end of the month."

"Is that why you're doing this?" his father accused.

Carson stilled. "Doing what?"

"Marrying the Langley woman."

Carson clenched his teeth and gripped the bottle of wine. "I'm marrying her because I want to and because we are in love. If you aren't happy with our reasons or if you have some hang-up, then that's your problem. I love you, Dad, but Lana is my fiancée and we're out to dinner right now, so I'll have to call you tomorrow."

He disconnected the call and pulled in a deep breath, then another, to calm his nerves before he headed back inside. The moment he stepped into the dining room, Lana turned to smile, but quickly tipped her head.

"Everything okay?" she asked, her eyebrows drawn in.

And wasn't that something. How she could pick up on his tension in just a fraction of a second absolutely floored him. Was she that in tune with his emotions and frustrations?

"Everything is fine," he assured her, leaning down to kiss her on the cheek.

Maybe the kiss was a show of their affection for Cammie and Drake, maybe the kiss was to convince her he was indeed all right, or maybe he'd kissed her because he just wanted to feel that simple touch. Odd that the very brief call with his dad had him wanting to get closer to Lana. That was something he'd have to think about later, not when he was in the midst of a dinner party hosted by great friends.

Carson circled the table and handed the bottle to Drake before going back around to take a seat next to Lana. Her leg brushed his, reminding him that he'd been at her place before this. He'd stopped by a little early, which only ended up with them in her bedroom, but not quite making it to the bed. He'd taken her right there against the wall inside the doorway.

When she'd answered the door in that damn dress with those spiky heels, he hadn't been able to resist. He still couldn't decide whether that whole girl-next-door vibe, or her killer curves in dresses, was his favorite look.

Either way, he couldn't wait to get back to her place and slide that dress up that shapely body and toss it aside. He hadn't quite taken the time he really wanted to, but now that he had her thigh against his, that only reminded him that he wasn't finished with her.

Only two and a half weeks left until they would ultimately go their separate ways...at least in their personal lives. They would still be working together in regard to the women's wing she wanted to complete.

Cammie had handed the baby off to Drake and then got all of the food ready and settled in at the table. All the while Drake started feeding Micah a bottle. The two seemed to work flawlessly with their temporary family.

"How is life with a little one?" Lana asked. "You all seem to be doing really well with him."

Cammie beamed. "He is an absolute joy to have. I've always wanted children, but Drake was more career-oriented. Micah is a wonderful influence, though, and Drake is doing really well with the adjustment. Taking care of his teenage stepsister was quite different than caring for an infant. He sees the joy there can be with children now and wouldn't change this for anything."

"He's definitely opened my eyes to future possibilities," Drake added as he rocked gently side to side while feeding the baby. "This experience might be tragic, but we are getting a good idea of how we would be as parents."

Carson reached for his wineglass. "Parenting looks good on you."

"Well, love looks good on you two." Cammie smiled across the table, her eyes darting between Carson and Lana. "Tell me all about the engagement. Your ring is absolutely stunning, by the way. But more importantly, I'm so glad we're going to finally put this Wentworth-Langley feuding in the past where it belongs."

"Thank you and I completely agree," Lana replied, as she stared down at the pearl and diamonds. "We actually had a nontraditional engagement. I asked Carson."

He couldn't help but laugh as he shook his head. "That's not exactly how it went."

She shifted in her seat and quirked an eyebrow his way. Damn that was sexy. Her attitude used to annoy him, but now he found everything about her a challenge and he never turned down an intriguing challenge.

"I believe I'm the one who got down on one knee," she reminded him.

"But I already had the ring in hand when you did that."

"Oh, man, you two are seriously made to be together," Drake laughed. "You're both so hardheaded and determined. It's no wonder you fell for each other."

That's not the first time he'd heard that and he wondered if he and Lana were just that good at convincing, or if other people saw something Carson wasn't aware of.

"So do you have any wedding details yet?" Cammie asked as she passed the bowl of fresh bread. "I love weddings. There's nothing more magical."

"I don't have wedding details yet, but I do have engagement-party plans."

Lana took a piece of bread, then set down the bowl. Were her hands shaking? Maybe she hadn't been kidding when she'd told him how much she hated lying and was terrible at it. But if he could keep this conversation on the party and not the wedding, then Lana should be just fine, because the party was a legit event that was going to happen.

"Oh, tell me all about the party," Cammie begged. "I hope it's going to be big and lavish. That just seems perfect for the two of you. You guys are the most dynamic power couple the club has ever seen."

They would be an epic power couple if this union between them was on the up-and-up. There would be no stopping him and Lana in anything they set their minds to.

But that joint venture wasn't meant to be for the long-term.

"So, when is the party?" Cammie asked.

"The end of the month," Lana replied. "You will be receiving a formal invitation in a couple of days. We plan on having it at the clubhouse in the new ballroom."

Drake shifted Micah up onto his shoulder and patted his back, immediately ridding the infant of air bubbles.

"This kid is one hell of an eater," Drake laughed. "He loves bottle time."

Carson glanced to Lana and saw that wistful look in her eyes. He'd not discussed kids with her, and why would he? It's not like this arrangement had to be taken that far. Thankfully a Wentworth-Langley baby hadn't been part of Harmon's deal.

He couldn't help but imagine what type of mother she would be. Hands on, for sure. Lana wouldn't want anyone else aiding in the raising of her child. She wouldn't be the type of parent who pawned off her baby to a nanny. She'd be the woman who put a nursery corner in her office and showed everyone exactly how multitasking worked.

An immediate image of a little girl with Lana's long, dark hair and wide, expressive eyes popped into his head. No doubt her child would be a go-getter and let nothing stand in the way of dreams and goals.

Something stirred deep in his gut and he didn't like this uncomfortable, unwanted sensation. He had no clue what had him so... Hell, he couldn't even put a label on this overwhelming emotion.

Lana's eyes went from Micah to him and she blinked, then suddenly shifted away. Whatever she'd seen in his eyes had been unwanted...and he wished like hell he knew what she'd seen.

Sure, Carson wanted children one day. He wanted to carry on the Wentworth name and have another generation to pass down the family's dynasty and legacy.

A cell chime echoed in the room and Drake immediately looked to Cammie.

"Go ahead," he told her.

Cammie offered an apologetic smile as she eased back from the table. "Excuse me. So sorry about this."

She grabbed the phone from the buffet table along the wall and stepped from the room.

"We have to take all the calls right now with Eve still recovering in rehab and with the social workers checking in." Drake took the baby and placed him in the swing next to the table and turned the device on low. "We're hoping Eve will be well enough soon to be able to be released. I know she wants to be reunited with Micah."

"How is she doing?" Lana asked.

"Last update we had she's doing really well," he replied. "I know she's very determined to get back. She wants to reconnect with that bond from her late sister."

Cammie stepped back into the room, but wasn't the smiling, bubbly woman she'd been only moments ago.

"Babe," Drake began. "What's wrong?"

"That was Officer Haley Lopez. She was calling to let me know that Eve is out of rehab now, but will require six more weeks of strenuous physical therapy."

"That's good…isn't it?" Drake asked, and Carson took note of his friend's confused tone.

"It is," Cammie replied as she took her seat on the other side of the high chair. "I just realized that now we have a deadline, and even though we've been preparing ourselves, knowing this was temporary, I hate the idea of seeing him go. He's been such a pleasure to have here."

Drake's demeanor shifted into something equally solemn as Cammie's. Carson wasn't good with comforting words. He was used to dealing with business and demands and goals. He didn't like the awkward silence that seemed to settle in the room.

"Well, you all know you have at least six weeks left," Lana offered in that upbeat tone of hers. "Micah has been the luckiest little boy to have the two of you care for him and I'm sure Eve will keep you involved in his life. She's going to be so grateful to you both."

Cammie pulled in a shaky breath and nodded. "I sure hope so. I can't imagine not seeing him grow up and reaching milestones."

"Let's not borrow worries," Drake told her. "We should enjoy our time together while we have him."

Micah let out a squeal and started crying from his swing. Drake reached for him, but Cammie stood up.

"I'll get him, you need to eat. You all go ahead. I'll just set him on my lap while we talk."

Carson watched the couple and wondered just how they would actually cope once the six weeks were over. Their temporary, life-altering arrangement would change them forever.

The parallels weren't lost on him. Without thinking, he reached beneath the table and slid his hand over Lana's thigh, giving her a gentle squeeze. His gesture had nothing at all to do with anything sexual, and everything to do with the fact that he wanted to sear every moment with her into his mind—to hold onto for the time when she was ultimately gone.

Thirteen

Lana reached for Carson's hand as he assisted her from his vehicle. They'd left their dinner party and headed back to her house in silence. She wasn't sure what had been on his mind, but she knew exactly what had been on hers.

Their time was limited. She'd known that all along, obviously. But seeing another couple facing an ending to a temporary arrangement really was like a slap in the face, and a dose of reality she needed.

The passion-filled nights would come to an end, their playful relationship in public would come to an end and the man who challenged her in the absolute best ways would come to an end.

"Hey."

She shifted her attention to his intense stare.

"You okay?" he asked.

Lana smiled. "Fine."

Carson tipped his head in that sexy, adorable way she'd come to find absolutely irresistible.

"You're a terrible liar," he told her with a grin.

"I told you that in the beginning," she reminded him. "But I seem to be doing okay where our engagement is concerned."

"You are," he agreed. "But I've gotten to know you pretty well and I can tell that you're lying."

Something warm and thrilling spread through her at his admission that he'd gotten to know her...because that meant he cared for her. He might not admit such feelings, but he did care.

So what did she do with that information? Did she call him out on it and tease? No, that's what the Lana from weeks ago would have done. Even though they were in this for the ultimate goal of money, she had to admit that she'd changed. In such a short time, he'd changed her and she wasn't even sure who she was anymore.

Her only option at this point was to be honest. Never in her life did she think she'd be opening up to her enemy, but right now there was nobody else she wanted this close to her.

"I guess just seeing them come to the realization that their time was limited really hit me," she admitted. "It just put our situation into perspective."

When Carson merely stared at her, Lana worried she might have gone too far, or exposed a side of herself that neither of them was ready for.

"Not that I'm in love with you," she continued. "I mean, you're a great guy, and honestly, we are compatible, but when I marry, I want to be completely head over heels and I want my guy to put me first in all things. I want to know I'm it for him."

"You deserve nothing less," Carson told her. "And he'll be a lucky man to have you by his side."

Lana was taken aback a bit. "You really think so? Because some men might think I'm too much to handle."

"Then they are missing out." Carson reached up, framed her face, and stared into her eyes. "Any man that doesn't want a strong, independent woman at his side is a damn fool."

There went those flutterings once again in her belly. Getting overly infatuated with Carson was a big no-no.

Why did the wrong man have all the right words?

"Can I put you down as a reference when the time comes?" she joked, desperately needing to keep things light between them.

Carson's lips quirked into a grin…which did nothing to help that curl of arousal inside her. Why did he have such control over her emotions when she'd told herself over and over to hold tight to her control?

Lana already despised the woman that would eventually come into his life. Jealousy had no place here, but Lana couldn't help the immediate reaction to the faceless lady who would step into Lana's role one day.

And that was it, wasn't it? All of this was a role. Short-term, fake, completely made up of lies and deceit—was there anything about any of that that appealed to her? And what good relationship could come from this situation? There was no real-life happily-ever-after—not for the two of them to actually end up together.

"I'm not discussing another man in your life as long as I'm the one in it." Carson's hands slid down over her shoulders and settled into the dip of her waist. He yanked her body against his. "And you're mine for the next few weeks."

His. She really shouldn't like the sound of that, but she did. Wasn't she supposed to be the strong, independent woman he'd mentioned? The deeper she fell with Carson, the more she wondered if she'd lost control somewhere.

Was she losing part of herself by getting wrapped up in all of this charade? Because that's what worried her most.

No, what worried her most was falling for Carson. That would be a complete disaster. His father was not on board with this and they were much too hardheaded to make this any longer than a month. Great sex helped to gloss over all of the anxiety and worry that kept flooding her mind. Carson was definitely good at distracting her.

"I can hear your mind working," he said, laughing. "I'm clearly not doing a good job here."

Lana placed her hands on his shoulders and tipped her head. "And here I was just thinking what a perfect distraction you were for everything going on."

"We're good for distracting each other." He leaned forward, feathering his lips over hers. "I'm about a second away from peeling you out of this dress right here in your driveway."

Just like she'd thought earlier…he had all the right words. Every word, every look, every touch held a promise of so much more to come.

"We'd better get inside," she told him, taking his hand and leading him up the brick steps to her porch.

As she glanced back, thunder rolled through the sky. Something about that ominous sound had her shivering, and not in the turned-on manner she'd become accustomed to. Between the reality hitting her hard from the dinner earlier and the storm brewing, she wanted to get inside and lock out any negativity or evil that could harm her or Carson. She had come to care for him—it would be impossible not to. But she had another sinking feeling that she might be falling for her enemy…no matter how many times she told herself that was a mistake.

And she still had over two weeks before letting him go for good.

Something had shifted. The light in Lana's eyes dimmed just enough for Carson to worry and wonder what was plaguing her mind, and what she was keeping bottled up inside. He wanted her to open up to him, to let him know what bothered her so he could fix any and all issues that bothered her. Never before had he wanted to wrap a woman in his protective embrace and slay anything that threatened her happiness.

And she would absolutely hate that he wanted to protect her. He knew full well that she could do everything herself, but she shouldn't have to. She deserved a man who would do anything she wanted, a man who would keep that smile on her face and that light shining in her eyes.

But he wasn't to be that man and he was an absolute fool for having such thoughts.

Carson took her key from her and opened her door

before he said something he might regret…like opening up about these unwanted, confusing feelings.

Sex. That's what they came back for and that's what they both seemed to understand.

Lana closed the door behind him. She went to the security panel and typed in her code, the quick succession of beeps echoing through the dark foyer.

Then she turned to face him and the accent lamp on the table lit up her face, and he saw that raw passion staring back at him. She didn't even need to say a word and he already knew what she needed. She needed him, and if she wanted to use him to forget everything, then he was more than ready to oblige.

"Is there more going on here?"

Her question sliced through his thoughts. He didn't want to assume he knew where her thought process was heading, but he had a pretty good idea. They'd been dancing around this for days. And by *this*, he meant the extra tension and unspoken emotions that had been swirling around them, pulling them closer and closer with each passing moment.

"More?" he asked.

"More than sex," she elaborated. "It just seems like for two people who were trained up to be enemies, we have a great deal in common, and other than the campaign, we haven't even bickered at each other."

"And why is that?"

Carson wasn't ready to admit anything and this might be one area he was more than willing to relinquish control. He definitely wanted to know what was in her head before he made any type of statement.

Maybe he was cut out for politics after all.

"I'd say because we think for ourselves." She

smiled and crossed her arms. "Neither one of us like to be told what to do, so the fact we're getting along, now that we're getting married, really just shows everyone how strong and determined we are."

Lana let out a soft laugh that tightened his gut and added another burst of arousal.

"I mean if we were actually getting married," she stated. "Can you imagine how crazy we would drive each other?"

Oh, he could imagine. She already drove him crazy on a daily basis…but in the most amazing of ways. He definitely couldn't admit that.

"I just don't want to get too swept up in the lies and start believing them myself."

Her smile faded and for the first time in this whole process, he saw a sliver of fear. These emotions were much too close to falling over into vulnerability and discomfort, which was something he had vowed not to let her experience.

Carson took a step forward, then another, closing the gap between them. He slid his hands up and over her shoulders, mimicking their stance from the driveway, but suddenly they'd gone from flirty and sexy to compassionate and caring.

"We're not getting swept up in anything," he assured her. "We're doing something to help the club, to help give Harmon peace of mind before he passes, and to prove our families can get along from here on out. We're breaking this toxic cycle."

He gave a gentle squeeze to her shoulders and rested his forehead against hers.

"The fact that we're involved intimately is just for

us," he whispered. "Nothing says we can't take what we both want without the guilt."

"And when all of this is over…"

Yeah, that was the part he was hoping to avoid. He didn't want to think of the time when he had to let her go and go back to dating random women. He'd gotten comfortable with Lana, maybe too comfortable, too fast, but he chalked it up to the fact he knew this wasn't permanent, so why should he get comfortable? There were no consequences here and nothing actually tying him down.

Carson didn't want to talk anymore, he didn't want to analyze his future or the feelings. He wanted to make her forget any worry or doubts. Their time together was too short to allow in any negativity, and if he had to help her overcome this small hurdle she couldn't get over on her own, then that's what he'd do.

They were a team, right? At least for the time being.

Lana lifted her head slightly, silently inviting him to kiss her. Clearly, she was done talking and worrying, too. How could they speak the same language without saying a word to each other?

He reached around her back and eased down the zipper. The material parted as he grazed his fingertips over her bare skin. The second she shivered beneath his touch, Carson peeled the dress from her arms and down her body, letting it glide effortlessly to the floor.

"Carson—"

He placed a fingertip over her lips, stared into those expressive eyes, and eased back slightly.

"Just let me show you," he murmured, sliding his

fingertip from her lips down her neck and to the valley between her breasts.

"Show me what?" she asked.

"Everything."

Carson lifted her and headed toward the staircase, wondering if he'd ever tire of carrying her up these steps. He wanted her in her bed, and he wanted to take his time. Every moment they'd been alone had been frantic and rushed. A woman like Lana deserved more than a few passion-filled moments. She deserved the entire night, she deserved...

A lifetime.

No. That couldn't be. There was no lifetime of them together and he wasn't even supposed to have those thoughts in his head. This situation and arrangement didn't have to be complicated.

Lana's head rested against his shoulder and something turned over in his chest. That simple, delicate gesture stemmed from nothing but trust. He'd never thought about a woman's trust before—it had never really mattered, apparently.

For reasons he didn't want to get into, Carson blocked any further emotion from entering this moment. All that mattered now was Lana. Even though they were both getting what they wanted for the club out of this situation, she'd ultimately agreed to this because of his great-grandfather.

Lana might be hard, strong, always showing her steely exterior, but there was a side to her that he liked to think only he knew. There was a side she kept hidden from the public, and she tried to hide from him, but he knew her little quirks and he knew she was fighting so hard to keep her emotions close to her chest.

Carson reached the double doors to her bedroom and used his toe to push them open. The darkened room only had a slash of moonlight falling across the bottom edge of the bed. He couldn't wait to mess up those perfectly placed blankets.

Lana's fingertips threaded through his hair at the nape of his neck. Her delicate touch never failed to turn him on. Everything about her made him want her more, from her touch to her quick banter.

This woman was the real deal. She might not give up all of her emotions, but she'd been right in admitting she couldn't lie. There was a sensitivity to her that she never showed and if he hadn't been so in tune with reading her body language and those expressive eyes, she would have fooled him into believing everything was just fine.

There was one emotion she couldn't hide, though. Desire.

Lana had to be the most passionate woman he'd ever known and in this short time, he'd come to value her even more. He found himself wanting to please her, wanting to uncover more layers to get to know her even better.

Carson crossed the dimly lit room and gently placed her on the bed. As she lay there completely bare—she hadn't worn anything under her dress— she stared up at him, and that clench in his chest happened once again.

He couldn't put a label on that and thinking too much on anything more than physical scared the hell out of him.

With her wide eyes locked on him, Carson shed himself of every piece of clothing. He reached for her foot, running his thumb along the arch. He grabbed her other foot and did the same before bending her knees and placing her feet flat on the bed.

There was never a more beautiful sight than Lana splayed out before him.

"I'm staying all night."

A wide smile spread across her face as she reached up for him. "I hadn't planned on letting you leave."

He didn't know if she meant for tonight...or at the end of the month.

Fourteen

A week of pretty much spending all of his time at Lana's home had led Carson to believe that they were even more compatible than he'd first thought. He knew they meshed in nearly all areas, but the longer he stayed, the more he wanted to.

Which was why he was back in his home. Wanting too much from Lana and this "relationship" could be detrimental to the entire process. They'd made a deal, a verbally binding agreement for a month. Nothing more.

They just needed to secure the funds from Harmon, end the feud between the Wentworths and the Langleys and move on with club business. Then they could each move on in their private lives as well.

But moving on didn't seem as exciting as it once had, and as their end date grew closer, there was a

new level of anxiety he hadn't experienced before…
and he wasn't quite sure what to make of it.

He needed to clear his mind a bit and circle back
to focus on why he was in this position. Besides, they
were a little over a week from the engagement party
and that really narrowed the gap in bringing this fake
engagement to an end.

Carson made his way upstairs toward his bedroom.
He just wanted a shower and to do a few things before he went to see his father later. He'd not spoken
to him since the phone call that interrupted Cammie
and Drake's dinner party and he wanted to check in.

He told Lana he'd get in touch with her later. He
wasn't sure if he should go to her house, or if he should
start putting that gap between them. They were falling
into an easy pattern that couldn't become the norm.

Stripping out of his clothes, he started heading toward his en suite. As he passed by his bed, something
seemed off. He did a double take at his nightstand and
noticed Arielle Martin's diary had been moved.
It wasn't in the same spot he kept it.

Since Sierra had loaned it to him, the diary always
sat beneath another book he'd been reading, but now
the diary was on top and the stack had shifted.

Carson picked up the diary, then scanned through
Arielle's words where she interviewed Harmon. The
ragged edge from one section gave him pause.

What the hell was this? He looked closer and realized pages had been torn out. The diary had been
completely intact when he'd last looked inside…which
was before he went to Lana's yesterday.

Who the hell had been in his home and messed

with the diary? Or had pages just been loose that he hadn't noticed? Maybe they'd slipped out.

He checked beneath the bed, in case the pages had fallen there, and he even looked in the top drawer of his nightstand. Where the hell had those pages gone? Someone had to have come in and taken them. What was on those pages that was so important?

Carson sank down on the edge of his bed and raked his hand through his hair. He hadn't seen one single thing out of place or missing other than those pages. How the hell could anyone get into his house with all the security?

It had to be someone who knew him, someone who came and went freely…someone Carson trusted to be here.

His first thought was Lana, but he really didn't believe she'd take it. Would she? Who else had been here? He certainly hadn't invited anyone else.

The thoughts weighed heavy on his mind as he went to grab a shower. He had to find out what happened to those pages and he had to figure out who the hell took them…and why.

"This party is going to be the most amazing event this club has ever seen."

Lana laughed as Abby gushed over the engagement party. Lana had asked her best friend to meet her in the ballroom so they could finalize some of the plans. She couldn't believe that in just over a week, this engagement would come and go like a wrinkle in her path of life. She and Carson would have to go back to their regularly scheduled days, and act as if they hadn't turned each other's worlds upside down and inside out.

She honestly had no clue how she was supposed to jump into the dating scene and not compare any man to Carson Wentworth.

"Well, if this is the event of the year, then it's all because you helped," Lana stated. "One thing is for sure—the night will be memorable."

As if this entire month hadn't been memorable? Lana had squeezed in years of memories with Carson in such a short time. No doubt the engagement party would also be a night she'd never forget. It was all the events that would follow that Lana wasn't looking forward to.

"I think we have everything down here," Abby stated as she did a slow turn, as if she was already seeing the space fully decorated. "Can you think of anything else we're missing?"

An actual engaged couple?

"I'm confident we've covered all the bases," Lana replied. "Do you want to see my ideas for the new women's area?"

Abby clasped her hands and let out a little squeal. "You know I do."

"Follow me." Lana gestured toward the hallway and led Abby toward her back office. "Now, nothing is finalized, Carson and I have been busy doing other things, but I'm thrilled with the vision."

"I imagine being engaged to a sexy man and planning to take over the world is time-consuming."

Lana laughed as she unlocked her office door and flipped on the light. "We're not taking over the world, but perhaps just the clubhouse."

"Well, with the way you gush when talking about him, I'm not sure how you two get anything done."

Lana paused and turned to face her best friend. "I don't gush."

Abby snickered. "Oh, girl. You most definitely gush. You mention his name and your face gets this pretty pink tint, your voice changes just a bit, and you smile like nothing I've seen before."

"What do you mean?"

What did Abby see? Obviously too much, but Lana had no clue she was giving off anything other than fake vibes. But if Abby was picking up all of that, what did that say about Lana's true feelings?

The feelings she didn't want to face. She knew they were there, under the surface. She hadn't wanted to admit it, she hadn't wanted to face the truth. But now that Abby had called her out...

"I'm just saying I'm really glad you're happy," Abby replied. "It shows and I just hope you two are always in this state."

Oh, they'd be happy once the farce came to an end. Then they could stop the public affection—but she didn't know if she wanted to. She wasn't even going to bother lying to herself at this point. She'd miss Carson's touch, his kisses…their nights together. That had nothing to do with a fake engagement and everything to do with their bond they'd formed.

When she'd tried to call him on it and bring it out in the open the night of Cammie's dinner party, the question had been somewhat dodged—in true president mode—and they'd ended up in bed. But that night there had been a shift between them, a shift that had almost brought them even closer together.

"We'll be happy," Lana assured her.

They'd be apart, but they'd create their own happiness. They were too much alike to stay together long-term, or at least that's what Lana kept telling herself. Even if they buried the feud, would that dark cloud still hover around them?

She didn't know how they could make things work, not with both of them having that type A personality. They'd get along for a while, but what happened when a problem hit them head on? What happened when they wanted to approach something major but had a difference of opinion?

That Wentworth-Langley battle mode would come back into play and Lana didn't want to risk hating him again. She liked where they were, but moving in the direction of a fully committed relationship wasn't the smartest move.

"I was hoping to run these plans by you and get your input." Lana circled back around to the original topic and moved to her desk to fire up her computer. "I think you are going to love them, but since you are the pioneer of the women's membership, I definitely want to know if you think I've missed anything."

"I'm sure you thought of all the perfect elements to add in," Abby assured her.

Lana took her laptop to the sofa and settled in beside Abby. She opened the file and started scrolling through, pointing out various upgrades, new amenities, and special perks for members only.

Abby beamed. "You nailed it. I can't believe how detailed this is, Lana. The women are going to absolutely love this."

"That's my goal."

"Is all of this in the budget?" Abby asked. "It seems rather over-the-top, even for the club."

"It's all in the budget." Just as soon as this engagement party was over and Harmon released the funds. "I've gotten bids and they are all similar, but Carson is making the final call on that."

Abby tapped on the screen a few more times, going back through the mock-up images. "These are all just so amazing. I can't wait to see it brought to life. You, my friend, are a genius."

Lana shrugged. "I don't know about that, but I do know what I like and I can't help but have expensive taste."

"That's nothing to apologize for," Abby added. "I love that you are a bold woman who knows what she wants and doesn't defend herself for it. That's why we're such good friends, even stronger than family."

Yeah, well, Lana didn't feel so bold right now. And she certainly should be apologizing for lying because that wasn't a good friend. But even after all of this was over, Lana still could never tell Abby the full truth. That thought really hit her hard because she never kept anything from Abby.

Now Lana's only sounding board was her enemy-turned-lover, her current fiancé who would ultimately become her ex. The man wore too many hats in her life to not be involved permanently, but that had been the agreement and she wouldn't be the one to break that deal.

"Is it silly that I'm more excited for your engagement party than I was my own?" Abby asked with a soft laugh. "Don't get me wrong, I love my husband, but I'm just so excited for you and Carson."

Another niggle of guilt hit Lana when she realized she'd have to tell her sister-in-law next week that this epic engagement would officially be called off. She hoped Abby understood that she was only trying to live up to her legacy and continue to grow the women's aspect of the club.

All too soon, everything would go back to being as it was before.

Only everything had changed and nobody outside of her and Carson would fully be able to grasp that concept. Even when they called things off, they would still have this bond they'd formed and Lana didn't know if anything, not even time or distance, could sever that.

Fifteen

Carson pulled into the ranch, the first time he'd been back since the dinner with his dad a few weeks ago. He'd been dodging his calls, not on purpose, but Carson had actually been busy each time his father had called. They'd texted, but there was still that rift between them that had started the second his father had found out about the engagement.

He'd stopped by to see his great-grandfather earlier, but had only stayed a minute. Harmon had looked tired and Carson wanted to let him rest. He'd check back in before the engagement party on Saturday.

Carson couldn't believe the month was nearly over. His time with Lana would be over in a few short days. At first this entire idea of pretending to be engaged had been preposterous and a month seemed like a lifetime, but now that he was staring down the end, he wasn't in such a hurry to see it all go.

How could either of them go back to how they were before? Nothing between them was the same. They'd forged a unique connection that only the two of them could understand and appreciate because nobody else knew of this ruse. This was something he and Lana would share forever, no matter what happened between them or who they ultimately ended up with.

The idea of another man in her life didn't sit well with Carson. An image of her laughing or sharing her secrets with another seemed so wrong. No way in hell did he want her sharing her bed with some other guy.

On the flip side of all of that, he wasn't so sure any woman would compare to Lana. He didn't know how he would ever get her far enough to the back of his mind in order to fully move on.

Because somewhere along the way, this whole ordeal went from being fake to feeling all too real, and he had no idea what the hell to do with that glaring, realistic fact.

So he'd ignore it. They had an arrangement, one he fully intended to uphold, and telling her his feelings had shifted would make him look like an utter fool. They'd shifted…so what? He didn't know anything beyond that. He didn't know what he wanted to do with all of these unwanted emotions. All of this was completely foreign territory for him.

But the business side? Yeah. That's what he understood, what he knew in his gut was right. So that's the angle he would continue pursuing. None of this emotional nonsense that he couldn't quite explain.

Pushing aside his thoughts, Carson stepped from

his car and realized there was another in the drive. He'd been so absorbed with his own issues, he'd totally missed that familiar vehicle.

Sierra Morgan was here. No doubt she was still trying to uncover the veiled secrets from the diary. Carson half wondered if it was his own father who had taken the pages from Arielle's diary, but he still wasn't sure. There were a limited number of people who would have had the opportunity to sneak into his house. But no matter who had stolen those pages, someone Carson trusted had betrayed him by doing so.

Tamping down the anger, Carson entered his father's home. Voices echoed from the den off the foyer. Carson stepped through the wide, arched entryway and spotted his father standing against the bay window, his grandfather, Troy, seated in one of the leather club chairs, while Sierra sat in another chair with her notepad and pen.

Carson met his father's gaze. "Is this a bad time?"

Hank shook his head. "Not at all. Sierra just got here. She wanted to interview me about what I know regarding the Wentworth family, as well as Royal's history, since our family has been here since the beginning."

Sierra crossed her legs and smiled at Carson from across the room. "Perfect timing," she said. "Three generations of Wentworths all in one room at my disposal."

Carson respected Sierra and her position—the woman was trying to do her job—but that didn't mean he was in the mood for any Q&A session. He'd come here to talk to his father and try to smooth over any animosity where Lana was concerned.

Which was going to be a moot point in a few days, when he and Lana called off the engagement. But there was something that just irked the hell out of him that his father wouldn't approve of the nuptials.

Damn it. He hated passive-aggressive people and he was doing it to himself with all of these juxtaposing thoughts.

"I was just telling Hank that I'm so excited about the engagement party on Saturday," Sierra added. "That's all anyone around town can talk about."

Just wait until he and Lana broke things off—that would really give people something to talk about.

Carson's eyes shifted to his father, who continued to lean against the window frame.

"It's sure to be a memorable night," Carson stated. "Lana has put a great deal of work into making everything perfect."

"She's a hardworking woman," Sierra agreed. "So do you care to answer some of my questions? I've got so many puzzle pieces that don't fit."

If he fled now he'd look like he was afraid, and nothing ever scared Carson...save for these jumbled-up emotions he couldn't quite get a hold of.

Before he could answer, Tate stepped into the room.

"Oh, I didn't realize we had company."

The teen started to turn, but Sierra called him back.

"I'd love for you to stay," she told him. "I'd be interested in getting your opinion as well."

Tate looked as uncomfortable as Carson felt, but Carson was at least older and more experienced in controlling his outward emotions.

When Tate's eyes landed on Carson, his stepbrother ultimately made his way into the room and took a seat on the leather sofa next to Carson.

"I don't want to keep you all here longer than necessary," Sierra began. "I know you're all busy men and this was a long time ago, but I'd like to discuss Violetta Ford. Her name appears in Arielle's diary. She fascinates me. I'd love to know more about her life. Does anyone know why she disappeared right after she was denied clubhouse membership?"

Carson's grandfather, Troy, scoffed and shook his head. "We have no clue. That's not something we were ever privy to. But she was probably pissed off."

"As far as Violetta, I don't know much about her," Hank admitted.

Sierra pursed her lips. "Okay. Back to your family. How about the breakup between Eloisa Langley and Dean Wentworth?"

Hank raked his hand over the back of his neck. "Listen, we don't want to be rude, but as you said, we are busy. These are questions we simply cannot answer."

"Can't or won't?" she pressed.

Tension fell over the room and Carson had a sinking feeling he was about to play referee or some sort of calming middleman. Sierra was a no-nonsense reporter, and even though she'd come to really embrace the community, she was still hell-bent on doing her job. But Carson knew his grandfather and father weren't about to sit here and pull their family's name through any more scandal than necessary.

What mattered at the end of the day was Harmon. He wanted the century-old feud buried and in order to do that, the secrets needed to come out. Keeping everything hidden and buried was no way to move forward with a clean slate.

Not only that, but Harmon might also keep his funds from the club if there was any hint that the fighting hadn't stopped once and for all.

Not to mention, Carson and Lana were on the same page in thinking it was time for both families to move on and live at peace here in Royal.

"I think we can trust Sierra with what we know," Carson stated. "She's not here out of any malicious intent. She's been in town long enough to know all the key players and the scandals that have shaped us. I believe her pursuing the truth is going to be the best thing for Royal, not to mention the Langleys and the Wentworths."

Hank's silver eyebrows rose in shock. Troy let out a deep sigh as his focus shifted from Carson back to Sierra.

"And for Harmon's birth mother, I heard rumors she had been in Royal for a little while, then there was a scandal surrounding her and she fled," Hank went on. "We don't know her name."

Sierra's pen moved in a flurry across her notepad and for the first time, Carson also noticed a tiny, old-school tape recorder on the table before her. This reporter covered all her bases.

"So where was Harmon left as a baby?" she asked, glancing back to Hank. "That location might help us figure out some tie to the woman who left him there."

"He was left on the doorstep of his father, Dean Wentworth," Hank told her. "The story goes that he had been in love with Eloisa Langley and was set on marrying her, but something happened and she broke things off. He had some flings and the next thing he knew, a baby showed up, but no mother."

"Dean would never discuss it, and we knew better than to ask," Carson's grandfather added.

Carson listened, soaking up each word, and he was starting to feel a twinge of remorse for Dean Wentworth. Carson was well aware what it was like to fall under the spell of a Langley woman. He knew exactly what that was like, to want to be with someone and…

No, that's not right. He and Dean had nothing in common. Dean actually loved Eloisa, right? Carson didn't love Lana. He valued her, he appreciated her, he enjoyed their time together, but there was no way in hell he could love her. That wasn't in the cards for either of them.

"Once Dean was left with a baby and no mother, he was shunned by the family for a while," Carson's grandfather went on. "After several years, people came around. A baby will do that to people, I guess. But Dean never got over losing Eloisa and Dean had a black mark associated with his name. The mess and feud spawned from there and still carries on to this day."

"Well, that will soon come to an end." Sierra smiled and glanced to Carson. "You have to feel a little pressure, but a whole lot of relief knowing you're obliterating this rivalry started so long ago."

Pressure, yes. Relief…not so much. He wasn't relieved about lying to his family or deceiving anyone and he certainly wasn't relieved about letting Lana go. That actually bothered him more than anything, which was so odd. Since when had she moved to the top slot of priorities in his life?

"Lana and I are both glad we can be the couple to help put this fighting aside and pave the way for the next generation," Carson answered.

At least that was honest. He was glad this all would come to an end between the families. Just because he and Lana weren't going to be married didn't mean that in the future, the families couldn't be civil and cordial toward each other. Royal was a small town with big-city vibes and it was well past time.

"Well, thank you all for sharing your family's history with me," Sierra announced. "The diary pieces are starting to fall into place."

Carson pulled in a deep breath and stretched his arm along the back of the sofa. "Interestingly enough, I discovered Arielle's diary in my bedroom with pages missing."

"What?"

"Are you serious?"

Carson's grandfather and father spoke up at the same time. He tried to gauge their reactions, wondering if either of them had gone into his house and taken those pages.

"Oh, I'm very serious," Carson stated. "Something was on those pages that someone didn't want people to see. Which really makes no sense because I've already read through the diary and so has Sierra. What was so important that pages had to be ripped out?"

Sierra's wide eyes mimicked exactly how he felt. This was absolutely absurd and something he didn't have the time or mental capacity for. He just wanted to get through this engagement party, figure out how to gently call off the engagement, and make the best use of the inheritance the club would be getting from Harmon.

"So you're saying someone came into your house and tore out pages?" Sierra asked. "Who would do such a thing?"

Carson shrugged. "I have no clue, but it would have to be a limited number of family members. No one else had access to my house. I'm so sorry, Sierra. I know Eve loaned it to me in good faith. I'll apologize to her."

"That is so strange," Sierra murmured. "I'm sure the pages will turn up or someone will fess up."

Carson didn't care so much about the missing pages as he did the reason why someone felt the need to sneak into his home and steal.

"I hear there's a surprise to be announced at the engagement party." Sierra wiggled her eyebrows and smiled, clearly ready to move on. "Any chance you want to give me an exclusive?"

Carson shook his head. "I'd like to keep the announcement a surprise."

Sierra nodded. "I can understand that, but I had to try."

She went on to ask several more questions and Tate even joined the conversation when prompted. Finally, Sierra seemed satisfied with her interview and gathered her things.

"This has just been a real pleasure," she told them as she went around the room and shook each man's hand. "The public has been so fascinated with all of my findings in Royal and I just know they are going to eat up this engagement party, the mysterious surprise, and all of this backstory with Harmon's birth mother. That whole misplaced baby is strangely familiar to everything going on now."

"They always say history repeats itself," Carson's grandfather added. "Thank you for stopping by. We'll be seeing you this Saturday at the party."

Once Troy had shown Sierra out, the men were left in the den and Carson got to his feet. He shoved his hands in his pockets and waited until his grandfather came back in.

"Do any of you want to tell me why you took those pages?" he asked, his attention shifting between his father and grandfather.

Both men scoffed, but his grandfather spoke up first.

"Boy, I've never stolen a damn thing in my life so don't start accusing me now."

Carson believed him, so he nodded and showed respect. "My apologies, but you have to understand where I'm coming from. I don't take kindly to someone I trust just taking something from my house without my permission."

He shifted his focus to his father, who remained silent. Carson merely raised his eyebrows.

"What?" his father asked. "You think I did it? Why would I? If I wanted the diary, I would have just told you."

"You're the one upset about this wedding because you've been ingrained to hate the Langleys," Carson growled. "Maybe you took something from the diary that you think would hurt our family name. I don't know. You tell me."

Hank's lips thinned. "There's nothing to tell, so take your accusations and get out."

So much for smoothing things over.

Carson sighed and turned to Tate. "I'll see you Saturday."

Tate merely nodded and remained silent, likely afraid to get involved in this drama. Smart kid. Hopefully by the time he got older and had a little more gumption to stand up for himself, he'd be able to hold his own and choose who the hell he wanted to be with for the rest of his life.

Granted, Carson didn't plan on being with Lana his entire life, but somehow in the last month, his mind had started believing his own lies.

Carson let himself out of the estate and headed to his SUV.

He hadn't seen Lana since last night and he was starting to get cranky. Who knew that faking a relationship could mess with his mind so much?

With the party closing in on them, Carson knew he needed to really make these last days count, because once they had the funds secured, there would be no reason to continue his relationship—fake or otherwise—with Lana Langley.

Sixteen

Lana took Carson's hand as he assisted her from the car. A jumble of nerves curled all through her as she was just steps away from her engagement party.

"You look absolutely stunning," he murmured as he leaned in close. "Green is my favorite color."

She smiled and rested her hand against his freshly shaved cheek. "I remembered and that's why I wore this dress."

The way his warm breath tickled her cheek had her ready to hop back into his car and head back to his house, or hers, she didn't care. She wanted more time alone—she didn't want this to come to an end. She didn't want to go inside that ballroom and smile and lie to everyone she cared about.

But more than anything else, she didn't want to

admit that she'd fallen in love with Carson. That was certainly never part of this plan.

"You look like you're ready to run," he joked, easing back to study her face.

Lana stared up into those emerald eyes she'd come to love. Funny how that word bounced around so freely inside her mind, but she couldn't even fathom saying it out loud. Carson would think she'd just gotten caught up in the whirlwind of events, but she knew her feelings for him had changed drastically. She'd gotten to know the real Carson, not the one she'd always been told to hate.

"I'm nervous," she admitted.

"You? I didn't think anything scared you."

Losing him forever scared her in a way she'd never imagined possible. But he wasn't technically hers to lose, which made this entire situation that much more complex and painful. She simply couldn't tell him the full truth of her feelings just yet...and she didn't know if she ever could.

"You know I'm not good at lying," she reminded him. "I just can't stand the thought of going in there and spending hours schmoozing and pretending we're in love."

Okay, well, there would be no pretending on her end.

"You'll do great," he assured her. "We're almost done and then we'll both get what we want. Don't lose sight of that."

Right. Their goal hinged on this business arrangement, not on her unexpected emotions.

"Ready?" he asked, giving her hand a gentle squeeze.

"Just stay close," she told him. "I need your support."

He blinked, as if shocked by her admission.

"You'll always have my support, Lana," he assured her. "Even after tonight."

She wanted to say something more, but words failed her and Carson turned, urging her with him as he held on to her hand. He led her across the lot and toward the main entrance to the clubhouse and the moment was lost. If she was ever going to confess how she felt, that would have been the time.

So perhaps it was for the best that she didn't say anything. She couldn't risk losing Harmon's very generous funding, but she also didn't want to see any of this come to an end.

Lana stopped, giving a tug on Carson for him to wait.

"Come home with me tonight."

Carson glanced over his shoulder, then slowly turned to face her. "What?"

Nerves were getting the best of her and if she wasn't careful, she'd end up losing that strong control she'd had on this arrangement…and she'd end up with a broken heart.

"I know we're supposed to be slowing down and ending things soon, but I'm not ready yet. Just…stay tonight."

His lids lowered as he closed the minuscule gap between them. Carson framed her face and slid his lips over hers, his touch feathering and arousing, yet so gentle.

"I hadn't planned on being anywhere else tonight," he whispered.

Oh, she was in trouble. More trouble than she'd realized and she didn't know how long she could keep her feelings bottled up inside.

As they reached the entryway, Hank and Harmon were coming up the ramp. Lana hadn't realized Harmon would be here in person.

"There's the happy couple." Harmon held on to the rail as he made his way slowly toward the door. "This is a monumental evening."

"It's so good to see you here," Carson stated, releasing her hand to assist his great-grandfather. "I had no clue you'd be showing up or if you'd feel up to it."

Harmon smiled. "After all this time, you think I'd miss the night we celebrate joining two families? Nothing short of death would keep me away."

Lana went ahead and held the door open for the men, and once Hank took Harmon's hand and led him forward, Carson rested his hand on the small of her back and ushered her inside.

She'd worn an emerald halter with a very low back and a long skirt with a slit—perfectly comfortable, yet enough to hopefully drive Carson mad with need.

As soon as they hit the entryway to the ballroom, Lana nearly choked up on her emotions. All the people mingling already, the green decor accented in gold, the music, the laughter... This was all for her and Carson.

Tears threatened and Lana closed her eyes for a moment. What was wrong with her? She didn't get worked up like this over anything. She hadn't cried over losing the TCC presidency and she'd desperately wanted that title.

But losing the title of Carson Wentworth's fiancée

was something else entirely. This was so much more personal, so much more heartbreaking.

And that was the crux of everything that had culminated in this moment. She'd gone and let her heart get involved when she'd sworn not to let that happen.

The DJ spotted them and cut the music, making an announcement about the couple. Everyone broke in to cheers and claps, with a few whistles and yells.

Carson waved and laughed and she had no clue how he was so casual, so…okay with this. They'd worked toward this moment for the last month, but now that it was here, she wasn't feeling as confident as she had been.

"Thank you all for coming," Carson said as the cheers died down. "Lana and I are thrilled everyone is here to support this new chapter in our lives. We hope you enjoy yourselves all evening and stick around for a special announcement later."

The crowd cheered again and Lana could only smile. She hoped nobody could read her stiff body language or her forced grin. Since when did she stand by her man and say nothing at all? That wasn't her personality and she wondered where she'd changed along the way.

Granted, if this had been a real engagement party, she'd be all over making her own announcement and much more comfortable with the atmosphere.

Before her mind could keep winding down that path of unwanted thoughts, various guests started showering her and Carson with love. So many hugs and smiles, so many people genuinely happy for this union.

The DJ made another announcement for a special

dance with the happy couple to start off the evening.
Carson led her to the dance floor and embraced her
as they swayed to a song she hadn't chosen.

"This isn't the song I picked," she muttered.

"No, I did," he told her, staring down into her eyes.
"You were doing everything for this and I wanted to
pick a song that reminded us of our time together. Do
you like it?"

She loved the song, but she actually loved more that
he had taken the initiative to change what she'd chosen. He'd actually put some thought into this moment.
Did that mean he cared more than he was willing to
admit? Did he see her as more than a bargaining tool
to get the funds for the club?

On one hand, Lana wished she knew exactly how
he felt and what he was thinking where they were
concerned, but on the other hand...

Yeah, maybe it was best that she didn't know. If he
told her everything between them over the last month
had only been to pass the time, she would be even
more crushed. Better to walk away with her head high
than to be ashamed and even more broken.

She rested one hand on Carson's shoulder and the
other in his hand as they swayed to the music. Lana
blocked out all the people staring and concentrated
on the man holding her.

"We've never danced before," she commented.
"This is nice."

"Do you like to dance?" he asked.

She stared into those green eyes and found herself
slipping even more. "With the right partner."

"Am I the right partner, Lana?"

She nearly tripped, but thankfully he had a strong,

firm hold on her. He wasn't asking about the dance, and she hadn't been, either.

But Lana didn't respond. Anything she said would give away her true feelings and this was not the place.

The irony of not being able to tell her fake fiancé at their engagement party that she loved him was not lost on her.

Once the song ended, the crowd cheered once again and the DJ pumped up the music to something more upbeat. Lana needed a minute to herself—she needed to regroup and take a breather. For some reason, being intimate with Carson had been easy, and it was the dancing, the hand-holding, the intense stare, and soft words that were really starting to mess with her head.

"I'll be right back," she told him.

He looked like he wanted to say something, but Tate stepped up to them right at that moment.

"Can I talk to Carson?" he asked.

Lana nodded. "Take your time."

Despite Carson's worried look, Lana excused herself and made her way out of the ballroom and toward her office, where she could lock the door for just a moment. If she didn't get control of herself, their ruse would be up and they could kiss the inheritance goodbye.

Why did there have to be such a fine line between love and money?

"What's up?" Carson asked Tate as his brother pulled him toward the back of the ballroom.

Something had upset Lana and he wanted nothing more than to go after her, but he knew she needed a minute and there was obviously something on Tate's mind.

Carson was going to have to seriously focus on what Tate wanted to talk about, because all he could think of was how perfect Lana had felt in his arms. This night might be all about the sham they'd created, but for reasons he was scared to admit, everything felt so very real.

"I have a confession," Tate stated, cutting into Carson's thoughts.

Carson shifted, his back to the ballroom, and really tuned in to his brother. "What's wrong? And was it illegal?"

Tate glanced away, clearly not impressed with Carson's joke. Something was definitely wrong for his brother to look so solemn.

"Hey, whatever it is, we can get through it," Carson assured him. "Is your girlfriend pregnant?"

Tate jerked. "What? No. It's…the diary."

"What about it?"

Tate squared his shoulders and pulled in a deep breath. "I took those pages."

"What? Why would you need them?"

"There's more," he added. "I overheard you and Lana in your office the other day and I know you've been lying about all of this."

Carson didn't know what he was more frustrated and shocked about—the fact that his brother had stolen from him, or that Tate knew their secret.

"Why didn't you say anything about knowing before now?" Carson asked, crossing his arms over his chest.

Tate shrugged. "I was upset that you were lying about the engagement and I didn't want you to ruin things for the family. So I went to your house when

I knew you weren't home. I was going to take the diary, but thought that would look too suspicious, so I just tore two pages out. I didn't think you'd notice."

The music continued on behind him as people laughed and mingled. Yet all the while Carson could not believe what he was hearing.

"What was on those pages that made you take them?" Carson asked.

"I read about Harmon wondering about his birth mother and how he wished his dad had told someone or had written it down. It got me thinking. Maybe he did. I ended up digging around in Grandpa's attic. I found some letters in an old lockbox."

"Are you kidding? I had no idea all of this was going on," Carson admitted, still stunned at this revelation.

"Nobody did, but I couldn't just let all of these lies keep going. Between the families feuding and then you and Lana lying, this had to come to an end."

Part of Carson was proud of the courageous step Tate had taken, but that didn't trump the sneaky way he went about it.

"So what did you find in the letters?"

Tate glanced around, likely making sure nobody was approaching them, then shifted his focus back to Carson.

"Dean Wentworth was supposed to marry Eloise Langley."

"Right," Carson said. "But she called it off."

"Yes, but he told everyone he was to blame for it. Eloisa had fallen in love with someone else and asked Dean to say calling off the engagement was his fault. Because he loved her, he did. Then when the baby turned up, which was Harmon, the Langley family, already really hating Dean because they thought he'd cheated on Eloise, had more proof he was no good because he had gotten some unknown woman pregnant."

And thus started a century-long battle between the families. What a mess, all because Dean had been trying to do the right thing on all accounts.

"But that's not all. According to the letters, *Violetta Ford* was Harmon's birth mother," Tate revealed.

"What?" Carson gasped. "No, that can't be right. She left town after being denied membership into the TCC."

Tate smiled. "It gets better. She never left, never sold her land. She started posing as a male rancher under the guise of Vincent Fenwick. 'Vincent' was the one who bought her land."

Tate paused to catch his breath. Carson could see how excited he was at this discovery.

"When Dean and Eloise ended their relationship, Dean turned to Violetta for comfort and that's when she got pregnant. She couldn't reveal her true identity, so she trusted Dean to raise their child. Can you believe it?"

Carson tried to process everything Tate had said. The truth had been found in an attic by a boy who was invested in this situation far more than Carson knew.

Still, Carson wasn't thrilled about the stolen pages, but in the end, that was nothing if the act revealed the truth once and for all.

"I'm done with lies, Carson. I don't like it and it's done nothing but cause drama and heartache for everyone for years." Tate glanced to his boots, then back up. "And because I think you and Lana really love each other."

Carson was taken aback. "Excuse me?" He couldn't help but laugh at this absurdity. "And where do you get that from? You don't know what's going on between Lana and me."

"Maybe I don't, but when I said I was sick of all the lying, I meant it," Tate went on. "I see the way you guys are with each other. Maybe you're actually meant to be together."

That was just crazy. Carson wasn't about to take relationship advice from a teenage kid. No matter how close he and Tate were, this was Carson's life.

"I'm not discussing this here," Carson stated between clenched teeth. "But we will talk later about privacy. And for someone who doesn't like lying, you've done a good bit yourself."

Tate shook his head. "Listen, I did everything to help put an end to all of this drama. I wouldn't have made a move had I not overheard you and Lana talking."

Carson rested his hand on the back of his neck and rolled around all the information he'd just been handed. Despite the fact Tate took the pages, that he'd known about the fake engagement and kept it to himself, none of that shook Carson more than what Tate thought he saw when he looked at Lana and Carson together. Was there something more than Carson was ready to admit?

All he knew was that he didn't want to delve into anything new where his emotions were concerned. He and Lana had a deal and he didn't intend on going back on his word of letting her go once their commitment was fulfilled.

"Everything okay here?"

Carson turned to see Harmon standing there. Carson opened his mouth to speak, but Tate beat him to it.

"Everything is fine. How are you feeling? Do you want me to get you a seat?"

Harmon waved his wrinkled hand through the air, blowing off the gesture. "Nah, I'm fine, son. It feels good to be out, enjoying life again here at the clubhouse."

"You look really good," Carson told him. "We should break you out more often."

Should he tell Harmon what Tate had discovered? No, tomorrow was soon enough. He'd let Harmon enjoy the party.

Harmon laughed. "I don't know if I have the energy for all of that, but tonight is nice. I never thought this would happen and to know it took a hundred years for the families to join back together, it's just a real dream come true."

Tate's eyes met Carson's and that guilt he'd tried to ignore over the past month came bubbling up with a vengeance. Tate was tired of the lies and maybe Carson should consider taking a chapter from his little brother's book and come clean with absolutely everything.

Seventeen

The knock on her office door had Lana jerking her attention toward the closed door. There was only one person who would come after her.

She pulled in a deep breath and crossed the room, flicked the lock, and twisted the knob. As soon as the door opened, Carson met her gaze with those deep green eyes.

"Are you hiding?" he asked as he stepped in and closed the distance between them.

Lana shrugged. "Maybe for a minute or two."

He rested his hands on her shoulders and rested his forehead against hers. "I don't want to be out there without you."

Lana eased back, surprised by his admission. She slid her hands up around his neck, threading her fingers through his hair.

"Tate knows," he added.

"Knows what?"

"The truth about us."

Shocked, Lana stilled. "How?"

"He claims he overheard us in my office last week," Carson explained. "He also said he's done with all the lying and he thinks…"

Lana waited for him to finish, but he closed his eyes and seemed to be waging some internal battle with himself.

"Carson."

His lids lifted slowly as he refocused on her. "I need to tell Harmon the truth."

"What? Why? We've worked so hard to make sure we secured this money for the club."

All of this hard work would be for nothing. She hadn't gone through all of this just to end up with no funds for her women's wing and a broken heart. She had to have something good come from these lies and all the manipulation.

"Tate got me thinking when he said he was over the lies," Carson went on. "He also said he thinks you and I are meant to be together."

Lana's breath caught in her throat. But she didn't know where Carson stood, so she tried to blow that off.

"He's a teenager. He hasn't had enough life lessons to come to this conclusion."

Carson shook his head. "Probably not, but he still got me thinking. I need to tell my great-grandfather the truth. I'll find out a way to still get your women's wing. I won't take that from you, but I need to be honest."

Lana waited for him to say something about them.

She wanted for him to add in something more, aside from their business agreement. But he didn't.

And that wasn't all she noticed missing from this conversation. She wanted Carson to open up about his feelings for her. If he was done with all the lying, wasn't he referring to everything? She'd never pegged him as a man like her father, but if he couldn't admit there was something more here, then maybe she didn't know him like she thought.

"I'll stand behind whatever you think is best," she finally told him, her heart breaking just a bit more. "If you think Harmon will understand. But I do want him to understand you and I are still friends, that we can make sure the families are merging together from here on out. We can do that without a wedding, right?"

Something came over his face, his lids lowered slightly and his lips thinned. Lana didn't know what he was thinking or feeling or if he planned on letting her in on any of his thoughts.

"Let's wait until after the party," he told her. "He's so happy to be here tonight and everyone is here."

Lana nodded. "I agree. Let's go out and have a good night. We can worry about all the rest tomorrow."

Carson's eyes dropped to her lips. "You're one amazing woman, do you know that?"

She couldn't help but smile. "I'm aware of how awesome I am, but I think you're pretty great, too. That love for your family is pretty amazing."

He slid his lips over hers and everything shifted. There was something in that kiss that seemed...different. But she couldn't quite put her finger on what was happening. They weren't engaged, they weren't even going to pretend after tonight, yet she felt closer and stronger with him than ever.

So what did that mean and how was she going to handle this new chapter when he couldn't even admit how he truly felt?

Carson had planned on talking to Harmon today, but his great-grandfather had called and pretty much demanded Carson meet him at the assisted-living facility.

So Carson stood outside the door to the room and wondered why Harmon was so adamant about this meeting. Regardless of what he wanted, Carson promised Lana he'd come clean today.

He'd spent the night again at her house, and it really should have been the last one, but he wasn't ready to tell her goodbye. He wasn't ready to cut those ties and go back to just being acquaintances.

But that was something he'd have to discuss with her later—right now he had other business to tend to first.

Carson let himself into the suite and closed the door behind him. Across the spacious room, Harmon sat in his chair next to the window. He had a cup of coffee on the table and the local news channel on his television. As soon as he saw Carson, he pointed the remote to the TV and clicked off his program.

"Good morning," Harmon greeted. "Are you alone today?"

Carson stepped into the living area and sank down onto the love seat. "I am. Your call sounded urgent so I came straight here."

Harmon reached for his coffee mug and took a sip,

clearly not in a hurry to get this conversation going…
which made Carson a bit nervous.

"That party last night was a big hit," he began,
turning his attention to Carson. "The crowd seemed
to love you and Lana together and they were even
more excited about the funds coming to the club for
even more renovations and amenities."

Carson had to admit that Harmon's funds would
push Cattleman's into something even grander and
greater. Every generation always wanted to take the
club into a new direction and all eyes were on Carson now that he was the new president and they had
an exorbitant amount of funds.

"Lana seemed upset a bit last night," he added. "I
saw you go toward her office."

Carson relaxed further on the sofa and stretched his
arm across the back. "She's nervous about this whole
process," he admitted.

Harmon's eyes met Carson's. "And what process
is that, exactly? Would that be the fake engagement
or that you two are actually in love?"

Carson stilled. "Excuse me?"

He knew? Not only did his great-grandfather know
about the ruse and the lies, but he also seemed to think
Carson and Lana were in love.

That made him the second person to point that out
in the span of about twelve hours.

Harmon smiled, the gesture deepening the wrinkles around his eyes and mouth. "I'm no fool, Carson. The two of you went from enemies and at each
other during the campaign, to engaged in the span of,
what, a few weeks? Besides, I overheard you talking

in her office while I was trying to find a quiet corner to catch my breath. So I know everything."

Damn it. He'd been so focused on making sure Lana was okay, plus he was reeling from the bomb dropped by Tate, that he hadn't even noticed anyone else in the hallway.

"I was going to tell you," Carson admitted. "That's what Lana and I were discussing last night. She's having a difficult time lying and I started having a change of heart as well."

Harmon nodded. "I overheard everything. I'm well aware of your intentions."

"I fully intend to fund the project Lana wants," Carson went on. "I can reconfigure the budget for her. We don't feel right about taking your money when there will be no marriage."

Harmon's bushy white eyebrows drew together. "No marriage? Why the hell not?"

Confused, Carson leaned forward. "You said you knew the truth, that this was all a sham. So the engagement wasn't authentic."

"Maybe not," Harmon agreed. "But just because this started out as a hoax, doesn't mean you two didn't get closer. Am I right?"

Well, yeah, he was right, but could Carson admit such a thing? If he said the words out loud, that would take everything from hypothetical to realistic in a flash.

"Listen."

Harmon winced as he adjusted himself in his chair.

"Are you okay?" Carson asked, starting to stand.

"I'm fine, relax," he insisted. "I'm old and my joints

are cranky sometimes. But we're focusing on you and Ms. Langley right now."

Carson didn't like that his great-grandfather was getting older and that he wouldn't be around forever. Harmon Wentworth wasn't just a staple in Royal, he was in the Cattleman's Club as well.

And he had always been a solid part of Carson's life. He valued what Harmon had to say and had always looked for his opinion on matters.

This was no different, but Carson just didn't know if he was ready to hear all of this.

"As I was saying," Harmon went on. "What I overheard made me so damn proud of you."

Confused, Carson asked, "Proud? I lied to you. We lied to everyone around us."

"You did," Harmon agreed, then shrugged. "But you two overcame your differences and came together. You were putting others' needs first, whether you realize that or not. You put my needs and the needs of the club members first. Not only that, you also realized that what you did wasn't right and you were ready to come clean and confess. All of that makes me realize what a fine man you are and I'm proud you're a Wentworth."

Carson couldn't believe what the man was saying. Out of everything that his great-grandfather would have mentioned, the word *proud* never crossed Carson's mind.

"I still plan on funding the clubhouse."

Another wave of shock overcame Carson. "You do?"

Harmon's smile widened. "Of course. I love that club and I love you. As the president, I want to do everything I can to help you out. Besides, I know the Langley-Wentworth feud is coming to an end."

"How are you so sure of that?"

"It's simple, really. You and Lana will end up together. Maybe not right now—you'll probably be stubborn like us Wentworth men can be, you'll let her go thinking it's for the best. But you won't be able to deny your feelings much longer."

Carson took in all the advice, all the *truth* being handed out freely. Wasn't truth the whole theme as of late? This whole sham started on a misunderstanding that had quickly flipped into a lie. Carson had pulled Lana right along with him.

He'd taken his sworn enemy and pulled her into his drama, and she'd agreed when she could have easily told him no and found other ways to get what she wanted for the club. Never once had he asked her how this whole situation affected her or how she felt. He assumed she was just fine, riding the wave of deceit right along with him.

Carson suddenly realized that Lana wasn't his enemy whatsoever. No, his enemy in all of this was her discomfort and all of the lies. Lana was his...

Everything.

He shifted his gaze back to his still smiling great-grandfather. No, Carson wasn't ready to admit anything, not to Harmon or anyone else. Not until he spoke with Lana and told her everything. Above anyone, she deserved to know where his head was and she deserved to have her own say-so with all of this.

They had something, that much he knew. But did their bond go beyond the loyalties to each other during this temporary process, or was there more…something they could actually build on.

"I appreciate you wanting to tell me the truth," Harmon stated after a bit. "I know your heart is in the right place and I know you will do right by Lana. I'm comfortable with giving up the funds for the club. I want to see it go to the proper place before I pass."

Relief washed over Carson and he couldn't help but smile back. "I need to tell you something else. Tate is the one who stole pages from the diary."

Harmon's eyebrows rose. "Is that right? Why did he do that?"

"He was done with the lies and the animosity between the families," Carson explained. "He didn't want that in place as he got older and he just wanted to smooth things over."

"Another strong Wentworth man."

"That he is," Carson agreed. "The diary gave him a clue that we'd all missed. He found a lockbox with some of Dean's letters up in the attic of the estate."

Harmon shifted in his seat, focusing more on Carson. "A lockbox? I recall my dad having one a long time ago. Forgot where I put the thing. Letters from my dad were in there?"

Carson nodded. "That's what Tate found. The letters fully explained how the feud started."

Carson gave Harmon a brief summary of what Tate told him. He took a deep breath before continuing.

"Harmon, the letters also say that Violetta Ford was your birth mother."

Silence filled the room and Carson wondered if this was too shocking. As much as Harmon was in good health for his age, he was still one hundred years old and his mind wasn't what it used to be.

"Violetta," Harmon whispered. "She was my biological mother? But she left town."

"Violetta was an amazing woman. In the letters it says after Dean and Eloisa broke up, Dean turned to Violetta. But friendship turned to more. After the brief affair she discovered she was pregnant. But here's the shocker—Violetta didn't leave Royal after being denied membership into the TCC. She transformed herself into Vincent Fenwick and continued to run the ranch. She knew Dean would take wonderful care of you, so she dropped you off on his doorstep."

Harmon blew out a sigh. "It's crazy," he muttered. "But in an odd way it makes sense. My dad used to tell me what a great rancher Violetta was, and how she sold her land to an equally great rancher, Vincent Fenwick. Wow, this will take a bit of time to sink in."

Carson was glad Harmon finally got some answers. Carson didn't know a more loyal family than his own and they'd be there to help Harmon adjust to this revelation. The Wentworths might bicker now and then, but they all always had each other's backs. Carson knew at any time his family would do anything for him.

There was someone else who would do anything for him and he was getting more anxious to get back to her. He'd left her bed this morning, wondering where they would go from here. He didn't know if he'd be welcomed back or if they were going to just stop everything once their secret was out.

"Don't you think you should be going?"

His great-grandfather's question pulled Carson from his own thoughts. "Going where?"

"Back to Ms. Langley. You don't want to stay here with me all day. I know your secret, and I'm still donating the funds. There's no reason to keep the inheritance until I pass. I know you and Lana will do what's right for both families and the clubhouse now."

Carson didn't know what to feel at this moment. There was more than relief. There was a sense of calm that overcame him, knowing that for once in his life, he knew exactly what he wanted...who he wanted.

Nothing stood in his way because he wouldn't let it. He wanted to hear what Lana had to say, but he also had quite a bit to tell her as well.

And he was going to start with "I love you."

Eighteen

Lana smoothed her hand over her cream duvet and fluffed her throw pillows into place. She stood back and stared at the perfectly made bed, and all she could think of was how imperfect she and Carson could make it.

When he'd left earlier, she'd lain around and opted to have a lazy Sunday. She'd stayed in bed for a bit, scrolling on social media. So many friends had posted photos from last night and, of course, they'd all tagged her.

When social media became too much, she'd gotten a shower and pulled her hair up in a smooth topknot. She put on her favorite strapless maxi dress that was a vibrant shade of blue. As she stood in her walk-in closet at the island in the middle looking over her earrings, she heard the chime from the security system at the end of her driveway.

She wasn't expecting anyone...unless Carson came back.

They hadn't said much this morning. What was there to say? He'd told her he was going to see Harmon and he would come clean with everything they'd been doing over the past month. Perhaps he was coming back to tell her how the meeting went.

She shouldn't be nervous, but she was. This past month she knew where she stood with Carson. She was his business partner, fake fiancée, and temporary lover. Things were as simple and as complicated as that.

Padding barefoot through her room, she went down the hallway toward her staircase. As she reached the top landing, her front door opened.

Lana stared down into the foyer as Carson stepped inside. His eyes immediately went up, meeting hers and holding her in place.

"I need to get that spare key back," she murmured.

Should her heart flutter like a teenage girl with her first crush? Shouldn't she be over the intensity of his stare by now? The man caused too many strong emotions within her, emotions no man had ever stirred up before. So how was she supposed to cut ties?

On the other hand, all of this was built on lies. Everything they had stemmed from a scandal, and nothing was real. They were both so strong-willed, how could they ever make things work in the real world?

She couldn't stand the silence another second, but she remained at the top of the landing as she rested her hand on the banister.

"Did you see Harmon?"

Carson nodded as he closed the door behind him, but he remained still. "He already knew we were faking the engagement."

"What? How?"

"He overheard us last night talking in your office," Carson explained. "He also overheard us discussing coming clean with him and telling the truth. He said he's proud of our honesty."

Stunned, Lana didn't quite know what to say. The ruse was officially over. This was the moment they'd both been working toward for the past month, but now that it was here, she didn't feel thrilled or excited one bit. There was a little piece of her that felt almost broken. Which was absurd, right? They had nothing solid between them other than their end goal of getting the inheritance.

"Is he keeping the money?" she asked.

"No, he's still donating because he said we had good intentions and we planned on doing the right thing."

Well, at least something right came out of all of this. That was the sole intent of the engagement…so why did she still have that empty pit in her stomach?

"He said something else," Carson added.

"What was that?"

Carson started up the steps, and with each one he kept his eyes locked on hers. Lana's heart beat a little fast as Carson slowly closed that gap between them.

When he reached the top of the landing, he placed his hands on her bare shoulders and turned her to face him fully. There was a light in his eyes she hadn't seen before. Perhaps he was relieved the lies were over.

Maybe he was glad to be done with all of this so he could move on with his life.

"He said we belong together."

Lana's breath caught in her throat. "No, he didn't."

Carson offered her a wide smile that had her heart doing a flip. "He absolutely did."

"Why would he say something like that?"

Carson's hands slid up over the column of her throat and up to her face. He held her firmly in that gentle grip as he leaned in closer.

"Because we do," he whispered. "You and I, Lana, we're cut from the same cloth. We complement each other in every way."

Panic set in. Those nerves coursing through her only intensified. The risk of making this real would only end in bigger heartache if they failed. Not to mention, last night Carson didn't include his feelings for her when he was laying out his plan of honesty. Shouldn't she just remove herself now to save that pain later down the road?

"We can't be together," she told him. "We would drive each other crazy. You and I both know we want our way all the time. We're so hardheaded and we'd just end up fighting all the time."

"Have we fought any over the past month?" he asked.

"Well, no."

He slid his thumb along her bottom lip, slowly trying to wear her down, and damn it, it was working.

"I don't want this," she told him, knowing her fear was talking.

Now that the possibility stared her in the face, she couldn't help but be terrified.

"You're lying." He had the audacity to laugh. "You always said you were a terrible liar and I see that now. You know you want to be with me."

Lana flattened her hands against his chest. "That's pretty arrogant even for you."

"Not arrogant," he insisted. "Confident. And I'm certain that you're worried this will all fall apart later down the road. Am I right?"

Lana shrugged, closing her eyes because she didn't want to see the future in front of her. Was he her future? Was this even a possibility? He seemed so sure of this relationship. Even Harmon saw something between them, but had he just been seeing the ruse, or something more authentic?

"What if we fail?" she whispered as tears clogged her throat.

"Look at me," he demanded.

Lana opened her eyes. Carson's smile had vanished, and now that stare was more intense than ever.

"You and I have never failed at anything we put our minds to," he told her. "And I've never wanted anything more than this right here. I love you, Lana."

Everything around her stilled, her breath caught in her throat and those tears she'd been willing away started welling up even more.

"You can't say that."

"Oh, I can and I did," he assured her. "I know you feel the same."

"How could you possibly know that?"

He said nothing as he leaned in, grazing his lips across hers. Carson coaxed her lips apart, gently, softly. Lana opened for him. Her hands on his chest curled in, gripping his T-shirt.

Carson slid his hands down to the top of her strapless dress. He continued making love to her mouth as he eased down the fabric, ultimately sending the material into a puddle at her feet.

Suddenly his hands were everywhere on her, removing her bra and panties in a flurry. His actions were hurried, but his touch gentle.

And then he stepped back, staring at her, raking that emerald gaze over her bare body. Not only was she physically stripped bare, but her raw emotions were also on display.

And she was wearing absolutely nothing now but his ring.

"Tell me you love me," he murmured.

There was no more hiding. She might be afraid of everything that could go wrong, but what if everything went right?

"You know I do," she admitted.

Carson smiled, the brightness reaching his eyes and making her heart melt even more.

"There's no more feud between our families," he told her. "We're not living in the past anymore. I want a future, with you, for real this time."

"Wait…you want to marry me?"

Carson laughed. "Did you think I just wanted to keep sleeping with you? Honey, you should know better than that. I'm all in with you. That ring on your finger isn't just a prop anymore. It's real, just like the life I want with you."

Lana refused to deny herself anymore. She'd always gone after what she wanted and tried to live up to Abby's legacy, so maybe it was a good thing she had that fear in her. That strong emotion would only make her want to work even harder at making this work.

"Are you going to stand there or take me back to bed?" she asked with a smile.

"Are you going to marry me?"

Lana wrapped her arms around him and smacked a kiss on his lips. "I wanted to be TCC president, but I can handle being the first lady."

Carson laughed as he lifted her in his arms and carried her to her bedroom. Lana might have had a different idea for her life, but that was nothing compared to the thrilling one she'd just been handed. From now on, she and Carson would be side by side in absolutely everything...and nothing could stop them.

* * * * *

COMING SOON!

We really hope you enjoyed reading this book. If you're looking for more romance, be sure to head to the shops when new books are available on

Thursday 3rd February

To see which titles are coming soon, please visit

millsandboon.co.uk/nextmonth

MILLS & BOON

THE HEART OF ROMANCE

A ROMANCE FOR EVERY READER

MODERN

Prepare to be swept off your feet by sophisticated, sexy and seductive heroes, in some of the world's most glamourous and romantic locations, where power and passion collide.

HISTORICAL

Escape with historical heroes from time gone by. Whether your passion is for wicked Regency Rakes, muscled Vikings or rugged Highlanders, awaken the romance of the past.

MEDICAL

Set your pulse racing with dedicated, delectable doctors in the high-pressure world of medicine, where emotions run high and passion, comfort and love are the best medicine.

True Love

Celebrate true love with tender stories of heartfelt romance, from the rush of falling in love to the joy a new baby can bring, and a focus on the emotional heart of a relationship.

Desire

Indulge in secrets and scandal, intense drama and plenty of sizzling hot action with powerful and passionate heroes who have it all: wealth, status, good looks…everything but the right woman.

HEROES

Experience all the excitement of a gripping thriller, with an intense romance at its heart. Resourceful, true-to-life women and strong, fearless men face danger and desire - a killer combination!

To see which titles are coming soon, please visit

millsandboon.co.uk/nextmonth

LET'S TALK
Romance

For exclusive extracts, competitions
and special offers, find us online:

 facebook.com/millsandboon

 @MillsandBoon

@MillsandBoonUK

Get in touch on 01413 063232

For all the latest titles coming soon, visit
millsandboon.co.uk/nextmonth

MILLS & BOON

HEROES

At Your Service

Experience all the excitement of a
gripping thriller, with an intense romance
at its heart. Resourceful, true-to-life
women and strong, fearless men face
danger and desire - a killer combination!

MILLS & BOON
MEDICAL
Pulse-Racing Passion

Set your pulse racing with dedicated, delectable doctors in the high-pressure world of medicine, where emotions run high and passion, comfort and love are the best medicine.